ACTIVE SERVICE

STEPHEN CRANE

1st WORLD
LIBRARY
Literary Society

Active Service

Stephen Crane

© 1st World Library – Literary Society, 2005
PO Box 2211
Fairfield, IA 52556
www.1stworldlibrary.org
First Edition

LCCN: 2006930800

Softcover ISBN: 1-4218-2201-6
Hardcover ISBN: 1-4218-2101-X
eBook ISBN: 1-4218-2301-2

Purchase *"Active Service"*
as a traditional bound book at:
www.1stWorldLibrary.org/purchase.asp?ISBN=1-4218-2201-6

1st World Library Literary Society is a nonprofit
organization dedicated to promoting literacy by:

- Creating a free internet library accessible from any
  computer worldwide.
- Hosting writing competitions and offering book
  publishing scholarships.

Readers interested in supporting literacy
through sponsorship, donations or
membership please contact:
literacy@1stworldlibrary.org
Check us out at: www.1stworldlibrary.ORG
and start downloading free ebooks today.

CHAPTER I

MARJORY walked pensively along the hall. In the cool shadows made by the palms on the window ledge, her face wore the expression of thoughtful melancholy expected on the faces of the devotees who pace in cloistered gloom. She halted before a door at the end of the hall and laid her hand on the knob. She stood hesitating, her head bowed. It was evident that this mission was to require great fortitude.

At last she opened the door. "Father," she began at once. There was disclosed an elderly, narrow-faced man seated at a large table and surrounded by manuscripts and books. The sunlight flowing through curtains of Turkey red fell sanguinely upon the bust of dead-eyed Pericles on the mantle. A little clock was ticking, hidden somewhere among the countless leaves of writing, the maps and broad heavy tomes that swarmed upon the table.

Her father looked up quickly with an ogreish scowl.

Go away!" he cried in a rage. "Go away. Go away. Get out" "He seemed on the point of arising to eject the visitor. It was plain to her that he had been interrupted in the writing of one of his sentences, ponderous, solemn and endless, in which wandered multitudes of homeless and friendless prepositions, adjectives looking for a parent, and quarrelling nouns, sentences which no longer symbolised the language-form of thought but which had about them a quaint aroma from the dens of long-dead scholars. "Get out," snarled the professor.

Father," faltered the girl. Either because his formulated thought was now completely knocked out of his mind by his own emphasis in defending it, or because he detected something of portent in her expression, his manner suddenly changed, and with a petulant glance at his writing he laid down his pen and sank back in his chair to listen. "Well, what is it, my child ?"

The girl took a chair near the window and gazed out upon the snow-stricken campus, where at the moment a group of students returning from a class room were festively hurling snow-balls. "I've got something important to tell you, father," said she, but I don't quite know how to say it."

"Something important?" repeated the professor. He was not habitually interested in the affairs of his family, but this proclamation that something important could be connected with them, filled his mind with a capricious interest. "Well, what is it, Marjory?"

She replied calmly: "Rufus Coleman wants to marry me."

"What?" demanded the professor loudly. "Rufus Coleman. What do you mean? "

The girl glanced furtively at him. She did not seem to be able to frame a suitable sentence.

As for the professor, he had, like all men both thoughtless and thoughtful, told himself that one day his daughter would come to him with a tale of this kind. He had never forgotten that the little girl was to be a woman, and he had never forgotten that this tall, lithe creature, the present Marjory, was a woman. He had been entranced and confident or entranced and apprehensive according' to the time. A man focussed upon astronomy, the pig market or social progression, may nevertheless have a secondary mind which hovers like a spirit over his dahlia tubers and dreams upon the mystery of their slow and tender revelations. The professor's secondary mind had dwelt always with his daughter and watched with a faith and delight the changing to a woman of a certain fat and mumbling babe. However, he now saw this machine, this self-sustaining, self-operative love, which had run with the ease of a clock, suddenly crumble to ashes and leave the mind of a great scholar staring at a calamity. "Rufus Coleman," he repeated, stunned. Here was his daughter, very obviously desirous of marrying Rufus Coleman. "Marjory," he cried in amazement and fear, "what possesses, you? Marry Rufus Colman?"

The girl seemed to feel a strong sense of relief at his prompt recognition of a fact. Being freed from the necessity of making a flat declaration, she simply hung her head and blushed impressively. A hush fell upon them. The professor stared long at his daugh. ter. The shadow of unhappiness deepened upon his face. "Marjory, Marjory," he murmured at last. He had tramped heroically upon his panic and devoted his strength to bringing thought into some kind of attitude toward this terrible fact. "I am - I am surprised," he began. Fixing her then with a stern eye, he asked: "Why do you wish to marry this man? You, with your opportunities of meeting persons of intelligence. And you want to marry -" His voice grew tragic. "You want to marry the Sunday editor of the New York Eclipse."

"It is not so very terrible, is it?" said Marjory sullenly.

"Wait a moment; don't talk," cried the professor. He arose and walked nervously to and fro, his hands flying in the air. He was very red behind the ears as when in the Classroom some student offended him. "A gambler, a sporter of fine clothes, an expert on champagne, a polite loafer, a witness knave who edits the Sunday edition of a great outrage upon our sensibilities. You want to marry him, this man? Marjory, you are insane. This fraud who asserts that his work is intelligent, this fool comes here to my house and-"

He became aware that his daughter was regarding him coldly. "I thought we had best have all this part of it over at once," she remarked.

He confronted her in a new kind of surprise. The little keen-eyed professor was at this time imperial, on the verge of a majestic outburst. "Be still," he said. "Don't be clever with your father. Don't be a dodger. Or, if you are, don't speak of it to me. I suppose this fine young man expects to see me personally?"

"He was coming to-morrow," replied Marjory. She began to weep. "He was coming to-morrow."

"Um," said the professor. He continued his pacing while Marjory wept with her head bowed to the arm of the chair. His brow made the three dark vertical crevices well known to his students. Some. times he glowered murderously at the photographs of ancient temples which adorned the walls. "My poor child," he said once, as he paused near her, "to think I never knew you were a fool. I have been deluding myself. It has been my fault as much as it has been yours. I will not readily forgive myself."

The girl raised her face and looked at him. Finally, resolved to disregard the dishevelment wrought by tears, she presented a desperate front with her wet eyes and flushed cheeks. Her hair was disarrayed. "I don't see why you can call me a fool," she said. The pause before this sentence had been so portentous of a wild and rebellious speech that the professor almost laughed now. But still the father for the first time knew that he was being un-dauntedly faced by his child in his own library, in the presence of 372 pages of the book that was to be his masterpiece. At the back of his mind he felt a great awe as if his own youthful spirit had come from the past and challenged him with a glance. For a moment he was almost a defeated man. He dropped into a chair. "Does your mother know of this " "he asked mournfully.

"Yes," replied the girl. "She knows. She has been trying to make me give up Rufus."

"Rufus," cried the professor rejuvenated by anger.

"Well, his name is Rufus," said the girl.

"But please don't call him so before me," said the father with icy dignity. "I do not recognise him as being named Rufus. That is a contention of yours which does not arouse my interest. I know him very well as a gambler and a drunkard, and if incidentally, he is named Rufus, I fail to see any importance to it."

"He is not a gambler and he is not a drunkard," she said.

"Um. He drinks heavily - that is well known. He gambles. He plays cards for money - more than he possesses - at least he did when he was in college."

"You said you liked him when he was in college."

"So I did. So I did," answered the professor sharply. "I often find myself liking that kind of a boy in college. Don't I know them-those lads with their beer and their poker games in the dead of the night with a towel hung over the keyhole. Their habits are often vicious enough, but something remains in them through it all and they may go away and do great things. This happens. We know it. It happens with confusing insistence. It destroys theo ries. There - there isn't much to say about it. And sometimes we like this kind of a boy better than we do the - the others. For my part I know of many a pure, pious and fine-minded student that I have positively loathed from a personal point-of-view. But," he added, "this Rufus Coleman, his life in college and his life since, go to prove how often we get off the track. There is no gauge of collegiate conduct whatever, until we can get evidence of the man's work in the world. Your precious scoundrel's evidence is now all in and he is a failure, or worse."

"You are not habitually so fierce in judging people," said the girl.

"I would be if they all wanted to marry my daughter," rejoined the professor. "Rather than let that man make love to you-or even be within a short railway journey of you, I'll cart you off to Europe this winter and keep you there until you forget. If you persist in this silly fancy, I shall at once become medieval."

Marjory had evidently recovered much of her composure. "Yes, father, new climates are alway's supposed to cure one," she remarked with a kind of lightness.

"It isn't so much the old expedient," said the professor musingly, "as it is that I would be afraid to leave you herewith no protection against that drinking gambler and gambling drunkard."

"Father, I have to ask you not to use such terms in speaking of the man that I shall marry."

There was a silence. To all intents, the professor remained unmoved. He smote the tips of his fingers thoughtfully together. "Ye-es," he observed. "That sounds reasonable from your standpoint." His eyes studied her face in a long and steady glance. He arose and went into the hall. When he returned he wore his hat and great coat. He took a book and some papers from the table and went away.

Marjory walked slowly through the halls and up to her room. From a window she could see her father making his way across the campus labouriously against the wind and whirling snow. She watched it, this little black figure, bent forward, patient, steadfast. It was an inferior fact that her father was one of the famous scholars of the generation. To her, he was now a little old man facing the wintry winds. Recollect. ing herself and Rufus Coleman she began to weep again, wailing amid the ruins of her tumbled hopes. Her skies had turned to paper and her trees were mere bits of green sponge. But amid all this woe appeared the little black image of her father making its way against the storm.

CHAPTER II

IN a high-walled corrider of one of the college buildings, a crowd of students waited amid jostlings and a loud buzz of talk. Suddenly a huge pair of doors flew open and a wedge of young men inserted itself boisterously and deeply into the throng. There was a great scuffle attended by a general banging of books upon heads. The two lower classes engaged in herculean play while members of the two higher classes, standing aloof, devoted themselves strictly to the encouragement of whichever party for a moment lost ground or heart. This was in order to prolong the conflict.

The combat, waged in the desperation of proudest youth, waxed hot and hotter. The wedge had been instantly smitten into a kind of block of men. It had crumpled into an irregular square and on three sides it was now assailed with remarkable ferocity.

It was a matter of wall meet wall in terrific rushes, during which lads could feel their very hearts leaving them in the compress of friends and foes. They on the outskirts upheld the honour of their classes by squeezing into paper thickness the lungs of those of their fellows who formed the centre of the melee.

In some way it resembled a panic at a theatre.

The first lance-like attack of the Sophomores had been formidable, but the Freshmen outnumbering their enemies and smarting from continual Sophomoric oppression, had swarmed to the front like drilled collegians and given the arrogant foe the first serious check of the year. Therefore the tall Gothic windows which lined one side of the corridor looked down upon as incomprehensible and enjoyable a tumult as could mark the steps of advanced education. The Seniors and juniors cheered themselves ill. Long freed from the joy of such meetings, their only means for this kind of recreation was to involve the lower classes, and they had never seen the victims fall to with such vigour and courage. Bits of printed leaves, torn note-books, dismantled collars and cravats, all floated to the floor beneath the feet of the warring hordes. There were no blows; it was a battle of pressure. It was a deadly pushing where the leaders on either side often suffered the most cruel and sickening agony caught thus between phalanxes of shoulders with friend as well as foe contributing to the pain.

Charge after charge of Freshmen beat upon the now compact and organised Sophomores. Then, finally, the rock began to give slow way. A roar came from the Freshmen and they hurled themselves in a frenzy upon their betters.

To be under the gaze of the juniors and Seniors is to be in sight of all men, and so the Sophomores at this important moment laboured with the desperation of the half-doomed to stem the terrible Freshmen.

In the kind of game, it was the time when bad tempers came strongly to the front, and in many Sophomores' minds a thought arose of the incomparable insolence of the Freshmen. A blow was struck; an infuriated Sophomore had swung an arm high and smote a Freshman.

Although it had seemed that no greater noise could be made by the given numbers, the din that succeeded this manifestation surpassed everything. The juniors and Seniors immediately set up an angry howl. These veteran classes projected themselves into the middle of the fight, buffeting everybody with small thought as to merit. This method of bringing peace was as militant as a landslide, but they had much trouble before they could separate the central clump of antagonists into its parts. A score of Freshmen had cried out: "It was Coke. Coke punched him. Coke." A dozen of them were tempestuously endeavouring to register their protest against fisticuffs by means of an introduction of more fisticuffs.

The upper classmen were swift, harsh and hard. "Come, now, Freshies, quit it. Get back, get back, d'y'hear?" With a wrench of muscles they forced themselves in front of Coke, who was being blindly defended by his classmates from intensely earnest attacks by outraged Freshmen.

These meetings between the lower classes at the door of a recitation room were accounted quite comfortable and idle affairs, and a blow delivered openly and in hatred fractured a sharply defined rule of conduct. The corridor was in a hubbub. Many Seniors and Juniors, bursting from old and iron discipline, wildly clamoured that some Freshman should be given the privilege of a single encounter with Coke. The Freshmen themselves were frantic. They besieged the tight and dauntless circle of men that encompassed

Coke. None dared confront the Seniors openly, but by headlong rushes at auspicious moments they tried to come to quarters with the rings of dark-browed Sophomores. It was no longer a festival, a game; it was a riot. Coke, wild-eyed, pallid with fury, a ribbon of blood on his chin, swayed in the middle of the mob of his classmates, comrades who waived the ethics of the blow under the circumstance of being obliged as a corps to stand against the scorn of the whole college, as well as against the tremendous assaults of the Freshmen. Shamed by their own man, but knowing full well the right time and the wrong time for a palaver of regret and disavowal, this battalion struggled in the desperation of despair. Once they were upon the verge of making unholy campaign against the interfering Seniors. This fiery impertinence was the measure of their state.

It was a critical moment in the play of the college. Four or five defeats from the Sophomores during the fall had taught the Freshmen much. They had learned the comparative measurements, and they knew now that their prowess was ripe to enable them to amply revenge what was, according to their standards, an execrable deed by a man who had not the virtue to play the rough game, but was obliged to resort to uncommon methods. In short, the Freshmen were almost out of control, and the Sophomores debased but defiant, were quite out of control. The Senior and junior classes which, in American colleges dictate in these affrays, found their dignity toppling, and in consequence there was a sudden oncome of the entire force of upper classmen football players naturally in advance. All distinctions were dissolved at once in a general fracas. The stiff and still Gothic windows surveyed a scene of dire carnage.

Stephen Crane

Suddenly a voice rang brazenly through the tumult. It was not loud, but it was different. " Gentlemen! Gentlemen!'" Instantly there was a remarkable number of haltings, abrupt replacements, quick changes. Prof. Wainwright stood at the door of his recitation room, looking into the eyes of each member of the mob of three hundred. "Ssh!" said the mob. "Ssh! Quit! Stop! It's the Embassador! Stop!" He had once been minister to Austro-Hungary, and forever now to the students of the college his name was Embassador. He stepped into the corridor, and they cleared for him a little respectful zone of floor. He looked about him coldly. "It seems quite a general dishevelment. The Sophomores display an energy in the halls which I do not detect in the class room." A feeble murmur of appreciation arose from the outskirts of the throng. While he had been speaking several remote groups of battling men had been violently signaled and suppressed by other students. The professor gazed into terraces of faces that were still inflamed. "I needn't say that I am surprised," he remarked in the accepted rhetoric of his kind. He added musingly: "There seems to be a great deal of torn linen. Who is the young gentleman with blood on his chin?"

The throng moved restlessly. A manful silence, such as might be in the tombs of stern and honourable knights, fell upon the shadowed corridor. The subdued rustling had fainted to nothing. Then out of the crowd Coke, pale and desperate, delivered himself.

"Oh, Mr. Coke," said the professor, "I would be glad if you would tell the gentlemen they may retire to their dormitories." He waited while the students passed out to the campus.

The professor returned to his room for some books, and then began his own march across the snowy campus. The wind twisted his coat-tails fantastically, and he was obliged to keep one hand firmly on the top of his hat. When he arrived home he met his wife in the hall. "Look here, Mary," he cried. She followed him into the library. "Look here," he said. "What is this all about? Marjory tells me she wants to marry Rufus Coleman."

Mrs. Wainwright was a fat woman who was said to pride herself upon being very wise and if necessary, sly. In addition she laughed continually in an inexplicably personal way, which apparently made everybody who heard her feel offended. Mrs. Wainwright laughed.

"Well," said the professor, bristling, "what do you mean by that ?"

"Oh, Harris," she replied. "Oh, Harris."

The professor straightened in his chair. "I do not see any illumination in those remarks, Mary. I understand from Marjory's manner that she is bent upon marrying Rufus Coleman. She said you knew of it."

"Why, of course I knew. It was as plain -"

"Plain !" scoffed the professor. "Plain!"

Why, of course," she cried. "I knew it all along."

There was nothing in her tone which proved that she admired the event itself. She was evidently carried away by the triumph of her penetration. "I knew it all along," she added, nodding.

The professor looked at her affectionately. "You knew it all along, then, Mary? Why didn't you tell me, dear?"

"Because you ought to have known it," she answered blatantly.

The professor was glaring. Finally he spoke in tones of grim reproach. "Mary, whenever you happen to know anything, dear, it seems only a matter of partial recompense that you should tell me."

The wife had been taught in a terrible school that she should never invent any inexpensive retorts concerning bookworms and so she yawed at once. "Really, Harris. Really, I didn't suppose the affair was serious. You could have knocked me down with a feather. Of course he has been here very often, but then Marjory gets a great deal of attention. A great deal of attention." The professor had been thinking. "Rather than let my girl marry that scalawag, I'll take you and her to Greece this winter with the class. Separation. It is a sure cure that has the sanction of antiquity."

"Well," said Mrs. Wainwright, "you know best, Harris. You know best." It was a common remark with her, and it probably meant either approbation or disapprobation if it did not mean simple discretion.

CHAPTER III

THERE had been a babe with no arms born in one of the western counties of Massachusetts. In place of upper limbs the child had growing from its chest a pair of fin-like hands, mere bits of skin-covered bone. Furthermore, it had only one eye. This phenomenon lived four days, but the news of the birth had travelled up this country road and through that village until it reached the ears of the editor of the Michaelstown Tribune. He was also a correspondent of the New York Eclipse. On the third day he appeared at the home of the parents accompanied by a photographer. While the latter arranged his, instrument, the correspondent talked to the father and mother, two coweyed and yellow-faced people who seemed to suffer a primitive fright of the strangers. Afterwards as the correspondent and the photographer were climbing into their buggy, the mother crept furtively down to the gate and asked, in a foreigner's dialect, if they would send her a copy of the photograph. The correspondent carelessly indulgent, promised it. As the buggy swung away, the father came from behind an apple tree, and the two semi-humans watched it with its burden of glorious strangers until it rumbled across the bridge and disappeared. The correspondent was elate; he told the photographer that the Eclipse would probably pay fifty dollars for the article and the photograph.

Stephen Crane

The office of the New York Eclipse was at the top of the immense building on Broadway. It was a sheer mountain to the heights of which the interminable thunder of the streets arose faintly. The Hudson was a broad path of silver in the distance. Its edge was marked by the tracery of sailing ships' rigging and by the huge and many-coloured stacks of ocean liners. At the foot of the cliff lay City Hall Park. It seemed no larger than a quilt. The grey walks patterned the snow-covering into triangles and ovals and upon them many tiny people scurried here and there, without sound, like a fish at the bottom of a pool. It was only the vehicles that sent high, unmistakable, the deep bass of their movement. And yet after listening one seemed to hear a singular murmurous note, a pulsation, as if the crowd made noise by its mere living, a mellow hum of the eternal strife. Then suddenly out of the deeps might ring a human voice, a newsboy shout perhaps, the cry of a faraway jackal at night.

From the level of the ordinary roofs, combined in many plateaus, dotted with short iron chimneys from which curled wisps of steam, arose other mountains like the Eclipse Building. They were great peaks, ornate, glittering with paint or polish. Northward they subsided to sun-crowned ranges.

From some of the windows of the Eclipse office dropped the walls of a terrible chasm in the darkness of which could be seen vague struggling figures. Looking down into this appalling crevice one discovered only the tops of hats and knees which in spasmodic jerks seemed to touch the rims of the hats. The scene represented some weird fight or dance or carouse. It was not an exhibition of men hurrying along a narrow street.

It was good to turn one's eyes from that place to the vista of the city's splendid reaches, with spire and spar shining in the clear atmosphere and the marvel of the Jersey shore, pearl-misted or brilliant with detail. From this height the sweep of a snow-storm was defined and majestic. Even a slight summer shower, with swords of lurid yellow sunlight piercing its edges as if warriors were contesting every foot of its advance, was from the Eclipse office something so inspiring that the chance pilgrim felt a sense of exultation as if from this peak he was surveying the worldwide war of the elements and life. The staff of the Eclipse usually worked without coats and amid the smoke from pipes.

To one of the editorial chambers came a photograph and an article from Michaelstown, Massachusetts. A boy placed the packet and many others upon the desk of a young man who was standing before a window and thoughtfully drumming upon the pane. He turned at the thudding of the packets upon his desk. "Blast you," he remarked amiably. "Oh, I guess it won't hurt you to work," answered the boy, grinning with a comrade's Insolence. Baker, an assistant editor for the Sunday paper, took scat at his desk and began the task of examining the packets. His face could not display any particular interest because he had been at the same work for nearly a fortnight.

The first long envelope he opened was from a woman. There was a neat little manuscript accompanied by a letter which explained that the writer was a widow who was trying to make her living by her pen and who, further, hoped that the generosity of the editor of the Eclipse would lead him to give her article the opportunity which she was sure it deserved. She hoped that the editor would pay her as well as possible for it, as she needed the money greatly. She added that her brother was a reporter on the Little Rock Sentinel and he had declared that her literary style was excellent. Baker really did not read this note. His vast experience of a fortnight had enabled him to detect its kind in two glances. He unfolded the manuscript, looked at it woodenly and then tossed it with the letter to the top of his desk, where it lay with the other corpses. None could think of widows in Arkansas, ambitious from the praise of the reporter on the Little Rock Sentinel, waiting for a crown of literary glory and money. In the next envelope a man using the note-paper of a Boston journal begged to know if the accompanying article would be acceptable; if not it was to be kindly returned in the enclosed stamped envelope. It was a humourous essay on trolley cars. Adventuring through the odd scraps that were come to the great mill, Baker paused occasionally to relight his pipe.

As he went through envelope after envelope, the desks about him gradually were occupied by young men who entered from the hall with their faces still red from the cold of the streets. For the most part they bore the unmistakable stamp of the American college. They had that confident poise which is easily brought from the athletic field. Moreover, their clothes were quite in the way of being of the newest fashion. There was an air of precision about their cravats and linen. But on the other hand there might be with them some indifferent westerner who was obliged to resort to irregular means and harangue startled shop-keepers in order to provide himself with collars of a strange kind. He was usually very quick and brave of eye and noted for his inability to perceive a distinction between his own habit and the habit of others, his western character preserving itself inviolate amid a confusion of manners.

The men, coming one and one, or two and two, flung badinage to all corners of the room. Afterward, as they wheeled from time to time in their chairs, they bitterly insulted each other with the utmost good-nature, taking unerring aim at faults and riddling personalities with the quaint and cynical humour of a newspaper office. Throughout this banter, it was strange to note how infrequently the men smiled, particularly when directly engaged in an encounter.

A wide door opened into another apartment where were many little slanted tables, each under an electric globe with a green shade. Here a curly-headed scoundrel with a corncob pipe was hurling paper balls the size of apples at the head of an industrious man who, under these difficulties, was trying to draw a picture of an awful wreck with ghastly-faced sailors frozen in the rigging. Near this pair a lady was challenging a German artist who resembled Napoleon III. with having been publicly drunk at a music hall on the previous night. Next to the great gloomy corridor of this sixteenth floor was a little office presided over by an austere boy, and here waited in enforced patience a little dismal band of people who wanted to see the Sunday editor.

Baker took a manuscript and after glancing about the room, walked over to a man at another desk, Here is something that. I think might do," he said. The man at the desk read the first two pages. "But where is the photogragh", "he asked then. "There should be a photograph with this thing."

"Oh, I forgot," said Baker. He brought from his desk a photograph of the babe that had been born lacking arms and one eye. Baker's superior braced a knee against his desk and settled back to a judicial attitude. He took the photograph and looked at it impassively. "Yes," he said, after a time, "that's a pretty good thing. You better show that to Coleman when he comes in."

In the little office where the dismal band waited, there had been a sharp hopeful stir when Rufus Coleman, the Sunday editor, passed rapidly from door to door and vanished within the holy precincts. It had evidently been in the minds of some to accost him then, but his eyes did not turn once in their direction. It was as if he had not seen them. Many experiences had taught him that the proper manner of passing through this office was at a blind gallop.

The dismal band turned then upon the austere office boy. Some demanded with terrible dignity that he should take in their cards at once. Others sought to ingratiate themselves by smiles of tender friendliness. He for his part employed what we would have called his knowledge of men and women upon the group, and in consequence blundered and bungled vividly, freezing with a glance an annoyed and importunate Arctic explorer who was come to talk of illustrations for an article that had been lavishly paid for in advance. The hero might have thought he was again in the northern seas. At the next moment the boy was treating almost courteously a German from the cast side who wanted the Eclipse to print a grand full page advertising description of his invention, a gun which was supposed to have a range of forty miles and to be able to penetrate anything with equanimity and joy. The gun, as a matter of fact, had once been induced to go off when it had hurled itself passionately upon its back, incidentally breaking its inventor's leg. The projectile had wandered some four hundred yards seaward, where it dug a hole in the water which was really a menace to navigation. Since then there had been nothing tangible save the inventor, in splints and out of splints, as the fortunes of science decreed. In short, this office boy mixed his business in the perfect manner of an underdone lad dealing with matters too large for him, and throughout he displayed the pride and assurance of a god.

As Coleman crossed the large office his face still wore the stern expression which he invariably used to carry him unmolested through the ranks of the dismal band. As he was removing his London overcoat he addressed the imperturbable back of one of his staff, who had a desk against the opposite wall. "Has Hasskins sent in that drawing of the mine accident yet? "The man did not lift his head from his work-, but he answered at once: "No; not yet." Coleman was laying his hat on a chair. "Well, why hasn't he?" he demanded. He glanced toward the door of the room in which the curly-headed scoundrel with the corncob pipe was still hurling paper balls at the man who was trying to invent the postures of dead mariners frozen in the rigging. The office boy came timidly from his post and informed Coleman of the waiting people. "All right," said the editor. He dropped into his chair and began to finger his letters, which had been neatly opened and placed in a little stack by a boy. Baker came in with the photograph of the miserable babe.

It was publicly believed that the Sunday staff of the Eclipse must have a kind of aesthetic delight in pictures of this kind, but Coleman's face betrayed no emotion as he looked at this specimen. He lit a fresh cigar, tilted his chair and surveyed it with a cold and stony stare. "Yes, that's all right," he said slowly. There seemed to be no affectionate relation between him and this picture. Evidently he was weighing its value as a morsel to be flung to a ravenous public, whose wolf-like appetite, could only satisfy itself upon mental entrails, abominations. As for himself, he seemed to be remote, exterior. It was a matter of the Eclipse business.

Suddenly Coleman became executive. "Better give it to Schooner and tell him to make a half-page - or, no, send him in here and I'll tell him my idea. How's the article? Any good? Well, give it to Smith to rewrite."

An artist came from the other room and presented for inspection his drawing of the seamen dead in the rigging of the wreck, a company of grizzly and horrible figures, bony-fingered, shrunken and with awful eyes. "Hum," said Coleman, after a prolonged study, " that's all right. That's good, Jimmie. But you'd better work 'em up around the eyes a little more." The office boy was deploying in the distance, waiting for the correct moment to present some cards and names.

The artist was cheerfully taking away his corpses when Coleman hailed him. "Oh, Jim, let me see that thing again, will you? Now, how about this spar? This don't look right to me."

"It looks right to me," replied the artist, sulkily.

"But, see. It's going to take up half a page. Can't you change it somehow "

How am I going to change it?" said the other, glowe-ring at Coleman. "That's the way it ought to be. How am I going to change it? That's the way it ought to be."

"No, it isn't at all," said Coleman. "You've got a spar sticking out of the main body of the drawing in a way that will spoil the look of the whole page."

The artist was a man of remarkable popular reputation and he was very stubborn and conceited of it, constantly making himself unbearable with covert, threats that if he was not delicately placated at all points, he would freight his genius over to the office of the great opposition journal.

"That's the way it ought to be," he repeated, in a tone at once sullen and superior. "The spar is all right. I can't rig spars on ships just to suit you."

"And I can't give up the whole paper to your accursed spars, either," said Coleman, with animation. "Don't you see you use about a third of a page with this spar sticking off into space? Now, you were always so clever, Jimmie, in adapting yourself to the page. Can't you shorten it, or cut it off, or something? Or, break it- that's the thing. Make it a broken spar dangling down. See? "

"Yes, I s'pose I could do that," said the artist, mollified by a thought of the ease with which he could make the change, and mollified, too, by the brazen tribute to a part of his cleverness.

"Well, do it, then," said the Sunday editor, turning abruptly away. The artist, with head high, walked majestically back to the other room. Whereat the curly-headed one immediately resumed the rain of paper balls upon him. The office boy came timidly to Coleman and suggested the presence of the people in the outer office. "Let them wait until I read my mail," said Coleman. He shuffled the pack of letters indifferently through his hands. Suddenly he came upon a little grey envelope. He opened it at once and scanned its contents with the speed of his craft. Afterward he laid it down before him on the desk and surveyed it with a cool and musing smile. "So?" he remarked. "That's the case, is it?"

He presently swung around in his chair, and for a time held the entire attention of the men at the various desks. He outlined to them again their various parts in the composition of the next great Sunday edition. In a few brisk sentences he set a complex machine in proper motion. His men no longer thrilled with admiration at the precision with which he grasped each obligation of the campaign toward a successful edition. They had grown to accept it as they accepted his hat or his London clothes. At this time his face was lit with something of the self-contained enthusiasm of a general. Immediately afterward he arose and reached for his coat and hat.

The office boy, coming circuitously forward, presented him with some cards and also with a scrap of paper upon which was scrawled a long and semicoherent word. "What are these?" grumbled Coleman.

"They are waiting outside," answered the boy, with trepidation. It was part of the law that the lion of the ante-room should cringe like a cold monkey, more or less, as soon as he was out of his private jungle. "Oh, Tallerman," cried the Sunday editor, "here's this Arctic man come to arrange about his illustration. I wish you'd go and talk it over with him." By chance he picked up the scrap of paper with its cryptic word. "Oh," he said, scowling at the office boy. "Pity you can't remember that fellow. If you can't remember faces any better than that you should be a detective. Get out now and tell him to go to the devil." The wilted slave turned at once, but Coleman hailed him. "Hold on. Come to think of it, I will see this idiot. Send him in," he commanded, grimly.

Coleman lapsed into a dream over the sheet of grey note paper. Presently, a middle-aged man, a palpable German, came hesitatingly into the room and bunted among the desks as unmanageably as a tempest-tossed scow. Finally he was impatiently towed in the right direction. He came and stood at Coleman's elbow and waited nervously for the engrossed man to raise his eyes. It was plain that this interview meant important things to him. Somehow on his commonplace countenance was to be found the expression of a dreamer, a fashioner of great and absurd projects, a fine, tender fool. He cast hopeful and reverent glances at the man who was deeply contemplative of the grey note. He evidently believed himself on the threshold of a triumph of some kind, and he awaited his fruition with a joy that was only made sharper by the usual human suspicion of coming events.

Coleman glanced up at last and saw his visitor.

"Oh, it's you, is it?" he remarked icily, bending upon the German the stare of a tyrant. "So you've come again, have you?" He wheeled in his chair until he could fully display a contemptuous, merciless smile. "Now, Mr. What's-your-name, you've called here to see me about twenty times already and at last I am going to say something definite about your invention." His listener's face, which had worn for a moment a look of fright and bewilderment, gladdened swiftly to a gratitude that seemed the edge of an outburst of tears. "Yes," continued Coleman, "I am going to say something definite. I am going to say that it is the most imbecile bit of nonsense that has come within the range of my large newspaper experience. It is simply the aberration of a rather remarkable lunatic. It is no good; it is not worth the price of a cheese sandwich. I understand that its one feat has been to break your leg; if it ever goes off again, persuade it to break your neck. And now I want you to take this nursery rhyme of yours and get out. And don't ever come here again. Do You understand ? You understand, do you ?" He arose and bowed in courteous dismissal.

The German was regarding him with the surprise and horror of a youth shot mortally. He could not find his tongue for a moment. Ultimately he gasped: "But, Mister Editor" - Coleman interrupted him tigerishly. "You heard what I said? Get out." The man bowed his head and went slowly toward the door.

Coleman placed the little grey note in his breast pocket. He took his hat and top coat, and evading the dismal band by a shameless manoeuvre, passed through the halls to the entrance to the elevator shaft. He heard a movement behind him and saw that the German was also waiting for the elevator. Standing in the gloom of the corridor, Coleman felt the mournful owlish eyes of the German resting upon him. He took a case from his pocket and elaborately lit a cigarette. Suddenly there was a flash of light and a cage of bronze, gilt and steel dropped, magically from above. Coleman yelled: "Down!" A door flew open. Coleman, followed by the German, stepped upon the elevator. "Well, Johnnie," he said cheerfully to the lad who operated this machine, "is business good?" "Yes, sir, pretty good," answered the boy, grinning. The little cage sank swiftly; floor after floor seemed to be rising with marvellous speed; the whole building was winging straight into the sky. There were soaring lights, figures and the opalescent glow of ground glass doors marked with black inscriptions. Other lifts were springing heavenward. All the lofty corridors rang with cries. "Up!" "Down!" "Down!" "Up!" The boy's hand grasped a lever and his machine obeyed his lightest movement with sometimes an unbalancing swiftness.

Coleman discoursed briskly to the youthful attendant. Once he turned and regarded with a quick stare of insolent annoyance the despairing countenance of the German whose eyes had never left him. When the elevator arrived at the ground floor, Coleman departed with the outraged air of a man who for a time had been compelled to occupy a cell in company with a harmless spectre.

He walked quickly away. Opposite a corner of the City Hall he was impelled to look behind him. Through the hordes of people with cable cars marching like panoplied elephants, he was able to distinguish the German, motionless and gazing after him. Coleman laughed. "That's a comic old boy," he said, to himself.

In the grill-room of a Broadway hotel he was obliged to wait some minutes for the fulfillment of his orders and he spent the time in reading and studying the little grey note. When his luncheon was served he ate with an expression of morose dignity.

CHAPTER IV

MARJORY paused again at her father's door. After hesitating in the original way she entered the library. Her father almost represented an emblematic figure, seated upon a column of books. "Well," he cried. Then, seeing it was Marjory, he changed his tone. "Ah, under the circumstances, my dear, I admit your privilege of interrupting me at any hour of the day. You have important business with me." His manner was satanically indulgent.

The girl fingered a book. She turned the leaves in absolute semblance of a person reading. "Rufus Coleman called."

"Indeed," said the professor.

"And I've come to you, father, before seeing him."

The professor was silent for a time. "Well, Marjory," he said at last, "what do you want me to say?" He spoke very deliberately. "I am sure this is a singular situation. Here appears the man I formally forbid you to marry. I am sure I do not know what I am to say."

"I wish to see him," said the girl.

"You wish to see him?" enquired the professor. "You

wish to see him "Marjory, I may as well tell you now that with all the books and plays I've read, I really don't know how the obdurate father should conduct himself. He is always pictured as an exceedingly dense gentleman with white whiskers, who does all the unintelligent things in the plot. You and I are going to play no drama, are we, Marjory? I admit that I have white whiskers, and I am an obdurate father. I am, as you well may say, a very obdurate father. You are not to marry Rufus Coleman. You understand the rest of the matter. He is here ; you want to see him. What will you say to him when you see him? "

"I will say that you refuse to let me marry him, father and -" She hesitated a moment before she lifted her eyes fully and formidably to her father's face. "And that I shall marry him anyhow."

The professor did not cavort when this statement came from his daughter. He nodded and then passed into a period of reflection. Finally he asked: "But when? That is the point. When?"

The girl made a sad gesture. "I don't know. I don't know. Perhaps when you come to know Rufus better -"

"Know him better. Know that rapscallion better? Why, I know him much better than he knows himself. I know him too well. Do you think I am talking offhand about this affair? Do you think I am talking without proper information?"

Marjory made no reply.

"Well," said the professor, "you may see Coleman on condition that you inform him at once that I forbid your marriage to him. I don't understand at all how to manage these situations. I don't know what to do. I suppose I should go myself and - No, you can't see him, Majory."

Still the girl made no reply. Her head sank forward and she breathed a trifle heavily. "Marjory," cried the professor, it is impossible that you should think so much of this man." He arose and went to his daughter. "Marjory, many wise children have been guided by foolish fathers, but we both suspect that no foolish child has ever been guided by a wise father. Let us change it. I present myself to you as a wise father. Follow my wishes in this affair and you will be at least happier than if you marry this wretched Coleman."

She answered: "He is waiting for me."

The professor turned abruptly from her and dropped into his chair at the table. He resumed a grip on his pen. "Go," he said, wearily. "Go. But if you have a remnant of sense, remember what I have said to you. Go" He waved his hand in a dismissal that was slightly scornful. "I hoped you would have a minor conception of what you were doing. It seems a pity." Drooping in tears, the girl slowly left the room.

Coleman had an idea that he had occupied the chair for several months. He gazed about at the pictures and the odds and ends of a drawing-room in an attempt to take an interest in them. The great garlanded paper shade over the piano lamp consoled his impatience in a mild degree because he knew that Marjory had made it. He noted the clusters of cloth violets which she had pinned upon the yellow paper and he dreamed over the fact. He was able to endow this shade with certain qualities of sentiment that caused his stare to become almost a part of an intimacy, a communion. He looked as if he could have unburdened his soul to this shade over the piano lamp.

Upon the appearance of Marjory he sprang up and came forward rapidly. "Dearest," he murmured, stretching out both hands. She gave him one set of fingers with chilling convention. She said something which he understood to be "Good-afternoon." He started as if the woman before him had suddenly drawn a knife. "Marjory," he cried, "what is the matter?" They walked together toward a window. The girl looked at him in polite enquiry. "Why?" she said. "Do I seem strange?" There was a moment's silence while he gazed into her eyes, eyes full of innocence and tranquillity. At last she tapped her foot upon the floor in expression of mild impatience. "People do not like to be asked what is the matter when there is nothing the matter. What do you mean ?"

Coleman's face had gradually hardened. " Well, what is wrong?" he demanded, abruptly. "What has happened? What is it, Marjory ? "

She raised her glance in a perfect reality of wonder. "What is wrong? What has happened? How absurd! Why nothing, of course." She gazed out of the window. "Look," she added, brightly, the students are rolling somebody in a drift. Oh, the poor Man!"

Coleman, now wearing a bewildered air, made some pretense of being occupied with the scene. "Yes," he said, ironically. "Very interesting, indeed."

"Oh," said Marjory, suddenly, "I forgot to tell you.

Father is going to take mother and me to Greece this winter with him and the class."

Coleman replied at once. "Ah, indeed ? That will be jolly."

"Yes. Won't it be charming?"

"I don't doubt it," he replied. His composure May have displeased her, for she glanced at him furtively and in a way that denoted surprise, perhaps.

"Oh, of course," she said, in a glad voice. "It will be more fun. We expect to nave a fine time. There is such a n ice lot of boys going Sometimes father chooses these dreadfully studious ones. But this time he acts as if he knew precisely how to make up a party."

He reached for her hand and grasped it vise-like. "Marjory," he breathed, passionately, "don't treat me so. Don't treat me -"

She wrenched her hand from him in regal indignation. "One or two rings make it uncomfortable for the hand that is grasped by an angry gentleman." She held her fingers and gazed as if she expected to find them mere debris. "I am sorry that you are not interested in the students rolling that man in the snow. It is the greatest scene our quiet life can afford."

He was regarding her as a judge faces a lying culprit. "I know," he said, after a pause. "Somebody has been telling you some stories. You have been hearing something about me."

"Some stories ?" she enquired. "Some stories about

you? What do you mean? Do you mean that I remember stories I may happen to hear about people?"

There was another pause and then Coleman's face flared red. He beat his hand violently upon a table. "Good God, Marjory! Don't make a fool of me. Don't make this kind of a fool of me, at any rate. Tell me what you mean. Explain -"

She laughed at him. "Explain? Really, your vocabulary is getting extensive, but it is dreadfully awkward to ask people to explain when there is nothing to explain."

He glanced at her, " I know as well as you do that your father is taking you to Greece in order to get rid of me."

"And do people have to go to Greece in order to get rid of you?" she asked, civilly. "I think you are getting excited."

"Marjory," he began, stormily. She raised her hand. "Hush," she said, "there is somebody coming." A bell had rung. A maid entered the room. "Mr. Coke," she said. Marjory nodded. In the interval of waiting, Coleman gave the girl a glance that mingled despair with rage and pride. Then Coke burst with half-tamed rapture into the room. "Oh, Miss Wainwright," he almost shouted, "I can't tell you how glad I am. I just heard to-day you were going. Imagine it. It will be more - oh, how are you Coleman, how are you"

Marjory welcomed the new-comer with a cordiality that might not have thrilled Coleman with pleasure. They took chairs that formed a triangle and one side of it vibrated with talk. Coke and Marjory engaged in a tumultuous conversation concerning the prospective trip to Greece. The Sunday editor, as remote as if the apex of his angle was the top of a hill, could only study the girl's clear profile. The youthful voices of the two others rang like bells. He did not scowl at Coke; he merely looked at him as if be gently disdained his mental calibre. In fact all the talk seemed to tire him; it was childish; as for him, he apparently found this babble almost insupportable.

"And, just think of the camel rides we'll have," cried Coke.

"Camel rides," repeated Coleman, dejectedly. "My dear Coke."

Finally he arose like an old man climbing from a sick bed. "Well, I am afraid I must go, Miss Wainwright." Then he said affectionately to Coke: "Good-bye, old boy. I hope you will have a good time."

Marjory walked with him to the door. He shook her hand in a friendly fashion. "Good-bye, Marjory,' he said. "Perhaps it may happen that I shan't see you again before you start for Greece and so I had best bid you God-speed - or whatever the term is now. You will have a charming time; Greece must be a delightful place. Really, I envy you, Marjory. And now my dear child "- his voice grew brotherly, filled with the patronage of generous fraternal love, "although I may never see you again let me wish you fifty as happy years as this last one has been for me." He smiled frankly into her eyes; then dropping her hand, he went away.

Coke renewed his tempest of talk as Marjory turned

toward him. But after a series of splendid eruptions, whose red fire illumined all of ancient and modem Greece, he too went away.

The professor was in his. library apparently absorbed in a book when a tottering pale-faced woman appeared to him and, in her course toward a couch in a corner of the room, described almost a semi-circle. She flung herself face downward. A thick strand of hair swept over her shoulder. "Oh, my heart is broken! My heart is broken!"

The professor arose, grizzled and thrice-old with pain. He went to the couch, but he found himself a handless, fetless man. "My poor child," he said. "My poor child." He remained listening stupidly to her convulsive sobbing. A ghastly kind of solemnity came upon the room.

Suddenly the girl lifted herself and swept the strand of hair away from her face. She looked at the professor with the wide-open dilated eyes of one who still sleeps. "Father," she said in a hollow voice, "he don't love me. He don't love me. He don't love me. at all. You were right, father." She began to laugh.

"Marjory," said the professor, trembling. "Be quiet, child. Be quiet."

"But," she said, " I thought he loved me - I was sure of it. But it don't - don't matter. I - I can't get over it. Women-women, the-but it don't matter."

"Marjory," said the professor. "Marjory, my poor daughter."

She did not heed his appeal, but continued in a dull whisper. "He was playing with me. He was - was-was flirting with me. He didn't care when I told him - I told him - I was going-going away." She turned her face wildly to the cushions again. Her young shoulders shook as if they might break. "Wo-men - women - they always -"

CHAPTER V

By a strange mishap of management the train which bore Coleman back toward New York was fetched into an obscure side-track of some lonely region and there compelled to bide a change of fate. The engine wheezed and sneezed like a paused fat man. The lamps in the cars pervaded a stuffy odor of smoke and oil. Coleman examined his case and found only one cigar. Important brakemen proceeded rapidly along the aisles, and when they swung open the doors, a polar wind circled the legs of the passengers. "Well, now, what is all this for? " demanded Coleman, furiously. "I want to get back to New York."

The conductor replied with sarcasm, "Maybe you think I'm stuck on it". I ain't running the road. I'm running this train, and I run it according to orders." Amid the dismal comforts of the waiting cars, Coleman felt all the profound misery of the rebuffed true lover. He had been sentenced, he thought, to a penal servitude of the heart, as he watched the dusky, vague ribbons of smoke come from the lamps and felt to his knees the cold winds from the brakemen's busy flights. When the train started with a whistle and a jolt, he was elate as if in his abjection his beloved's hand had reached to him from the clouds.

When he had arrived in New York, a cab rattled him to

an uptown hotel with speed. In the restaurant he first ordered a large bottle of champagne. The last of the wine he finished in sombre mood like an unbroken and defiant man who chews the straw that litters his prison house. During his dinner he was continually sending out messenger boys. He was arranging a poker party. Through a window he watched the beautiful moving life of upper Broadway at night, with its crowds and clanging cable cars and its electric signs, mammoth and glittering, like the jewels of a giantess.

Word was brought to him that the poker players were arriving. He arose joyfully, leaving his cheese. In the broad hall, occupied mainly by miscellaneous people and actors, all deep in leather chairs, he found some of his friends waiting. They trooped up stairs to Coleman's rooms, where as a preliminary, Coleman began to hurl books and papers from the table to the floor. A boy came with drinks. Most of the men, in order to prepare for the game, removed their coats and cuffs and drew up the sleeves of their shirts. The electric globes shed a blinding light upon the table. The sound of clinking chips arose; the elected banker spun the cards, careless and dexterous.

Later, during a pause of dealing, Coleman said: "Billie, what kind of a lad is that young Coke up at Washurst?" He addressed an old college friend.

"Oh, you mean the Sophomore Coke?" asked the friend. "Seems a decent sort of a fellow. I don't know. Why? "

"Well, who is he? Where does he come from? What do you know about him?"

"He's one of those Ohio Cokes - regular thing - father millionaire-used to be a barber-good old boy -why?"

"Nothin'," said Coleman, looking at his cards. "I know the lad. I thought he was a good deal of an ass. I wondered who his people were."

"Oh, his people are all right-in one way. Father owns rolling mills. Do you raise it, Henry? Well, in order to make vice abhorrent to the young, I'm obliged to raise back."

"I'll see it," observed Coleman, slowly pushing forward two blue chips. Afterward he reached behind him and took another glass of wine.

To the others Coleman seemed to have something bitter upon his mind. He played poker quietly, steadfastly, and, without change of eye, following the mathematical religion of the game. Outside of the play he was savage, almost insupportable. "What's the matter with you, Rufus?" said his old college friend. "Lost your job? Girl gone back on you? You're a hell of - a host. We don't get any. thing but insults and drinks."

Late at night Coleman began to lose steadily. In the meantime he drank glass after glass of wine. Finally he made reckless bets on a mediocre hand and an opponent followed him thoughtfully bet by bet, undaunted, calm, absolutely without emotion. Coleman lost; he hurled down his cards. "Nobody but a damned fool would have seen that last raise on anything less than a full hand."

"Steady. Come off. What's wrong with you, Rufus?"

Stephen Crane

cried his guests.

"You're not drunk, are you?" said his old college friend, puritanically.

"'Drunk' ?" repeated Coleman.

"Oh, say," cried a man, "let's play cards. What's all this gabbling ? "

It was when a grey, dirty light of dawn evaded the thick curtains and fought on the floor with the feebled electric glow that Coleman, in the midst of play, lurched his chest heavily upon the table. Some chips rattled to the floor. "I'll call you," he murmured, sleepily.

"Well," replied a man, sternly, " three kings."

The other players with difficulty extracted five cards from beneath Coleman's pillowed head. "Not a pair! Come, come, this won't do. Oh, let's stop playing. This is the rottenest game I ever sat in. Let's go home. Why don't you put him. to bed, Billie?"

When Coleman awoke next morning, he looked back upon the poker game as something that had transpired in previous years. He dressed and went down to the grill-room. For his breakfast he ordered some eggs on toast and a pint of champagne. A privilege of liberty belonged to a certain Irish waiter, and this waiter looked at him, grinning. "Maybe you had a pretty lively time last night, Mr Coleman? "

"Yes, Pat," answered Coleman, "I did. It was all because of an unrequited affection, Patrick." The man stood near, a napkin over his arm. Coleman went on impressively. "The ways of the modern lover are strange. Now, I, Patrick, am a modern lover, and when, yesterday, the dagger of disappointment was driven deep into my heart, I immediately played poker as hard as I could and incidentally got loaded. This is the modern point of view. I understand on good authority that in old times lovers used to. languish. That is probably a lie, but at any rate we do not, in these times, languish to any great extent. We get drunk. Do you understand, Patrick? "The waiter was used to a harangue at Coleman's breakfast time. He placed his hand over his mouth and giggled. "Yes sir."

"Of course," continued Coleman, thoughtfully. "It might be pointed out by uneducated persons that it is difficult to maintain a high standard of drunkenness for the adequate length of time, but in the series of experiments which I am about to make I am sure I can easily prove them to be in the wrong."

"I am sure, sir," said the waiter, " the young ladies would not like to be hearing you talk this way."

"Yes; no doubt, no doubt. The young ladies have still quite medieval ideas. They don't understand. They still prefer lovers to languish."

"At any rate, sir, I don't see that your heart is sure enough broken. You seem to take it very easy. "

"Broken! " cried Coleman. " Easy? Man, my heart is in fragments. Bring me another small bottle."

CHAPTER VI

Six weeks later, Coleman went to the office of the proprietor of the Eclipse. Coleman was one of those smooth-shaven old-young men who wear upon some occasions a singular air of temperance and purity. At these times, his features lost their quality of worldly shrewdness and endless suspicion and bloomed as the face of some innocent boy. It then would be hard to tell that he had ever encountered even such a crime as a lie or a cigarette. As he walked into the proprietor's office he was a perfect semblance of a fine, inexperienced youth. People usually concluded this change was due to a Turkish bath or some other expedient of recuperation, but it was due probably to the power of a physical characteristic.

"Boss in?" said Coleman.

"Yeh," said the secretary, jerking his thumb toward an inner door. In his private office, Sturgeon sat on the edge of the table dangling one leg and dreamily surveying the wall. As Coleman entered he looked up quickly. "Rufus," he cried, "you're just the man I wanted to see. I've got a scheme. A great scheme."He slid from the table and began to pace briskly to and fro, his hands deep in his trousers' pockets, his chin sunk in his collar, his light blue eyes afire with interest. " Now listen. This is immense. The Eclipse enlists a battalion of men to go to Cuba and fight the Spaniards under its own flag-the Eclipse flag. Collect trained officers from here and there enlist every young devil we see-drill 'em - best rifles-loads of ammunition-provisions-staff of doctors and nurses -a couple of dynamite guns- everything complete best in the world. Now, isn't that great ? What's the matter with that now ? Eh? Eh? Isn't that great? It's great, isn't it? Eh? Why, my boy, we'll free -"

Coleman did not seem to ignite. "I have been arrested four or five times already on fool matters connected with the newspaper business," he observed, gloomily, "but I've never yet been hung. I think your scheme is a beauty."

Sturgeon paused in astonishment. "Why, what happens to be the matter with you ? What are you kicking about ?"

Coleman made a slow gesture. "I'm tired," he answered. " I need a vacation."

"Vacation!" cried Sturgeon. "Why don't you take one then?"

"That's what I've come to see you about. I've had a pretty heavy strain on me for three years now, and I want to get a little rest."

"Well, who in thunder has been keeping you from it? It hasn't been me."

"I know it hasn't been you, but, of course, I wanted the paper to go and I wanted to have my share in its success, but now that everything is all right I think I might go away for a time if you don't mind."

"Mind!" exclaimed Sturgeon falling into his chair and reaching for his check book. "Where do you want to go? How long do you want to be gone? How much money do you want ?"

"I don't want very much. And as for where I want to go, I thought I might like to go to Greece for a while."

Sturgeon had been writing a check. He poised his pen in the air and began to laugh. " That's a queer place to go for a rest. Why, the biggest war of modern times - a war that may involve all Europe-is likely to start there at any moment. You are not likely to get any rest in Greece."

"I know that," answered Coleman. "I know there is likely to be a war there. But I think that is exactly what would rest me. I would like to report the war."

"You are a queer bird," answered Sturgeon deeply fascinated with this new idea. He had apparently forgotten his vision of a Cuban volunteer battalion. "War correspondence is about the most original medium for a rest I ever heard of."

"Oh, it may seem funny, but really, any change will be good for me now. I've been whacking at this old Sunday edition until I'm sick of it, and some,. times I wish the Eclipse was in hell."

That's all right," laughed the proprietor of the Eclipse. "But I still don't see how you 'are going to get any vacation out of a war that will upset the whole of Europe. But that's your affair. If you want to become the chief correspondent in the field in case of any such war, why, of course, I would be glad to have you. I couldn't get anybody better. But I don't see where your vacation comes in."

"I'll take care of that," answered Coleman. "When I take a vacation I want to take it my own way, and I think this will be a vacation because it will be different - don't you see - different?"

"No, I don't see any sense in it, but if you think that is the way that suits you, why, go ahead. How much money do you want ? "

"I don't want much. just enough to see me through nicely."

Sturgeon scribbled on his check book and then ripped a check from it. "Here's a thousand dollars. Will that do you to start with?"

"That's plenty."

"When do you want to start ?"

"To-morrow."

"Oh," said Sturgeon. "You're in a hurry." This impetuous manner of exit from business seemed to appeal to him. "To-morrow," he repeated smiling. In reality he was some kind of a poet using his millions romantically, spending wildly on a sentiment that might be with beauty or without beauty, according to the momentary vacillation. The vaguely-defined desperation in Coleman's last announcement appeared to delight him. He grinned and placed the points of his fingers together stretching out his legs in a careful attitude of indifference which might even mean disapproval. "To-morrow," he murmured teasingly.

"By jiminy," exclaimed Coleman, ignoring the other man's mood, "I'm sick of the whole business. I've got out a Sunday paper once a week for three years and I feel absolutely incapable of getting out another edition. It would be all right if we were running on ordinary lines, but when each issue is more or less of an attempt to beat the previous issue, it becomes rather wearing, you know. If I can't get a vacation now I take one later in a lunatic asylum."

"Why, I'm not objecting to your having a vacation. I'm simply marvelling at the kind of vacation you want to take. And 'to-morrow,' too, eh?" "Well, it suits me," muttered Coleman, sulkily.

"Well, if it suits you, that's enough. Here's your check. Clear out now and don't let me see you again until you are thoroughly rested, even if it takes a year." He arose and stood smiling. He was mightily pleased with himself. He liked to perform in this way. He was almost seraphic as he thrust the check for a thousand dollars toward Coleman.

Then his manner changed abruptly. "Hold on a minute. I must think a little about this thing if you are going to manage the correspondence. Of course it will be a long and bloody war."

"You bet."

"The big chance is that all Europe will be dragged into it. Of course then you would have to come out of

Greece and take up abetter position-say Vienna."

"No, I wouldn't care to do that," said Coleman positively. "I just want to take care of the Greek end of it."

"It will be an idiotic way to take a vacation," observed Sturgeon.

"Well, it suits me," muttered Coleman again. "I tell you what it is -" he added suddenly. "I've got some private reasons - see?"

Sturgeon was radiant with joy. "Private reasons." He was charmed by the sombre pain in Coleman's eyes and his own ability to eject it. "Good. Go now and be blowed. I will cable final instruction to meet you in London. As soon as you get to Greece, cable me an account of the situation there and we will arrange our plans." He began to laugh. " Private reasons. Come out to dinner with me."

"I can't very well," said Coleman. "If I go tomorrow, I've got to pack -"

But here the real tyrant appeared, emerging suddenly from behind the curtain of sentiment, appearing like a red devil in a pantomine. "You can't?" snapped Sturgeon. "Nonsense -"

CHAPTER VII

SWEEPING out from between two remote, half-submerged dunes on which stood slender sentry light. houses, the steamer began to roll with a gentle insinuating motion. Passengers in their staterooms saw at rhythmical intervals the spray racing fleetly past the portholes. The waves grappled hurriedly at the sides of the great flying steamer and boiled discomfited astern in a turmoil of green and white. From the tops of the enormous funnels streamed level masses of smoke which were immediately torn to nothing by the headlong wind. Meanwhile as the steamer rushed into the northeast, men in caps and ulsters comfortably paraded the decks and stewards arranged deck chairs for the reception of various women who were coming from their cabins with rugs.

In the smoking room, old voyagers were settling down comfortably while new voyagers were regarding them with a diffident respect. Among the passengers Coleman found a number of people whom he knew, including a wholesale wine merchant, a Chicago railway magnate and a New York millionaire. They lived practically in the smoking room. Necessity drove them from time to time to the salon, or to their berths. Once indeed the millionaire was absent, from the group while penning a short note to his wife.

When the Irish coast was sighted Coleman came on deck to look at it. A tall young woman immediately halted in her walk until he had stepped up to her. "Well, of all ungallant men, Rufus Coleman, you are the star," she cried laughing and held out her hand.

"Awfully sorry, I'm sure," he murmured. "Been playing poker in the smoking room all voyage. Didn't have a look at the passenger list until just now. Why didn't you send me word?" These lies were told so modestly and sincerely that when the girl flashed her, brilliant eyes full upon their author there was a mixt of admiration in the indignation.

"Send you a card " I don't believe you can read, else you would have known I was to sail on this steamer. If I hadn't been ill until to-day you would have seen me in the salon. I open at the Folly Theatre next week. Dear ol' Lunnon, y' know."

"Of course, I knew you were going," said Coleman. "But I thought you were to go later. What do you open in?"

"Fly by Night. Come walk along with me. See those two old ladies "They've been watching for me like hawks ever since we left New York. They expected me to flirt with every man on board. But I've fooled them. I've been just as g-o-o-d. I had to be."

As the pair moved toward the stern, enormous and radiant green waves were crashing futilely after the steamer. Ireland showed a dreary coast line to the north. A wretched man who had crossed the Atlantic eighty-four times was declaiming to a group of novices. A venerable banker, bundled in rugs, was asleep in his deck chair.

"Well, Nora," said Coleman, "I hope you make a hit in London. You deserve it if anybody does. You've worked hard."

"Worked hard," cried the girl. "I should think so. Eight years ago I was in the rear row. Now I have the centre of the stage whenever I want it. I made Chalmers cut out that great scene in the second act between the queen and Rodolfo. The idea! Did he think I would stand that ? And just because he was in love with Clara Trotwood, too."

Coleman was dreamy. "Remember when I was dramatic man for the Gazette and wrote the first notice ?"

"Indeed, I do," answered the girl affectionately. "Indeed, I do, Rufus. Ah, that was a great lift. I believe that was the first thing that had an effect on old Oliver. Before that, he never would believe that I was any good. Give me your arm, Rufus. Let's parade before the two old women." Coleman glanced at her keenly. Her voice had trembled slightly. Her eyes were lustrous as if she were about to weep.

"Good heavens," he said. "You are the same old Nora Black. I thought you would be proud and 'aughty by this time."

"Not to my friends," she murmured., "Not to my friends. I'm always the same and I never forget. Rufus."

"Never forget what? " asked Coleman.

"If anybody does me a favour I never forget it as long as I live," she answered fervently.

"Oh, you mustn't be so sentimental, Nora. You remember that play you bought from little Ben Whipple, just because he had once sent you some flowers in the old days when you were poor and happened to bed sick. A sense of gratitude cost you over eight thousand dollars that time, didn't it?" Coleman laughed heartily.

"Oh, it wasn't the flowers at all," she interrupted seriously. "Of course Ben was always a nice boy, but then his play was worth a thousand dollars. That's all I gave him. I lost some more in trying to make it go. But it was too good. That was what was the matter. It was altogether too good for the public. I felt awfully sorry for poor little Ben."

"Too good?" sneered Coleman. "Too good? Too indifferently bad, you mean. My dear girl, you mustn't imagine that you know a good play. You don't, at all."

She paused abruptly and faced him. This regal, creature was looking at him so sternly that Coleman felt awed for a moment as if he, were in the presence of a great mind. "Do you mean to say that I'm not an artist?" she asked.

Coleman remained cool. "I've never been decorated for informing people of their own affairs," he observed, "but I should say that you were about as much of an artist as I am."

Frowning slightly, she reflected upon this reply. Then, of a sudden, she laughed. "There is no use in being angry with you, Rufus. You always were a hopeless scamp. But," she added, childishly wistful, "have you ever seen Fly by Night? Don't you think my dance in the second act is artistic?"

"No," said Coleman, "I haven't seen Fly by Night yet, but of course I know that you are the most beautiful dancer on the stage. Everybody knows that."

It seemed that her hand tightened on his arm. Her face was radiant. "There," she exclaimed. "Now you are forgiven. You are a nice boy, Rufus - sometimes."

When Miss Black went to her cabin, Coleman strolled into the smoking room. Every man there covertly or openly surveyed him. He dropped lazily into a chair at a table where the wine merchant, the Chicago railway king and the New York millionaire were playing cards. They made a noble pretense of not being aware of him. On the oil cloth top of the table the cards were snapped down, turn by turn.

Finally the wine merchant, without lifting his head to address a particular person, said: "New conquest."

Hailing a steward Coleman asked for a brandy and soda.

The millionaire said: "He's a sly cuss, anyhow." The railway man grinned. After an elaborate silence the wine merchant asked: "Know Miss Black long, Rufus?" Coleman looked scornfully at his friends. "What's wrong with you there, fellows, anyhow?" The Chicago man answered airily. "Oh, nothin'. Nothin', whatever."

At dinner in the crowded salon, Coleman was aware that more than one passenger glanced first at Nora Black and then at him, as if connecting them in some train of thought, moved to it by the narrow horizon of shipboard and by a sense of the mystery that surrounds the lives of the beauties of the stage. Near the captain's right hand sat the glowing and splendid Nora, exhibiting under the gaze of the persistent eyes of many meanings, a practiced and profound composure that to the populace was terrfying dignity.

Strolling toward the smoking room after dinner, Coleman met the New York millionaire, who seemed agitated. He took Coleman fraternally by the arm. "Say, old man, introduce me, won't you ? I'm crazy to know her."

"Do you mean Miss Black?" asked Coleman.

"Why, I don't know that I have a right. Of course, you know, she hasn't been meeting anybody aboard. I'll ask her, though - certainly."

"Thanks, old man, thanks. I'd be tickled to death. Come along and have a drink. When will you ask her?" "Why, I don't know when I'll see her. To-morrow, I suppose -"

They had not been long in the smoking room, however, when the deck steward came with a card to Coleman. Upon it was written: "Come for' a stroll?" Everybody, saw Coleman read this card and then look up and whisper to the deck steward. The deck steward bent his head and whispered discreetly in reply. There was an abrupt pause in the hum of conversation. The interest was acute.

Coleman leaned carelessly back in his chair, puffing at his cigar. He mingled calmly in a discussion of the comparative merits of certain trans-Atlantic lines. After a time he threw away his cigar and arose. Men nodded. "Didn't I tell you?" His studiously languid exit was made dramatic by the eagle-eyed attention of the smoking room.

On deck he found Nora pacing to and fro. "You didn't hurry yourself," she said, as he joined her. The lights of Queenstown were twinkling. A warm wind, wet with the moisture of rain-stricken sod, was coming from the land.

"Why," said Coleman, "we've got all these duffers very much excited."

"Well what do you care?" asked hte girl. "You don't, care do you?"

"No, I don't care. Only it's rather absurd to be watched all the time." He said this precisely as if he abhorred being watched in this case. "Oh by the way," he added. Then he paused for a moment. "Aw - a friend of mine - not a bad fellow - he asked me for an introduction. Of course, I told him I'd ask you."

She made a contemptuous gesture. "Oh, another Willie. Tell him no. Tell him to go home to his family. Tell him to run away."

"He isn't a bad fellow. He - " said Coleman diffidently, "he would probably be at the theatre every night in a box."

"Yes, and get drunk and throw a wine bottle on the

stage instead of a bouquet. No," she declared positively, "I won't see him."

Coleman did not seem to be oppressed by this ultimatum. "Oh, all right. I promised him - that was all."

"Besides, are you in a great hurry to get rid of me?"

"Rid of you? Nonsense."

They walked in the shadow. "How long are you going to be in London, Rufus?" asked Nora softly.

"Who? I? Oh, I'm going right off to Greece. First train. There's going to be a war, you know."

"A war? Why, who is going to fight? The Greeks and the - the - the what?"

"The Turks. I'm going right over there."

"Why, that's dreadful, Rufus," said the girl, mournfull and shocked. "You might get hurt or something." Presently she asked: "And aren't you going to be in London any time at all?"

"Oh," he answered, puffing out his lips, "I may stop in Londom for three or four days on my way home. I'm not sure of it."

"And when will that be?"

"Oh, I can't tell. It may be in three or four months, or it may be a year from now. When the war stops."

There was a long silence as the walked up and down the swaying deck.

"Do you know," said Nora at last, "I like you, Rufus Coleman. I don't know any good reason for it either, unless it is because you are such a brute. Now, when I was asking you if you were to be in London you were perfectly detestable. You know I was anxious."

"I - detestable?" cried Coleman, feigning amazement. "Why, what did I say?"

"It isn't so much what you said -" began Nora slowlly. Then she suddenly changed her manner. "Oh, well, don't let's talk about it any more. It's too foolish. Only-you are a disagreeable person sometimes."

In the morning, as the vessel steamed up the Irish channel, Coleman was on deck, keeping furtive watch on the cabin stairs. After two hours of waiting, he scribbled a message on a card and sent it below. He received an answer that Miss Black had a headache, and felt too ill to come on deck. He went to the smoking room. The three card-players glanced up, grinning. "What's the matter?" asked the wine merchant. "You look angry." As a matter of fact, Coleman had purposely wreathed his features in a pleasant and satisfied expression, so he was for a moment furious at the wine merchant.

"Confound the girl," he thought to himself. "She has succeeded in making all these beggars laugh at me." He mused that if he had another chance he would show her how disagreeable or detestable or scampish he was under some circumstances. He reflected ruefully that the complacence with which he had accepted the comradeship of the belle of the voyage might have been somewhat overdone. Perhaps he had got a little out of proportion. He was annoyed at the stares of the other men in the smoking room, who seemed now to be reading his discomfiture. As for Nora Black he thought of her wistfully and angrily as a superb woman whose company was honour and joy, a payment for any sacrifices.

"What's the matter?" persisted the wine merchant. "You look grumpy." Coleman laughed. "Do I?"

At Liverpool, as the steamer was being slowly warped to the landing stage by some tugs, the passengers crowded the deck with their hand-bags. Adieus were falling as dead leaves fall from a great tree. The stewards were handling small hills of luggage marked with flaming red labels. The ship was firmly against the dock before Miss Black came from her cabin. Coleman was at the time gazing shoreward, but his three particular friends instantly nudged him. "What?" "There she is?" "Oh, Miss Black?" He composedly walked toward her. It was impossible to tell whether she saw him coming or whether it was accident, but at any rate she suddenly turned and moved toward the stern of the ship. Ten watchful gossips had noted Coleman's travel in her direction and more than half the passengers noted his defeat. He wheeled casually and returned to his three friends. They were colic-stricken with a coarse and yet silent merriment. Coleman was glad that the voyage was over.

After the polite business of an English custom house, the travellers passed out to the waiting train. A nimble little theatrical agent of some kind, sent from London, dashed forward to receive Miss Black. He had a first-class compartment engaged for her and he bundled her and her maid into it in an exuberance of enthusiasm and admiration. Coleman passing moodily along the line of coaches heard Nora's voice hailing him.

"Rufus." There she was, framed in a carriage window, beautiful and smiling brightly. Every near. by person turned to contemplate this vision.

"Oh," said Coleman advancing, "I thought I was not going to get a chance to say good-bye to you." He held out his hand. "Good-bye."

She pouted. "Why, there's plenty of room in this compartment." Seeing that some forty people were transfixed in observation of her, she moved a short way back. "Come on in this compartment, Rufus," she said.

"Thanks. I prefer to smoke," said Coleman. He went off abruptly.

On the way to London, he brooded in his corner on the two divergent emotions he had experienced when refusing her invitation. At Euston Station in London, he was directing a porter, who had his luggage, when he heard Nora speak at his shoulder. "Well, Rufus, you sulky boy," she said, "I shall be at the Cecil. If you have time, come and see me."

"Thanks, I'm sure, my dear Nora," answered Coleman effusively. "But honestly, I'm off for Greece."

A brougham was drawn up near them and the nimble little agent was waiting. The maid was directing the establishment of a mass of luggage on and in a four-wheeler cab. "Well, put me into my carriage, anyhow," said Nora. "You will have time for that."

Afterward she addressed him from the dark interior. Now, Rufus, you must come to see me the minute you strike London again - of She hesitated a moment and then smiling gorgeously upon him, she said: "Brute!"

CHAPTER VIII

As soon as Coleman had planted his belongings in a hotel he was bowled in a hansom briskly along the smoky Strand, through a dark city whose walls dripped like the walls of a cave and whose passages were only illuminated by flaring yellow and red signs.

Walkley the London correspondent of the Eclipse, whirled from his chair with a shout of joy and relief - at sight of Coleman. "Cables," he cried. "Nothin' but cables! All the people in New York are writing cables to you. The wires groan with them. And we groan with them too. They come in here in bales. However, there is no reason why you should read them all. Many are similar in words and many more are similar in spirit. The sense of the whole thing is that you get to Greece quickly, taking with you immense sums of money and enormous powers over nations."

"Well, when does the row begin?"

"The most astute journalists in Europe have been predicting a general European smash-up every year since 1878," said Walkley, "and the prophets weep. The English are the only people who can pull off wars on schedule time, and they have to do it in odd corners of the globe. I fear the war business is getting tuckered. There is sorrow in the lodges of the lone wolves, the war correspondents. However, my boy, don't bury your face in your blanket. This Greek business looks very promising, very promising." He then began to proclaim trains and connections. "Dover, Calais, Paris, Brindisi, Corfu, Patras, Athens. That is your game. You are supposed to sky-rocket yourself over that route in the shortest possible time, but you would gain no time by starting before to-morrow, so you can cool your heels here in London until then. I wish I was going along."

Coleman returned to his hotel, a knight impatient and savage at being kept for a time out of the saddle. He went for a late supper to the grill room and as he was seated there alone, a party of four or five people came to occupy the table directly behind him. They talked a great deal even before they arrayed them. selves at the table, and he at once recognised the voice of Nora Black. She was queening it, apparently, over a little band of awed masculine worshippers.

Either by accident or for some curious reason, she took a chair back to back with Coleman's chair. Her sleeve of fragrant stuff almost touched his shoulder and he felt appealing to him seductively a perfume of orris root and violet. He was drinking bottled stout with his chop; be sat with a face of wood.

"Oh, the little lord?" Nora was crying to some slave. "Now, do you know, he won't do at all. He is too awfully charming. He sits and ruminates for fifteen minutes and then he pays me a lovely compliment. Then he ruminates for another fifteen minutes and cooks up another fine thing. It is too tiresome. Do you know what kind of man. I like? "she asked softly and confidentially. And here she sank back in her chair until. Coleman knew from the tingle that her head was but a few inches from his head. Her, sleeve touched him. He turned more wooden under the spell of the orris root and violet. Her courtiers thought it all a graceful pose, but Coleman believed otherwise. Her voice sank to the liquid, siren note of a succubus. "Do you know what kind of a man I like? Really like? I like a man that a woman can't bend in a thousand different ways in five minutes. He must have some steel in him. He obliges me to admire him the most when he remains stolid; stolid to me lures. Ah, that is the only kind of a man who cap ever break a heart among us women of the world. His stolidity is not real; no; it is mere art, but it is a highly finished art and often enough we can't cut through it. Really we can't. And, then we may actually come to - er - care for the man. Really we may. Isn't it funny?"

Alt the end Coleman arose and strolled out of the. room, smoking a cigarette. He did not betray, a sign. Before. the door clashed softly behind him, Nora laughed a little defiantly, perhaps a little loudly. It made every man in the grill-room perk up his ears. As for her courtiers, they were entranced. In her description of the conquering man, she had easily contrived that each one of them wondered if she might not mean him. Each man was perfectly sure that he had plenty of steel in his composition and that seemed to be a main point.

Coleman delayed for a time in the smoking room and then went to his own quarters. In reality he was Somewhat puzzled in his mind by a projection of the beauties of Nora Black upon his desire for Greece and Marjory, His thoughts formed a duality. Once he was on the point of sending his card to Nora Black's parlour, inasmuch as Greece was very distant and he could not start until the morrow. But he suspected that he was holding the interest of the actress because of his recent appearance of impregnable serenity in the presence of her fascinations. If he now sent his card, it was a form of surrender and he knew her to be one to take a merciless advantage. He would not make this tactical mistake. On the contrary he would go to bed and think of war.

In reality he found it easy to fasten his mind upon the prospective war. He regarded himself cynically in most affairs, but he could not be cynical of war, because had he - seen none of it. His rejuvenated imagination began to thrill to the roll of battle, through his thought passing all the lightning in the pictures of Detaille, de Neuville and Morot; lashed battery horse roaring over bridges; grand cuirassiers dashing headlong against stolid invincible red-faced lines of German infantry; furious and bloody grapplings in the streets of little villages of northeastern France. There was one thing at least of which he could still feel the spirit of a debutante. In this matter of war he was not, too, unlike a young girl embarking upon her first season of opera. Walkely, the next morning, saw this mood sitting quaintly upon Coleman and cackled with astonishment and glee. Coleman's usual manner did not return until he detected Walkely's appreciation of his state and then he snubbed him according to the ritual of the Sunday editor of the New York Eclipse. Parenthetically, it might be said that if Coleman now recalled Nora Black to his mind at all, it was only to think of her for a moment with ironical complacence. He had beaten her.

When the train drew out of the station, Coleman felt himself thrill. Was ever fate less perverse? War and love-war and Marjory - were in conjunction both in

Greece - and he could tilt with one lance at both gods. It was a great fine game to play and no man was ever so blessed in vacations. He was smiling continually to himself and sometimes actually on the point of talking aloud. This was despite the presence in the compartment of two fellow passengers who preserved in their uncomfortably rigid, icy and uncompromising manners many of the more or less ridiculous traditions of the English first class carriage. Coleman's fine humour betrayed him once into addressing one of these passengers and the man responded simply with a wide look of incredulity, as if he discovered that he was travelling in the same compartment with a zebu. It turned Coleman suddenly to evil temper and he wanted to ask the man questions concerning his education and his present mental condition: and so until the train arrived at Dover, his ballooning soul was in danger of collapsing. On the packet crossing the channel, too, he almost returned to the usual Rufus Coleman since all the world was seasick and he could not get a cabin in which to hide himself from it. However he reaped much consolation by ordering a bottle of champagne and drinking it in sight of the people, which made them still more seasick. From Calais to Brindisi really nothing met his disapproval save the speed of the train, the conduct of some of the passengers, the quality of the food served, the manners of the guards, the temperature of the carriages, the prices charged and the length of the journey.

In time he passed as in a vision from wretched Brindisi to charming Corfu, from Corfu to the little war-bitten city of Patras and from Patras by rail at the speed of an ox-cart to Athens.

With a smile of grim content and surrounded in his

carriage with all his beautiful brown luggage, he swept through the dusty streets of the Greek capital. Even as the vehicle arrived in a great terraced square in front of the yellow palace, Greek recruits in garments representing many trades and many characters were marching up cheering for Greece and the king. Officers stood upon the little iron chairs in front of the cafes; all the urchins came running and shouting; ladies waved their handkerchiefs from the balconies; the whole city was vivified with a leaping and joyous enthusiasm. The Athenians - as dragomen or otherwise - had preserved an ardor for their glorious traditions, and it was as if that in the white dust which lifted from the plaza and floated across the old-ivory face of the palace, there were the souls of the capable soldiers of the past. Coleman was almost intoxicated with it. It seemed to celebrate his own reasons, his reasons of love and ambition to conquer in love.

When the carriage arrived in front of the Hotel D'Angleterre, Coleman found the servants of the place with more than one eye upon the scene in the plaza, but they soon paid heed to the arrival of a gentleman with such an amount of beautiful leather luggage, all marked boldly with the initials "R. C." Coleman let them lead him and follow him and conduct him and use bad English upon him without noting either their words, their salaams or their work. His mind had quickly fixed upon the fact that here was the probable headquarters of the Wainwright party and, with the rush of his western race fleeting through his veins, he felt that he would choke and die if he did not learn of the Wainwrights in the first two minutes. It was a tragic venture to attempt to make the Levantine mind understand something off the course, that the new arrival's first thought was to establish a knowlege of the whereabouts of some of his friends rather than to swarm helter-skelter into that part of the hotel for which he was willing to pay rent. In fact he failed to thus impress them; failed in dark wrath, but, nevertheless, failed. At last he was simply forced to concede the travel of files of men up the broad, redcarpeted stair-case, each man being loaded with Coleman's luggage. The men in the hotel-bureau were then able to comprehend that the foreign gentleman might have something else on his mind. They raised their eyebrows languidly when he spoke of the Wainwright party in gentle surprise that he had not yet learned that they were gone some time. They were departed on some excursion. Where? Oh, really - it was almost laughable, indeed - they didn't know. Were they sure? Why, yes-it was almost laughable, indeed - they were quite sure. Where could the gentleman find out about them ? Well, they - as they had explained - did not know, but - it was possible-the American minister might know. Where was he to be found? Oh, that was very simple. It was well known that the American minister had apartments in the hotel. Was he in? Ah, that they could not say. So Coleman, rejoicing at his final emanci-pation and with the grime of travel still upon him, burst in somewhat violently upon the secretary of the Hon. Thomas M. Gordner of Nebraska, the United States minister to Greece. From his desk the secretary arose from behind an accidental bulwark of books and govermental pamphets. "Yes, certainly. Mr. Gordner is in. If you would give me your card -"

Directly. Coleman was introduced into another room where a quiet man who was rolling a cigarette looked him frankly but carefully in the eye. "The Wainwrights" said the minister immediately after the question. "Why, I myself am immensely concerned about them at present. I'm afraid they've gotten themselves into trouble.'

"Really? " said Coleman.

"Yes. That little professor is ratherer - stubborn; Isn't he ? He wanted to make an expedition to Nikopolis and I explained to him all the possibilities of war and begged him to at least not take his wife and daughter with him."

"Daughter," murmured Coleman, as if in his sleep.

"But that little old man had a head like a stone and only laughed at me. Of course those villainous young students were only too delighted at a prospect of war, but it was a stupid and absurd. thing for the man to take his wife and daughter there. They are up there now. I can't get a word from them or get a word to them."

Coleman had been choking. "Where is Nikopolis? " he asked.

The minister gazed suddenly in comprehension of the man before him. "Nikopolis is in Turkey," he answered gently.

Turkey at that time was believed to be a country of delay, corruption, turbulence and massacre. It meant everything. More than a half of the Christians of the world shuddered at the name of Turkey. Coleman's lips tightened and perhaps blanched, and his chin moved out strangely, once, twice, thrice. "How can I get to Nikopolis?" he said.

The minister smiled. "It would take you the better part of four days if you could get there, but as a matter of fact you can't get there at the present time. A Greek army and a Turkish army are looking at each other from the sides of the river at Arta - the river is there the frontier-and Nikopolis happens to be on the wrong side. You can't reach them. The forces at Arta will fight within three days. I know it. Of course I've notified our legation at Constantinople, but, with Turkish methods of communication, Nikopolis is about as far from Constantinople as New York is from Pekin."

Coleman arose. "They've run themselves into a nice mess," he said crossly. "Well, I'm a thousand times obliged to you, I'm sure."

The minister opened his eyes a trifle. You are not going to try to reach them, are you?"

"Yes," answered Coleman, abstractedly. "I'm going to have a try at it. Friends of mine, you know -"

At the bureau of the hotel, the correspondent found several cables awaiting him from the alert office of the New York Eclipse. One of them read: "State Department gives out bad plight of Wainwright party lost somewhere; find them. Eclipse." When Coleman perused the message he began to smile with seraphic bliss. Could fate have ever been less perverse.

Whereupon he whirled himself in Athens. And it was to the considerable astonishment of some Athenians. He discovered and instantly subsidised a young Englishman who, during his absence at the front, would act as correspondent for the Eclipse at the capital. He took unto himself a dragoman and then bought three horses and hired a groom at a speed that caused a little crowd at the horse dealer's place to come out upon the pavement and watch this surprising young man ride back toward his hotel. He had already driven his dragoman into a curious state of Oriental bewilderment and panic in which he could only lumber hastily and helplessly here and there, with his face in the meantime marked with agony. Coleman's own field equipment had been ordered by cable from New York to London, but it was necessary to buy much tinned meats, chocolate, coffee, candles, patent food, brandy, tobaccos, medicine and other things.

He went to bed that night feeling more placid. The train back to Patras was to start in the early morning, and he felt the satisfaction of a man who is at last about to start on his own great quest. Before he dropped off to slumber, he heard crowds cheering exultantly in the streets, and the cheering moved him as it had done in the morning. He felt that the celebration of the people was really an accompaniment to his primal reason, a reason of love and ambition to conquer in love-even as in the theatre, the music accompanies the heroin his progress. He arose once during the night to study a map of the Balkan peninsula and get nailed into his mind the exact position of Nikopolis. It was important.

CHAPTER IX

COLEMAN'S dragoman aroused him in the blue before dawn. The correspondent arrayed himself in one of his new khaki suits-riding breeches and a tunic well marked with buttoned pockets - and accompanied by some of his beautiful brown luggage, they departed for the station.

The ride to Patras is a terror under ordinary circumstances. It begins in the early morning and ends in the twilight. To Coleman, having just come from Patras to Athens, this journey from Athens to Patras had all the exasperating elements of a forced recantation. Moreover, he had not come prepared to view with awe the ancient city of Corinth nor to view with admiration the limpid beauties of the gulf of that name with its olive grove shore. He was not stirred by Parnassus, a faraway snowfield high on the black shoulders of the mountains across the gulf. No; he wished to go to Nikopolis. He passed over the graves of an ancient race the gleam of whose mighty minds shot, hardly dimmed, through the clouding ages. No; he wished to go to Nikopolis. The train went at a snail's pace, and if Coleman bad an interest it was in the people who lined the route and cheered the soldiers on the train. In Coleman s compartment there was a greasy person who spoke a little English. He explained that he was a poet, a poet who now wrote of nothing but war. When a man is in pursuit of his love and success is known to be at least remote, it often relieves his strain if he is deeply bored from time to time.

The train was really obliged to arrive finally at Patras even if it was a tortoise, and when this happened, a hotel runner appeared, who lied for the benefit of the hotel in saying that there was no boat over to Mesalonghi that night. When, all too late, Coleman discovered the truth of the matter his wretched dragoman came in for a period of infamy and suffering. However, while strolling in the plaza at Patras, amid newsboys from every side, by rumour and truth, Coleman learned things to his advantage. A Greek fleet was bombarding Prevasa. Prevasa was near Nikopolis. The opposing armies at Arta were engaged, principally in an artillery duel. Arta was on the road from Nikopolis into Greece. Hearing this news in the sunlit square made him betray no weakness, but in the darkness of his room at the hotel, he seemed to behold Marjory encircled by insurmountable walls of flame. He could look out of his window into the black night of the north and feel every ounce of a hideous circumstance. It appalled him; here was no power of calling up a score of reporters and sending them scampering to accomplish everything. He even might as well have been without a tongue as far as it could serve him in goodly speech. He was alone, confronting the black ominous Turkish north behind which were the deadly flames; behind the flames was Marjory. It worked upon him until he felt obliged to call in his dragoman, and then, seated upon the edge of his bed and waving his pipe eloquently, he described the plight of some very dear friends who were cut off at Nikopolis in Epirus. Some of his talk was almost wistful in its wish for sympathy from his servant, but at the end he bade the dragoman understand that be, Coleman, was going to their rescue, and he defiantly asked the hireling if he was prepared to go with him. But he did not know the Greek nature. In two minutes the dragoman was weeping tears of enthusiasm, and, for these tears, Coleman was over-grateful, because he had not been told that any of the more crude forms of sentiment arouse the common Greek to the highest pitch, but sometimes, when it comes to what the Americans call a "show down," when he gets backed toward his last corner with a solitary privilege of dying for these sentiments, perhaps he does not always exhibit those talents which are supposed to be possessed by the bulldog. He often then, goes into the cafes and take's it out in oration, like any common Parisian.

In the morning A steamer carried them across the strait and landed them near Mesalonghi at the foot of the railroad that leads to Agrinion. At Agrinion Coleman at last began to feel that he was nearing his goal. There were plenty of soldiers in the town, who received with delight and applause this gentleman in the distingui-shed-looking khaki clothes with his revolver and his field glasses and his canteen and; his dragoman. The dragoman lied, of course, and vocifcrated that the gentleman in the distinguished-looking khaki clothes was an English soldier of reputation, who had, naturally, come to help the cross in its fight against, the crescent. He also said that his master had three superb horses coming from Athens in charge of a groom, and was undoubtedly going to join the cavalry. Whereupon the soldiers wished to embrace and kiss the gentleman in the distinguished-looking khaki clothes.

There was more or less of a scuffle. Coleman would

have taken to kicking and punching, but he found that by a - series of elusive movements he could dodge the demonstrations of affection without losing his popularity. Escorted by the soldiers, citizens, children and dogs, he went to the diligence which was to take him and others the next stage of the journey. As the diligence proceeded, Coleman's mind suffered another little inroad of ill-fate as to the success of his expedition. In the first place it appeared foolish to expect that this diligence would ever arrive anywhere. Moreover, the accommodations were about equal to what one would endure if one undertook to sleep for a night in a tree. Then there was a devil-dog, a little black-and-tan terrier in a blanket gorgeous and belled, whose duty it was to stand on the top of the coach and bark incessantly to keep the driver fully aroused to the enormity of his occupation. To have this cur silenced either by strangulation or ordinary clubbing, Coleman struggled with his dragoman as Jacob struggled with the angel, but in the first place, the dragoman was a Greek whose tongue could go quite drunk, a Greek who became a slave to the heralding and establishment of one certain fact, or lie, and now he was engaged in describing to every village and to all the country side the prowess of the gentleman in the distinguished-looking khaki clothes. It was the general absurdity of this advance to the frontier and the fighting, to the crucial place where he was resolved to make an attempt to rescue his sweetheart; it was this ridiculous aspect that caused to come to Coleman a premonition of failure. No knight ever went out to recover a lost love in such a diligence and with such a devil-dog, tinkling his little bells and yelping insanely to keep the driver awake. After night-fall they arrived at a town on the southern coast of the Gulf of Arta and the goaded dragoman was - thrust forth from the little inn into the street to find the first possible means of getting on to Arta. He returned at last to tremulously say that there was no single chance of starting for Arta that night. Where upon he was again thrust into the street with orders, strict orders. In due time, Coleman spread his rugs upon the floor of his little room and thought himself almost asleep,. when the dragoman entered with a really intelligent man who, for some reason, had agreed to consort with him in the business of getting the stranger off to Arta. They announced that there was a brigantine about to sail with a load of soldiers for a little port near Arta, and if Coleman hurried he could catch it, permission from an officer having already been obtained. He was up at once, and the dragoman and the unaccountably intelligent person hastily gathered his chattels. Stepping out into a black street and moving to the edge of black water and embarking in a black boat filled with soldiers whose rifles dimly shone, was as impressive to Coleman as if, really, it had been the first start. He had endured many starts, it was true, but the latest one always touched him as being conclusive.

There were no lights on the brigantine and the men swung precariously up her sides to the deck which was already occupied by a babbling multitude. The dragoman judiciously found a place for his master where during the night the latter had to move quickly everytime the tiller was shifted to starboard.

The craft raised her shadowy sails and swung slowly off into the deep gloom. Forward, some of the soldiers began to sing weird minor melodies. Coleman, enveloped in his rugs, - smoked three or four cigars. He was content and miserable, lying there, hearing these melodies which defined to him his own affairs.

At dawn they were at the little port. First, in the carmine and grey tints from a sleepy sun, they could see little mobs of soldiers working amid boxes of stores. And then from the back in some dun and green hills sounded a deep-throated thunder of artillery An officer gave Coleman and his dragoman positions in one of the first boats, but of course it could not be done without an almost endless amount of palaver. Eventually they landed with their traps. Coleman felt through the sole of his boot his foot upon the shore. He was within striking distance.

But here it was smitten into the head of Coleman's servant to turn into the most inefficient dragoman, probably in the entire East. Coleman discerned it immediately, before any blunder could tell him. He at first thought that it was the voices of the guns which had made a chilly inside for the man, but when he reflected upon the incompetency, or childish courier's falsity, at Patras and his discernible lack of sense from Agrinion onward, he felt that the fault was elemental in his nature. It was a mere basic inability to front novel situations which was somehow in the dragoman; he retreated from everything difficult in a smoke of gibberish and gesticulation. Coleman glared at him with the hatred that sometimes ensues when breed meets breed, but he saw that this man was indeed a golden link in his possible success. This man connected him with Greece and its language. If he destroyed him he delayed what was now his main desire in life. However, this truth did not prevent him from addressing the man in elegant speech.

The two little men who were induced to carry Coleman's luggage as far as the Greek camp were really procured by the correspondent himself, who

Stephen Crane

pantomined vigourously and with unmistakable vividness. Followed by his dragoman and the two little men, he strode off along a road which led straight as a stick to where the guns were at intervals booming. Meanwhile the dragoman and the two little men talked, talked, talked. - Coleman was silent, puffing his cigar and reflecting upon the odd things which happen to chivalry in the modern age.

He knew of many men who would have been astonished if they could have seen into his mind at that time, and he knew of many more men who would have laughed if they had the same privilege of sight. He made no attempt to conceal from himself that the whole thing was romantic, romantic despite the little tinkling dog, the decrepit diligence, the palavering natives, the super-idiotic dragoman. It was fine, It was from another age and even the actors could not deface the purity of the picture. However it was true that upon the brigantine the previous night he had unaccountably wetted all his available matches. This was momentous, important, cruel truth, but Coleman, after all, was taking - as well as he could forgeta solemn and knightly joy of this adventure and there were as many portraits of his lady envisioning. before him as ever held the heart of an armour-encased young gentleman of medieval poetry. If he had been travelling in this region as an ordinary tourist, he would have been apparent mainly for his lofty impatience over trifles, but now there was in him a positive assertion of direction which was undoubtedly one of the reasons for the despair of the accomplished dragoman.

Before them the country slowly opened and opened, the straight white road always piercing it like a lanceshaft. Soon they could see black masses of men marking the green knolls. The artillery thundered loudly and now vibrated augustly through the air. Coleman quickened his pace, to the despair of the little men carrying the traps. They finally came up with one of these black bodies of men and found it to be composed of a considerable number of soldiers who were idly watching some hospital people bury a dead Turk. The dragoman at once dashed forward to peer through the throng and see the face of the corpse. Then he came and supplicated Coleman as if he were hawking him to look at a relic and Coleman moved by a strong, mysterious impulse, went forward to look at the poor little clay-coloured body. At that moment a snake ran out from a tuft of grass at his feet and wriggled wildly over the sod. The dragoman shrieked, of course, but one of the soldiers put his heel upon the head of the reptile and it flung itself into the agonising knot of death. Then the whole crowd powwowed, turning from the dead man to the dead snake. Coleman signaled his contingent and proceeded along the road.

This incident, this paragraph, had seemed a strange introduction to war. The snake, the dead man, the entire sketch, made him shudder of itself, but more than anything he felt an uncanny symbolism. It was no doubt a mere occurrence; nothing but an occurrence; but inasmuch as all the detail of this daily life associated itself with Marjory, he felt a different horror. He had thought of the little devil-dog and Marjory in an interwoven way. Supposing Marjory had been riding in the diligence with the devil-dog-a-top ? What would she have said? Of her fund of expressions, a fund uncountable, which would she have innocently projected against the background of the Greek hills? Would it have smitten her nerves badly or would she have laughed? And supposing Marjory could have seen

Stephen Crane

him in his new khaki clothes cursing his dragoman as he listened to the devil-dog?

And now he interwove his memory of Marjory with a dead man and with a snake in the throes of the end of life. They crossed, intersected, tangled, these two thoughts. He perceived it clearly; the incongruity of it. He academically reflected upon the mysteries of the human mind, this homeless machine which lives here and then there and often lives in two or three opposing places at the same instant. He decided that the incident of the snake and the dead man had no more meaning than the greater number of the things which happen to us in our daily lives. Nevertheless it bore upon him.

On a spread of plain they saw a force drawn up in a long line. It was a flagrant inky streak on the verdant prairie. From somewhere near it sounded the timed reverberations of guns. The brisk walk of the next ten minutes was actually exciting to Coleman. He could not but reflect that those guns were being fired with serious purpose at certain human bodies much like his own.

As they drew nearer they saw that the inky streak was composed of cavalry, the troopers standing at their bridles. The sunlight flicked, upon their bright weapons. Now the dragoman developed in one of his extraordinary directions. He announced forsooth that an intimate friend was a captain of cavalry in this command. Coleman at first thought. that this was some kind of mysterious lie, but when he arrived where they could hear the stamping of hoofs, the clank of weapons, and the murmur of men, behold, a most dashing young officer gave a shout of joy and he and the dragoman hurled themselves into a mad embrace.

After this first ecstacy was over, the dragoman bethought him of his employer, and looking toward Coleman hastily explained him to the officer. The latter, it appeared, was very affable indeed. Much had happened. The Greeks and the Turks had been fighting over a shallow part of the river nearly opposite this point and the Greeks had driven back the Turks and succeeded in throwing a bridge of casks and planking across the stream. It was now the duty and the delight of this force of cavalry to cross the bridge and, passing, the little force of covering Greek infantry, to proceed into Turkey until they came in touch with the enemy.

Coleman's eyes dilated. Was ever fate less perverse? Partly in wretched French to the officer and partly in idiomatic English to the dragoman, he proclaimed his fiery desire to accompany the expedition. The officer immediately beamed upon him. In fact, he was delighted. The dragoman had naturally told him many falsehoods concerning Coleman, incidentally referring to himself more as a philanthropic guardian and, valuable friend of the correspondent than as, a plain, unvarnished. dragoman with an exceedingly good eye for the financial possibilities of his position.

Coleman wanted to ask his servant if there was any chance of the scout taking them near Nikopolis, but he delayed being informed upon this point until such time as he could find out, secretly, for himself. To ask the dragoman would be mere stupid questioning which would surely make the animal shy. He tried to be content that fate had given him this early opportunity of dealing with a Medieval situation with some show of proper form ; that is to say, armed, a-horseback, and in danger. Then he could feel that to the gods of the game he was not laughable, as when he rode to rescue his love in a diligence with a devil-dog yelping a-top.

With some flourish, the young captain presented him to the major who commanded the cavalry. This officer stood with his legs wide apart, eating the rind of a fresh lemon and talking betimes to some of his officers. The major also beamed upon Coleman when the captain explained that the gentleman in the distinguished-looking khaki clothes wished to accompany the expedition. He at once said that he would provide two troop horses for Coleman and the dragoman. Coleman thanked fate for his behaviour and his satisfaction was not without a vestige of surprise. At that time he judged it to be a remarkable amiability of individuals, but in later years he came to believe in certain laws which he deemed existent solely for the benefit of war correspondents. In the minds of governments, war offices and generals they have no function save one of disturbance, but Coleman deemed it proven that the common men, and many uncommon men, when they go away to the fighting ground, out of the sight, out of the hearing of the world known to them, and are eager to perform feats of war in this new place, they feel an absolute longing for a spectator. It is indeed the veritable coronation of this world. There is not too much vanity of the street in this desire of men to have some disinterested fellows perceive their deeds. It is merely that a man doing his best in the middle of a sea of war, longs to have people see him doing his best. This feeling is often notably serious if, in peace, a man has done his worst, or part of his worst. Coleman believed that, above everybody, young, proud and brave subalterns had this itch, but it existed, truly enough, from lieutenants to colonels. None wanted to conceal from his left hand that his right hand was performing a manly and valiant thing, although there might be times when an application of the principle would be immensely convenient. The war correspondent arises, then, to become a sort of a cheap telescope for the people at home; further still, there have been fights where the eyes of a solitary man were the eyes of the world; one spectator, whose business it was to transfer, according to his ability, his visual impressions to other minds.

Coleman and his servant were conducted to two saddled troop horses, and beside them, waited decently in the rear of the ranks. The uniform of the troopers was of plain, dark green cloth and they were well and sensibly equipped. The mounts, however, had in no way been picked; there were little horses and big horses, fat horses and thin horses. They looked the result of a wild conscription. Coleman noted the faces of the troopers, and they were calm enough save when a man betrayed himself by perhaps a disproportionate angry jerk at the bridle of his restive horse.

The major, artistically drooping his cloak from his left shoulder and tenderly and musingly fingering his long yellow moustache, rode slowly to the middle of the line and wheeled his horse to face his men. A bugle called attention, and then he addressed them in a loud and rapid speech, which did not seem to have an end. Coleman imagined that the major was paying tribute to the Greek tradition of the power of oratory. Again the trumpet rang out, and this parade front swung off into column formation. Then Coleman and the dragoman trotted at the tail of the squadron, restraining with difficulty their horses, who could not understand their new places in the procession, and worked feverishly to regain what they considered their positions in life.

Stephen Crane

The column jangled musically over the sod, passing between two hills on one of which a Greek light battery was posted. Its men climbed to the tops of their interenchments to witness the going of the cavalry. Then the column curved along over ditch and through hedge to the shallows of the river. Across this narrow stream was Turkey. Turkey, however, presented nothing to the eye but a muddy bank with fringes of trees back of it. It seemed to be a great plain with sparse collections of foliage marking it, whereas the Greek side, presented in the main a vista of high, gaunt rocks. Perhaps one of the first effects of war upon the mind, is a. new recognition and fear of the circumscribed ability of the eye, making all landscape seem inscrutable. The cavalry drew up in platoon formation on their own. bank of the stream and waited. If Coleman had known anything of war, he would have known, from appearances, that there was nothing in the immediate vicinity to, cause heart-jumping, but as a matter of truth he was deeply moved and wondered what was hidden, what was veiled by those trees. Moreover, the squadrons resembled art old picture of a body of horse awaiting Napoleon's order to charge. In the, meantime his mount fumed at the bit, plunging to get back to the ranks. The sky was, without a cloud, and the sun rays swept down upon them. Sometimes Coleman was on the verge of addressing the dragoman, according to his anxiety, but in the end he simply told him to go to the river and fill the canteens.

At last an order came, and the first troop moved with muffled tumult across the bridge. Coleman and his dragoman followed the last troop. The horses scrambled up the muddy bank much as if they were merely breaking out of a pasture, but probably all the men felt a sudden tightening of their muscles.

Coleman, in his excitement, felt, more than he saw, glossy horse flanks, green clothed men chumping in their saddles, banging sabres and canteens, and carbines slanted in line.

There were some Greek infantry in a trench. They were heavily overcoated, despite the heat, and some were engaged in eating loaves of round, thick bread. They called out lustily as the cavalry passed them. The troopers smiled slowly, somewhat proudly in response.

Presently there was another halt and Coleman saw the major trotting busily here and there, while troop commanders rode out to meet him. Spreading groups of scouts and flankers moved off and disappeared. Their dashing young officer friend cantered past them with his troop at his heels. He waved a joyful good-bye. It was the doings of cavalry in actual service, horsemen fanning out in all forward directions. There were two troops held in reserve, and as they jangled ahead at a foot pace, Coleman and his dragoman followed them.

The dragoman was now moved to erect many reasons for an immediate return. It was plain that he had no stomach at all for this business, and that he wished himself safely back on the other side of the river. Coleman looked at him askance. When these men talked together Coleman might as well have been a polar bear for all he understood of it. When he saw the trepidation of his dragoman, he did not know what it foreboded. In this situation it was not for him to say that the dragoman's fears were founded on nothing. And ever the dragoman raised his reasons for a retreat. Coleman spoke to himself. "I am just a trifle rattled," he said to his heart, and after he had communed for a time upon the duty of steadiness, he addressed the dragoman in cool language. "Now, my persuasive friend, just quit all that, because business is business, and it may be rather annoying business, but you will have to go through with it." Long afterward, when ruminating over the feelings of that morning, he saw with some astonishment that there was not a single thing within sound or sight to cause a rational being any quaking. He was simply riding with some soldiers over a vast tree-dotted prairie.

Presently the commanding officer turned in his saddle and told the dragoman that he was going to ride forward with his orderly to where he could see the flanking parties and the scouts, and courteously, with the manner of a gentleman entertaining two guests, he asked if the civilians cared to accompany him. The dragoman would not have passed this question correctly on to Coleman if he had thought he could have avoided it, but, with both men regarding him, he considered that a lie probably meant instant detection. He spoke almost the truth, contenting himself with merely communicating to Coleman in a subtle way his sense that a ride forward with the commanding officer and his orderly would be depressing and dangerous occupation. But Coleman immediately accepted the invitation mainly because it was the invitation of the major, and in war it is a brave man who can refuse the invitation of a commanding officer. The little party of four trotted away from the reserves, curving in single file about the water-holes. In time they arrived at where the plain lacked trees and was one great green lake of grass; grass and scrubs. On this expanse they could see the Greek horsemen riding, mainly appearing as little black dots. Far to the left there was a squad said to be composed of only twenty troopers, but in the distance their black mass seemed to be a regiment.

As the officer and his guests advanced they came in view of what one may call the shore of the plain. The rise of ground was heavily clad with trees, and over the tops of them appeared the cupola and part of the walls of a large white house, and there were glimpses of huts near it as if a village was marked. The black specks seemed to be almost to it. The major galloped forward and the others followed at his pace. The house grew larger and larger and they came nearly to the advance scouts who they could now see were not quite close to the village. There had been a deception of the eye precisely as occurs at sea. Herds of unguarded sheep drifted over the plain and little ownerless horses, still cruelly hobbled, leaped painfully away, frightened, as if they understood that an anarchy had come upon them. The party rode until they were very nearly up with the scouts, and then from low down at the very edge of the plain there came a long rattling noise which endured as if some kind of grinding machine had been put in motion. Smoke arose, faintly marking the position of an intrenchment. Sometimes a swift spitting could be heard from the air over the party.

It was Coleman's fortune to think at first that the Turks were not firing in his direction, but as soon as he heard the weird voices in the air he knew that war was upon him. But it was plain that the range was almost excessive, plain even to his ignorance. The major looked at him and laughed; he found no difficulty in smiling in response. If this was war, it could be withstood somehow. He could not at this time understand what a mere trifle was the present incident. He felt upon his cheek a little breeze which was moving the grass-blades. He had tied his canteen in a wrong place on the saddle and every time the horse moved quickly the canteen banged the correspondent, to his annoyance and distress, forcibly on the knee. He had forgotten about his dragoman, but happening to look upon that faithful servitor, he saw him gone white with horror. A bullet at that moment twanged near his head and the slave to fear ducked in a spasm. Coleman called the orderly's attention and they both laughed discreetly. They made no pretension of being heroes, but they saw plainly that they were better than this man. Coleman said to him: "How far is it now to Nikopolis?" The dragoman replied only, with a look of agonized impatience.

But of course there was no going to Nikopolis that day. The officer had advanced his men as far as was intended by his superiors, and presently they were all recalled and trotted back to the bridge. They crossed it to their old camp.

An important part of Coleman's traps was back with his Athenian horses and their groom, but with his present equipment he could at least lie smoking on his blankets and watch the dragoman prepare food. But he reflected that for that day he had only attained the simple discovery that the approach to Nikopolis was surrounded with difficulties.

CHAPTER X

The same afternoon Coleman and the dragoman rode up to Arta on their borrowed troop horses. The correspondent first went to the telegraph office and found there the usual number of despairing clerks. They were outraged when they found he was going to send messages and thought it preposterous that he insisted upon learning if there were any in the office for him. They had trouble enough with endless official communications without being hounded about private affairs by a confident young man in khaki. But Coleman at last unearthed six cablegrams which collective said that the Eclipse wondered why they did not hear from him, that Walkley had been relieved from duty in London and sent to join the army of the crown prince, that young Point, the artist, had been shipped to Greece, that if he, Coleman, succeeded in finding the Wainwright party the paper was prepared to make a tremendous uproar of a celebration over it and, finally, the paper wondered twice more why they did not hear from him.

When Coleman went forth to enquire if anybody knew of the whereabouts of the Wainwright party he thought first of his fellow correspondents. He found most of them in a cafe where was to be had about the only food in the soldier-laden town. It was a slothful den where even an ordinary boiled egg could be made unpalatable. Such a common matter as the salt men watched with greed and suspicion as if they were always about to grab it from each other. The proprietor, in a dirty shirt, could always be heard whining, evidently telling the world that he was being abused, but he had spirit enough remaining to charge three prices for everything with an almost Jewish fluency.

The correspondents consoled themselves largely upon black - bread and the native wines. Also there were certain little oiled fishes, and some green odds and ends for salads. The correspondents were practically all Englishmen. Some of them were veterans of journalism in the Sudan, in India, in South Africa; and there were others who knew as much of war as they could learn by sitting at a desk and editing the London stock reports. Some were on their own hook; some had horses and dragomen and some had neither the one nor the other; many knew how to write and a few had it yet to learn. The thing in common was a spirit of adventure which found pleasure in the extraordinary business of seeing how men kill each other.

They were talking of an artillery duel which had been fought the previous day between the Greek batteries above the town and the Turkish batteries across the river. Coleman took seat at one of the long tables, and the astute dragoman got somebody in the street to hold the horses in order that he might be present at any feasting.

One of the experienced correspondents was remarking that the fire of the Greek batteries in the engagement had been the finest artillery practice of the century. He spoke a little loudly, perhaps, in the wistful hope that some of the Greek officers would understand enough English to follow his meaning, for it is always good for a correspondent to admire the prowess on his own side of the battlefield. After a time Coleman spoke in a lull, and describing the supposed misfortunes of the Wainwright party, asked if anyone had news of them. The correspondents were surprised; they had none of them heard even of the existence of a Wainwright party. Also none of them seemed to care exceedingly. The conversation soon changed to a discussion of the probable result of the general Greek advance announced for the morrow.

Coleman silently commented that this remarkable appearance of indifference to the mishap of the Wainwrights, a little party, a single group, was a better definition of a real condition of war than that bit of long-range musketry of the morning. He took a certain despatch out of his pocket and again read it. "Find Wainwright party at all hazards; much talk here; success means red fire by ton. Eclipse." It was an important matter. He could imagine how the American people, vibrating for years to stories of the cruelty of the Turk, would tremble-indeed, was now trembling-while the newspapers howled out the dire possibilities. He saw all the kinds of people, from those who would read the Wainwright chapters from day to day as a sort of sensational novel, to those who would work up a gentle sympathy for the woe of others around the table in the evenings. He saw bar keepers and policemen taking a high gallery thrill out of this kind of romance. He saw even the emotion among American colleges over the tragedy of a professor and some students. It certainly was a big affair. Marjory of course was everything in one way, but that, to the world, was not a big affair. It was the romance of the Wainwright party in its simplicity that to the American world was arousing great sensation; one that in the old days would have made his heart leap like a colt.

Still, when batteries had fought each other savagely, and horse, foot and guns were now about to make a general advance, it was difficult, he could see, to stir men to think and feel out of the present zone of action; to adopt for a time in fact the thoughts and feelings of the other side of the world. It made Coleman dejected as he saw clearly that the task was wholly on his own shoulders.

Of course they were men who when at home manifested the most gentle and wide-reaching feelings; most of them could not by any possibility have slapped a kitten merely for the prank and yet all of them who had seen an unknown man shot through the head in battle had little more to think of it than if the man had been a rag-baby. Tender they might be; poets they might be; but they were all horned with a provisional, temporary, but absolutely essential callouse which was formed by their existence amid war with its quality of making them always think of the sights and sounds concealed in their own direct future.

They had been simply polite. "Yes?" said one to Coleman. "How many people in the party? Are they all Americans? Oh, I suppose it will be quite right. Your minister in Constantinople will arrange that easily. Where did you say? At Nikopolis? Well, we conclude that the Turks will make no stand between here and Pentepigadia. In that case your Nikopolis will be uncovered unless the garrison at Prevasa intervenes. That garrison at Prevasa, by the way, may make a deal of trouble. Remember Plevna."

"Exactly how far is it to Nikopolis? " asked Coleman.

"Oh, I think it is about thirty kilometers," replied the others. " There is a good miltary road as soon as you cross the Louros river. I've got the map of the Austrian general staff. Would you like to look at it?"

Coleman studied the map, speeding with his eye rapidly to and fro between Arta and Nikopolis. To him it was merely a brown lithograph of mystery, but he could study the distances.

He had received a cordial invitation from the commander of the cavalry to go with him for another ride into Turkey, and he inclined to believe that his project would be furthered if he stuck close to the cavalry. So he rode back to the cavalry camp and went peacefully to sleep on the sod. He awoke in the morning with chattering teeth to find his dragoman saying that the major had unaccountably withdrawn his loan of the two troop horses. Coleman of course immediately said to himself that the dragoman was lying again in order to prevent another expedition into ominous Turkey, but after all if the commander, of the cavalry had suddenly turned the light of his favour from the correspondent it was only a proceeding consistent with the nature which Coleman now thought he was beginning to discern, a nature which can never think twice in the same place, a gageous mind which drifts, dissolves, combines, vanishes with the ability of an aerial thing until the man of the north feels that when he clutches it with full knowledge of his senses he is only the victim of his ardent imagination. It is the difference in standards, in creeds, which is the more luminous when men call out that they are all alike.

So Coleman and his dragoman loaded their traps and moved out to again invade Turkey. It was not yet clear daylight, but they felt that they might well start early since they were no longer mounted men.

On the way to the bridge, the dragoman, although he was curiously in love with his forty francs a day and his opportunities, ventured a stout protest, based apparently upon the fact that after all this foreigner, four days out from Athens was somewhat at his mercy. "Meester Coleman," he said, stopping suddenly, "I think we make no good if we go there. Much better we wait Arta for our horse. Much better. I think this no good. There is coming one big fight and I think much better we go stay Arta. Much better."

"Oh, come off," said Coleman. And in clear language he began to labour with the man. "Look here, now, if you think you are engaged in steering a bunch of wooden-headed guys about the Acropolis, my dear partner of my joys and sorrows, you are extremely mistaken. As a matter of fact you are now the dragoman of a war correspondent and you were engaged and are paid to be one. It becomes necessary that you make good. Make good, do you understand? I'm not out here to be buncoed by this sort of game." He continued indefinitely in this strain and at intervals he asked sharply Do you understand ?

Perhaps the dragoman was dumbfounded that the laconic Coleman could on occasion talk so much, or perhaps he understood everything and was impressed by the argumentative power. At any rate he suddenly wilted. He made a gesture which was a protestation of martyrdom and picking up his burden proceeded on his way.

When they reached the bridge, they saw strong columns of Greek infantry, dead black in the dim light, crossing the stream and slowly deploying on the other shore. It was a bracing sight to the dragoman, who then went into one of his absurd babbling moods, in which he would have talked the head off any man who was not born in a country laved by the childish Mediterranean. Coleman could not understand what he said to the soldiers as they passed, but it was evidently all grandiose nonsense.

Two light batteries had precariously crossed the rickety bridge during the night, and now this force of several thousand infantry, with the two batteries, was moving out over the territory which the cavalry had reconnoitered on the previous day. The ground being familiar to Coleman, he no longer knew a tremour, and, regarding his dragoman, he saw that that invaluable servitor was also in better form. They marched until they found one of the light batteries unlimbered and aligned on the lake of grass about a mile from where parts of the white house appeared above the tree-tops. Here the dragoman talked with the captain of artillery, a tiny man on an immense horse, who for some unknown reason told him that this force was going to raid into Turkey and try to swing around the opposing army's right flank. He announced, as he showed his teeth in a smile, that it would be very, very dangerous work. The dragoman precipitated himself upon Coleman.

"This is much danger. The copten he tell me the trups go now in back of the Turks. It will be much danger. I think much better we go Arta wait for horse. Much better." Coleman, although be believed he despised the dragoman, could not help but be influenced by his fears. They were, so to speak, in a room with one window, and only the dragoman looked forth from the window, so if he said that what he saw outside frightened him, Coleman was perforce frightened also in a measure. But when the correspondent raised his eyes he saw the captain of the battery looking at him, his teeth still showing in a smile, as if his information, whether true or false, had been given to convince the foreigner that the Greeks were a very superior and brave people, notably one little officer of artillery. He had apparently assumed that Coleman would balk from venturing with such a force upon an excursion to trifle with the rear of a hard fighting Ottoman army. He exceedingly disliked that man, sitting up there on his tall horse and grinning like a cruel little ape with a secret. In truth, Coleman was taken back at the outlook, but he could no more refrain from instantly accepting this half-concealed challenge than he could have refrained from resenting an ordinary form of insult. His mind was not at peace, but the small vanities are very large. He was perfectly aware that he was, being misled into the thing by an odd pride, but anyhow, it easily might turn out to be a stroke upon the doors of Nikopolis. He nodded and smiled at the officer in grateful acknowledgment of his service.

The infantry was moving steadily a-field. Black blocks of men were trailing in column slowly over the plain. They were not unlike the backs of dominoes on a green baize table; they were so vivid, so startling. The correspondent and his servant followed them. Eventually they overtook two companies in command of a captain, who seemed immensely glad to have the strangers with him. As they marched, the captain spoke through the dragoman upon the virtues of his men, announcing with other news the fact that his first sergeant was the bravest man in the world.

A number of columns were moving across the plain parallel to their line of march, and the whole force seemed to have orders to halt when they reached a long ditch about four hundred yards from where the shore of the plain arose to the luxuriant groves with the cupola of the big white house sticking above them. The soldiers lay along the ditch, and the bravest man in the world spread his blanket on the ground for the captain, Coleman and himself. During a long pause Coleman tried to elucidate the question of why the Greek soldiers wore heavy overcoats, even in the bitter heat of midday, but he could only learn that the dews, when they came, were very destructive to the lungs, Further, he convinced himself anew that talking through an interpreter to the minds of other men was as satisfactory as looking at landscape through a stained glass window.

After a time there was, in front, a stir near where a curious hedge of dry brambles seemed to outline some sort of a garden patch. Many of the soldiers exclaimed and raised their guns. But there seemed to come a general understanding to the line that it was wrong to fire. Then presently into the open came a dirty brown figure, and Coleman could see through his glasses that its head was crowned with a dirty fez which had once been white. This indicated that the figure was that of one of the Christian peasants of Epirus. Obedient to the captain, the sergeant arose and waved invitation. The peasant wavered, changed his mind, was obviously terror-stricken, regained confidence and then began to advance circuitously toward the Greek lines. When he arrived within hailing distance, the captain, the sergeant, Coleman's dragoman and many of the soldiers yelled human messages, and a moment later he was seen to be a poor, yellow-faced stripling with a body which seemed to have been first twisted by an ill-birth and afterward maimed by either labour or oppression, these being often identical in their effects.

His reception of the Greek soldiery was no less fervid than their welcome of him to their protection. He threw his grimy fez in the air and croaked out cheers, while tears wet his cheeks. When he had come upon the right side of the ditch he ran capering among them and the captain, the sergeant, the dragoman and a number of soldiers received wild embraces and kisses. He made a dash at Coleman, but Coleman was now wary in the game, and retired dexterously behind different groups with a finished appearance of not noting that the young man wished to greet him.

Behind the hedge of dry brambles there were more indications of life, and the peasant stood up and made beseeching gestures. Soon a whole flock of miserable people had come out to the Greeks, men, women and children, in crude and comic smocks, prancing here and there, uproariously embracing and kissing their deliverers. An old, tearful, toothless hag flung herself rapturously into the arms of the captain, and Coleman's brick-and-iron soul was moved to admiration at the way in which the officer administered a chaste salute upon the furrowed cheek. The dragoman told the correspondent that the Turks had run away from the village on up a valley toward Jannina. Everybody was proud and happy. A major of infantry came from the rear at this time and asked the captain in sharp tones who were the two strangers in civilian attire. When the captain had answered correctly the major was immediately mollified, and had it announced to the correspondent that his battalion was going to move immediately into the village, and that he would be delighted to have his company.

The major strode at the head of his men with the group of villagers singing and dancing about him and looking upon him as if he were a god. Coleman and the dragoman, at the officer's request, marched one on either side of him, and in this manner they entered the village. From all sorts of hedges and thickets, people came creeping out to pass into a delirium of joy. The major borrowed three little pack horses with rope-bridles, and thus mounted and followed by the clanking column, they rode on in triumph.

It was probably more of a true festival than most men experience even in the longest life time. The major with his Greek instinct of drama was a splendid personification of poetic quality; in fact he was himself almost a lyric. From time to time he glanced back at Coleman with eyes half dimmed with appreciation. The people gathered flowers, great blossoms of purple and corn colour. They sprinkled them over the three horsemen and flung them deliriously under the feet of the little nags. Being now mounted Coleman had no difficulty in avoiding the embraces of the peasants, but he felt to the tips of his toes an abandonment to a kind of pleasure with which he was not at all familiar. Riding thus amid cries of thanksgiving addressed at him equally with the others, he felt a burning virtue and quite lost his old self in an illusion of noble be. nignity. And there continued the fragrant hail of blossoms. Miserable little huts straggled along the sides of the village street as if they were following at the heels of the great white house of the bey. The column proceeded northward, announcing laughingly to the glad villagers that they would never see another Turk. Before them on the road was here and there a fez from the head of a fled Turkish soldier and they lay like drops of blood from some wounded leviathan. Ultimately it grew cloudy. It even rained slightly. In the misty downfall the column of soldiers in blue was dim as if it were merely a long trail of low-hung smoke.

They came to the ruins of a church and there the major halted his battalion. Coleman worried at his dragoman to learn if the halt was only temporary. It was a long time before there was answer from the major, for he had drawn up his men in platoons and was addressing them in a speech as interminable as any that Coleman had heard in Greece. The officer waved his arms and roared out evidently the glories of patriotism and soldierly honour, the glories of their ancient people, and he may have included any subject in this wonderful speech, for the reason that he had plenty of time in which to do it. It was impossible to tell whether the oration was a good one or bad one, because the men stood in their loose platoons without discernible feelings as if to them this appeared merely as one of the inevitable consequences of a campaign, an established rule of warfare. Coleman ate black bread and chocolate tablets while the dragoman hovered near the major with the intention of pouncing upon him for information as soon as his lungs yielded to the strain upon them.

The dragoman at last returned with a very long verbal treatise from the major, who apparently had not been as exhausted after his speech to the men as one would think. The major had said that he had been ordered to halt here to form a junction with some of the troops coming direct from Arta, and that he expected that in the morning the army would be divided and one wing would chase the retreating Turks on toward Jannina, while the other wing would advance upon Prevasa because the enemy had a garrison there which had not retreated an inch, and, although it was cut off, it was necessary to send either a force to hold it in its place or a larger force to go through with the business of capturing it. Else there would be left in the rear of the left flank of a Greek advance upon Jannina a body of the enemy which at any moment might become active. The major said that his battalion would probably form part of the force to advance upon Prevasa. Nikopolis was on the road to Prevasa and only three miles away from it.

CHAPTER XI

Coleman spent a long afternoon in the drizzle Enveloped in his macintosh he sat on a boulder in the lee of one of the old walls and moodily smoked cigars and listened to the ceaseless clatter of tongues. A ray of light penetrated the mind of the dragoman and he laboured assiduously with wet fuel until he had accomplished a tin mug of coffee. Bits of cinder floated in it, but Coleman rejoiced and was kind to the dragoman.

The night was of cruel monotony. Afflicted by the wind and the darkness, the correspondent sat with nerves keyed high waiting to hear the pickets open fire on a night attack. He was so unaccountably sure that there would be a tumult and panic of this kind at some time of the night that he prevented himself from getting a reasonable amount of rest. He could hear the soldiers breathing in sleep all about him. He wished to arouse them from this slumber which, to his ignorance, seemed stupid. The quality of mysterious menace in the great gloom and the silence would have caused him to pray if prayer would have transported him magically to New York and made him a young man with no coat playing billiards at his club.

The chill dawn came at last and with a fine elation which ever follows a dismal night in war; an elation which bounds in the bosom as soon as day has knocked the shackles from a trembling mind. Although Coleman had slept but a short time he was now as fresh as a total abstainer coming from the bath. He heard the creak of battery wheels; he saw crawling bodies of infantry moving in the dim light like ghostly processions. He felt a tremendous virility come with this new hope in the daylight. He again took satisfaction in his sentimental journey. It was a shining affair. He was on active service, an active service of the heart, and he' felt that he was a strong man ready to conquer difficulty even as the olden heroes conquered difficulty. He imagined himself in a way like them. He, too, had come out to fight for love with giants, dragons and witches. He had never known that he could be so pleased with that kind of a parallel.

The dragoman announced that the major had suddenly lent their horses to some other people, and after cursing this versatility of interest, he summoned his henchmen and they moved out on foot, following the sound of the creaking wheels. They came in time to a bridge, and on the side of this bridge was a hard military road which sprang away in two directions, north and west. Some troops were creeping out the westward way and the dragoman pointing at them said: "They going Prevasa. That is road to Nikopolis." Coleman grinned from ear to car and slapped his dragoman violently on the shoulder. For a moment he intended to hand the man a louis of reward, but he changed his mind.

Their traps were in the way of being heavy, but they minded little since the dragoman was now a victim of the influence of Coleman's enthusiasm. The road wound along the base of the mountain range, sheering around the abutments in wide white curves and then circling into glens where immense trees spread their shade over it. Some of the great trunks were oppressed with vines green as garlands, and these vines even ran like verdant foam over the rocks. Streams of translucent water showered down from the hills, and made pools in which every pebble, every eaf of a water plant shone with magic lustre, and if the bottom of a pool was only of clay, the clay glowed with sapphire light. The day was fair. The country was part of that land which turned the minds of its ancient poets toward a more tender dreaming, so that indeed their nymphs would die, one is sure, in the cold mythology of the north with its storms amid the gloom of pine forests. It was all wine to Coleman's spirit. It enlivened him to think of success with absolute surety. To be sure one of his boots began soon to rasp his toes, but he gave it no share of his attention. They passed at a much faster pace than the troops, and everywhere they met laughter and confidence and the cry. "On to Prevasa!"

At midday they were at the heels of the advance battalion, among its stragglers, taking its white dust into their throats and eyes. The dragoman was waning and he made a number of attempts to stay Coleman, but no one could have had influence upon Coleman's steady rush with his eyes always straight to the front as if thus to symbolize his steadiness of purpose. Rivulets of sweat marked the dust on his face, and two of his toes were now paining as if they were being burned off. He was obliged to concede a privilege of limping, but he would not stop.

At nightfall they halted with the outpost batallion of the infantry. All the cavalry had in the meantirne come up and they saw their old friends. There was a village from which the Christian peasants came and cheered like a trained chorus. Soldiers were driving a great flock of fat sheep into a corral. They had belonged to a Turkish bey and they bleated as if they knew that they were now mere spoils of war. Coleman lay on the steps of the bey's house smoking with his head on his blanket roll. Camp fires glowed off in the fields. He was now about four miles from Nikopolis.

Within the house, the commander of the cavalry was writing dispatches. Officers clanked up and down the stairs. The dashing young captain came and said that there would be a general assault on Prevasa at the dawn of the next day. Afterward the dragoman descended upon the village and in some way wrenched a little grey horse from an inhabitant. Its pack saddle was on its back and it would very handily carry the traps. In this matter the dragoman did not consider his master; he considered his own sore back.

Coleman ate more bread and chocolate tablets and also some tinned sardines. He was content with the day's work. He did not see how he could have improved it. There was only one route by which the Wainwright party could avoid him, and that was by going to Prevasa and thence taking ship. But since Prevasa was blockaded by a Greek fleet, he conceived that event to be impossible. Hence, he had them hedged on this peninsula and they must be either at Nikopolis or Prevasa. He would probably know all early in the morning. He reflected that he was too tired to care if there might be a night attack and then wrapped in his blankets he went peacefully to sleep in the grass under a big tree with the crooning of some soldiers around their fire blending into his slumber.

And now, although the dragoman had performed a number of feats of incapacity, he achieved during the one hour of Coleman's sleeping a blunder which for real finish was simply a perfection of art. When Coleman, much later, extracted the full story, it appeared that ringing. events happened during that single hour of sleep. Ten minutes after he had lain down for a night of oblivion, the battalion of infantry, which had advanced a little beyond the village, was recalled and began a hurried night march back on the way it had so festively come. It was significant enough to appeal to almost any mind, but the dragoman was able to not understand it. He remained jabbering to some acquaintances among the troopers. Coleman had been asleep his hour when the dashing young captain perceived the dragoman, and completely horrified by his presence at that place, ran to him and whispered to him swiftly that the game was to flee, flee, flee. The wing of the army which had advanced northward upon Jannina had already been tumbled back by the Turks and all the other wing had been recalled to the Louros river and there was now nothing practically between him and his sleeping master and the enemy but a cavalry picket. The cavalry was immediately going to make a forced march to the rear. The stricken dragoman could even then see troopers getting into their saddles. He, rushed to, the, tree, and in. a panic simply bundled Coleman upon his feet before he was awake. He stuttered out his tale, and the dazed, correspondent heard it punctuated by the steady trample of the retiring cavalry. The dragoman saw a man's face then turn in a flash from an expression of luxurious drowsiness to an expression of utter malignancy. However, he was in too much of a hurry to be afraid of it; he ran off to the little grey horse and frenziedly but skilfully began to bind the traps upon the packsaddle.

He appeared in a moment tugging at the halter. He could only say: "Come! Come! Come! Queek! Queek! "They slid hurriedly down a bank to the road and started to do again that which they had accomplished with considerable expenditure of physical power during the day. The hoof beats of the cavalry had already died away and the mountains shadowed them in lonely silence. They were the rear guard after the rear guard.

The dragoman muttered hastily his last dire rumours. Five hundred Circassian cavalry were coming. The mountains were now infested with the dread Albanian irregulars, Coleman had thought in his daylight tramp that he had appreciated the noble distances, but he found that he knew nothing of their nobility until he tried this night stumbling. And the hoofs of the little horse made on the hard road more noise than could be made by men beating with hammers upon brazen cylinders. The correspondent glanced continually up at the crags. From the other side he could sometimes hear the metallic clink of water deep down in a glen. For the first time in his life he seriously opened the flap of his holster and let his fingers remain on the handle of his revolver. From just in front of him he could hear the chattering of the dragoman's teeth which no attempt at more coolness could seem to prevent. In the meantime the casual manner of the little grey horse struck Coleman with maddening vividness. If the blank darkness was simply filled with ferocious Albanians, the horse did not care a button; he leisurely put his feet down with a resounding ring. Coleman whispered hastily to the dragoman. "If they rush us, jump down the bank, no matter how deep it is. That's our only chance. And try to keep together."

All they saw of the universe was, in front of them, a place faintly luminous near their feet, but fading in six yards to the darkness of a dungeon. This represented the bright white road of the day time. It had no end. Coleman had thought that he could tell from the very feel of the air some of the landmarks of his daytime journey, but he had now no sense of location at all. He would not have denied that he was squirming on his belly like a worm through black mud. They went on and on. Visions of his past were sweeping through Coleman's mind precisely as they are said to sweep through the mind of a drowning person. But he had no regret for any bad deeds; he regretted merely distant hours of peace and protection. He was no longer a hero going to rescue his love. He was a slave making a gasping attempt to escape from the most incredible tyranny of circumstances. He half vowed to himself that if the God whom he had in no wise heeded, would permit him to crawl out of this slavery he would never again venture a yard toward a danger any greater than may be incurred from the police of a most proper metropolis. If his juvenile and uplifting thoughts of other days had reproached him he would simply have repeated and repeated: "Adventure be damned."

It became known to them that the horse had to be led. The debased creature was asserting its right to do as it had been trained, to follow its customs; it was asserting this right during a situation which required conduct superior to all training and custom. It was so grossly conventional that Coleman would have understood that demoniac form of anger which sometimes leads men to jab knives into warm bodies. Coleman from cowardice tried to induce the dragoman to go ahead leading the horse, and the dragoman from cowardice tried to induce Coleman to go ahead leading the horse.

Coleman of course had to succumb. The dragoman was only good to walk behind and tearfully whisper maledictions as he prodded the flanks of their tranquil beast.

In the absolute black of the frequent forests, Coleman could not see his feet and he often felt like a man walking forward to fall at any moment down a thousand yards of chasm. He heard whispers; he saw skulking figures, and these frights turned out to be the voice of a little trickle of water or the effects of wind among the leaves, but they were replaced by the same terrors in slightly different forms.

Then the poignant thing interpolated. A volley crashed ahead of them some half of a mile away and another volley answered from a still nearer point. Swishing noises which the correspondent had heard in the air he now know to have been from the passing of bullets. He and the dragoman came stock still. They heard three other volleys sounding with the abrupt clamour of a hail of little stones upon a hollow surface. Coleman and the dragoman came close together and looked into the whites of each other's eyes. The ghastly horse at that moment stretched down his neck and began placidly to pluck the grass at the roadside. The two men were equally blank with fear and each seemed to seek in the other some newly rampant manhood upon which he could lean at this time. Behind them were the Turks. In front of them was a fight in the darkness. In front it was mathematic to suppose in fact were also the Turks. They were barred; enclosed; cut off. The end was come.

Even at that moment they heard from behind them the sound of slow, stealthy footsteps. They both wheeled instantly, choking with this additional terror. Coleman saw the dragoman move swiftly to the side of the road, ready to jump into whatever abyss happened to be there. Coleman still gripped the halter as if it were in truth a straw. The stealthy footsteps were much nearer. Then it was that an insanity came upon him as if fear had flamed up within him until it gave him all the magnificent desperation of a madman. He jerked the grey horse broadside to the approaching mystery, and grabbing out his revolver aimed it from the top of his improvised bulwark. He hailed the darkness.

"Halt. Who's there?" He had expected his voice to sound like a groan, but instead it happened to sound clear, stern, commanding, like the voice of a young sentry at an encampment of volunteers. He did not seem to have any privilege of selection as to the words. They were born of themselves.

He waited then, blanched and hopeless, for death to wing out of the darkness and strike him down. He heard a voice. The voice said: " Do you speak English? "For one or two seconds he could not even understand English, and then the great fact swelled up and within him. This voice with all its new quavers was still undoubtedly the voice of Prof. Harrison B.Wainwright of Washurst College.

CHAPTER XII

A CHANGE flashed over Coleman as if it had come from an electric storage. He had known the professor long, but he had never before heard a quaver in his voice, and it was this little quaver that seemed to impel him to supreme disregard of the dangers which he looked upon as being the final dangers. His own voice had not quavered.

When he spoke, he spoke in a low tone, it was the voice of the master of the situation. He could hear his dupes fluttering there in the darkness. "Yes," he said, "I speak English. There is some danger. Stay where you are and make no noise." He was as cool as an iced drink. To be sure the circumstances had in no wise changed as to his personal danger, but beyond the important fact that there were now others to endure it with him, he seemed able to forget it in a strange, unauthorized sense of victory. It came from the professor's quavers.

Meanwhile he had forgotten the dragoman, but he recalled him in time to bid him wait. Then, as well concealed as a monk hiding in his cowl, he tip-toed back into a group of people who knew him intimately.

He discerned two women mounted on little horses and about them were dim men. He could hear them breathing hard. "It is all right" he began smoothly. "You only need to be very careful -"

Suddenly out of the blackness projected a half phosphorescent face. It was the face of the little professor. He stammered. "We-we-do you really speak English? "Coleman in his feeling of superb triumph could almost have laughed. His nerves were as steady as hemp, but he was in haste and his haste allowed him to administer rebuke to his old professor.

"Didn't you hear me?" he hissed through his tightening lips. "They are fighting just ahead of us on the road and if you want to save yourselves don't waste time."

Another face loomed faintly like a mask painted in dark grey. It belonged to Coke, and it was a mask figured in profound stupefaction. The lips opened and tensely breathed out the name: "Coleman." Instantly the correspondent felt about him that kind of a tumult which tries to suppress itself. He knew that it was the most theatric moment of his life. He glanced quickly toward the two figures on horseback. He believed that one was making foolish gesticulation while the other sat rigid and silent. This latter one he knew to be Marjory. He was content that she did not move. Only a woman who was glad he had come but did not care for him would have moved. This applied directly to what he thought he knew of Marjory's nature.

There was confusion among the students, but Coleman suppressed it as in such situation might a centurion. "S-s-steady!" He seized the arm of the professor and drew him forcibly close. "The condition is this," he whispered rapidly. "We are in a fix with this fight on up the road. I was sent after you, but I can't get you into the Greek lines to-night. Mrs. Wainwright and Marjory must dismount and I and my man will take the horses on and hide them. All the rest of you must go up about a hundred feet into the woods and hide. When I come back, I'll hail you and you answer low." The professor was like pulp in his grasp. He choked out the word "Coleman" in agony and wonder, but he obeyed with a palpable gratitude. Coleman sprang to the side of the shadowy figure of Marjory. "Come," he said authoritatively. She laid in his palm a little icy cold hand and dropped from her horse. He had an impulse to cling to the small fingers, but he loosened them immediately, imparting to his manner, as well as the darkness permitted him, a kind of casual politeness as if he were too intent upon the business in hand. He bunched the crowd and pushed them into the wood. Then he and the dragoman took the horses a hundred yards onward and tethered them. No one would care if they were stolen; the great point was to get them where their noise would have no power of revealing the whole party. There had been no further firing.

After he had tied the little grey horse to a tree he unroped his luggage and carried the most of it back to the point where the others had left the road. He called out cautiously and received a sibilant answer. He and the dragoman bunted among the trees until they came to where a forlorn company was seated awaiting them lifting their faces like frogs out of a pond. His first question did not give them any assurance. He said at once: "Are any of you armed?" Unanimously they lowly breathed: "No." He searched them out one by one and finally sank down by the professor. He kept sort of a hypnotic handcuff upon the dragoman, because he foresaw that this man was really going to be the key to the best means of escape. To a large neutral party wandering between hostile lines there was technically no danger, but actually there was a great deal. Both armies had too many irregulars, lawless hillsmen come out to fight in their own way, and if they were encountered in the dead of night on such hazardous ground the Greek hillsmen with their white cross on a blue field would be precisely as dangerous as the blood-hungry Albanians. Coleman knew that the rational way was to reach the Greek lines, and he had no intention of reaching the Greek lines without a tongue, and the only tongue was in the mouth of the dragoman. He was correct in thinking that the professor's deep knowledge of the ancient language would give him small clue to the speech of the modern Greek.

As he settled himself by the professor the band of students, eight in number pushed their faces close.

He did not see any reason for speaking. There were thirty seconds of deep silence in which he felt that all were bending to hearken to his words of counsel The professor huskily broke the stillness. Well * * * what are we to do now? "

Coleman was decisive, indeed absolute. "We'll stay here until daylight unless you care to get shot."

"All right," answered the professor. He turned and made a useless remark to his flock. "Stay here."

Coleman asked civilly, "Have you had anything to eat? Have you got anything to wrap around you?"

"We have absolutely nothing," answered the professor."

Our servants ran away and * * and then we left everything behind us * * and I've never been in such a position in my life."

Coleman moved softly in the darkness and unbuckled some of his traps. On his knee he broke the hard cakes of bread and with his fingers he broke the little tablets of chocolate. These he distributed to his people. And at this time he felt fully the appreciation of the conduct of the eight American college students They had not yet said a word with the exception of the bewildered exclamation from Coke. They all knew him well. In any circumstance of life which as far as he truly believed, they had yet encountered, they would have been privileged to accost him in every form of their remarkable vocabulary. They were as new to this game as, would have been eight newly-caught Apache Indians if such were set to run the elevators in the Tract Society Building. He could see their eyes gazing at him anxiously and he could hear their deep-drawn breaths. But they said no word. He knew that they were looking upon him as their leader, almost as their saviour, and he knew also that they were going to follow him without a murmur in the conviction that he knew ten-fold more than they knew. It occurred to him that his position was ludicrously false, but, anyhow, he was glad. Surely it would be a very easy thing to lead them to safety in the morning and he foresaw the credit which would come to him. He concluded that it was beneath his dignity as preserver to vouchsafe them many words. His business was to be the cold, masterful, enigmatic man. It might be said that these reflections were only half-thoughts in his mind. Meanwhile a section of his intellect was flying hither and thither, speculating upon the Circassian cavalry and the Albanian guerillas and even the

Greek outposts.

He unbuckled his blanket roll and taking one blanket placed it about the shoulders of the shadow which was Mrs. Wainwright. The shadow protested incoherently, but he muttered "Oh that's all right." Then he took his other blanket and went to the shadow which was Marjory. It was something like putting a wrap about the shoulders of a statue. He was base enough to linger in the hopes that he could detect some slight trembling but as far as lie knew she was of stone. His macintosh he folded around the body of the professor amid quite senile protest, so senile that the professor seemed suddenly proven to him as an old, old man, a fact which had never occurred to Washurst or her children. Then he went to the dragoman and pre-empted half of his blankets, The dragoman grunted but Coleman It would not do to have this dragoman develop a luxurious temperament when eight American college students were, without speech, shivering in the cold night.

Coleman really begun to ruminate upon his glory, but he found that he could not do this well without Smoking, so he crept away some distance from this fireless, encampment, and bending his face to the ground at the foot of a tree he struck a match and lit a cigar. His retun to the others would have been some-what in the manner of coolness as displayed on the stage if he had not been prevented by the necessity of making no noise. He saw regarding him as before the dimly visible eyes of the eight students and Marjory and her father and mother. Then he whispered the conventional words. "Go to sleep if you can. You'll need your strength in the morning. I and this man here will keep watch." Three of the college students of course crawled up to him and each said: "I'll keep watch, old man."

"No. We'll keep watch. You people try to sleep."

He deemed that it might be better to yield the dragoman his blanket, and So he got up and leaned against a tree, holding his hand to cover the brilliant point of his cigar. He knew perfectly well that none of them could sleep. But he stood there somewhat like a sentry without the attitude, but with all the effect of responsibility.

He had no doubt but what escape to civilisation would be easy, but anyhow his heroism should be preserved. He was the rescuer. His thoughts of Marjory were somewhat in a puzzle. The meeting had placed him in such a position that he had expected a lot of condescension on his own part. Instead she had exhibited about as much recognition of him as would a stone fountain on his grandfather's place in Connecticut. This in his opinion was not the way to greet the knight who had come to the rescue of his lady. He had not expected it so to happen. In fact from Athens to this place he had engaged himself with imagery of possible meetings. He was vexed, certainly, but, far beyond that, he knew a deeper adminiration for this girl. To him she represented the sex, and so the sex as embodied in her seemed a mystery to be feared. He wondered if safety came on the morrow he would not surrender to this feminine invulnerability. She had not done anything that he had expected of her and so inasmuch as he loved her he loved her more. It was bewitching. He half considered himself a fool. But at any rate he thought resentfully she should be thankful to him for having rendered her a great service.

However, when he came to consider this proposition he knew that on a basis of absolute manly endeavour he had rendered her little or no service.

The night was long.

CHAPTER XIII

COLEMAN suddenly found himself looking upon his pallid dragoman. He saw that he had been asleep crouched at the foot of the tree. Without any exchange of speech at all he knew there had been alarming noises. Then shots sounded from nearby. Some were from rifles aimed in that direction and some were from rifles opposed to them. This was distinguishable to the experienced man, but all that Coleman knew was that the conditions of danger were now triplicated. Unconsciously he stretched his hands in supplication over his charges. "Don't move! Don't move! And keep close to the ground!" All heeded him but Marjory. She still sat straight. He himself was on his feet, but he now knew the sound of bullets, and he knew that no bullets had spun through the trees. He could not see her distinctly, but it was known to him in some way that she was mutinous. He leaned toward her and spoke as harshly as possible. "Marjory, get down!" She wavered for a moment as if resolved to defy him. As he turned again to peer in the direction of the firing it went through his mind that she must love him very much indeed. He was assured of it. It must have been some small outpour between nervous pickets and eager hillsmen, for it ended in a moment. The party waited in abasement for what seemed to them a time, and the blue dawn began, to laggardly shift the night as they waited. The dawn itself seemed prodigiously long in arriving at anything like discernible landscape. When this was consummated, Coleman, in somewhat the manner of the father of a church, dealt bits of chocolate out to the others. He had already taken the precaution to confer with the dragoman, so he said: "Well, come ahead. We'll make a try for it." They arose at his bidding and followed him to the road. It was the same broad, white road, only that the white was in the dawning something like the grey of a veil. It took some courage to venture upon this thoroughfare, but Coleman stepped out-after looking quickly in both directions. The party tramped to where the horses had been left, and there they were found without change of a rope. Coleman rejoiced to see that his dragoman now followed him in the way of a good lieutenant. They both dashed in among the trees and had the horses out into the road in a twinkle. When Coleman turned to direct that utterly subservient, group he knew that his face was drawn from hardship and anxiety, but he saw everywhere the same style of face with the exception of the face of Marjory, who looked simply of lovely marble. He noted with a curious satisfaction, as if the thing was a tribute to himself, that his macintosh was over the professor's shoulder, that Marjory and her mother were each carrying a blanket, and that, the corps of students had dutifully brought all the traps which his dragoman had forgotten. It was grand.

He addressed them to say: "Now, approaching outposts is very dangerous business at this time in the morning. So my man, who can talk both Greek and Turkish, will go ahead forty yards, and I will follow somewhere between him and you. Try not to crowd forward."

He directed the ladies upon their horses and placed the professor upon the little grey nag. Then they took up

their line of march. The dragoman had looked somewhat dubiously upon this plan of having him go forty
yards in advance, but he had the utmost confidence in
this new Coleman, whom yesterday he had not known.
Besides, he himself was a very gallant man indeed, and
it befitted him to take the post of danger before the
eyes of all these foreigners. In his new position he was
as proud and unreasonable as a rooster. He was
continually turning his head to scowl back at them,
when only the clank of hoofs was sounding. An
impenetrable mist lay on the valley and the hill-tops
were shrouded. As for the people, they were like mice.
Coleman paid no attention to the Wainwright party,
but walked steadily along near the dragoman.

Perhaps the whole thing was a trifle absurd, but to a
great percentage, of the party it was terrible. For
instance, those eight boys, fresh from a school, could
in no wise gauge the dimensions. And if this was true
of the students, it was more distinctly true of Marjory
and her mother. As for the professor, he seemed
Weighted to the earth by his love and his
responsibility.

Suddenly the dragoman wheeled and made demoniac
signs. Coleman half-turned to survey the main body,
and then paid his attention swiftly to the front. The
white road sped to the top of a hill where it seemed to
make a rotund swing into oblivion. The top of the
curve was framed in foliage, and therein was a
horseman. He had his carbine slanted on his thigh, and
his bridle-reins taut. Upon sight of them he immediately wheeled and galloped down the other slope and
vanished.

The dragoman was throwing wild gestures into the air.

As Coleman looked back at the Wainwright party he saw plainly that to an ordinary eye they might easily appear as a strong advance of troops. The peculiar light would emphasize such theory. The dragoman ran to him jubilantly, but he contained now a form of intelligence which caused him to whisper; "That was one Greek. That was one Greek-what do you call - sentree?"

Coleman addressed the others. He said: "It's all right. Come ahead. That was a Greek picket. There is only one trouble now, and that is to approach them easy-do you see-easy."

His obedient charges came forward at his word. When they arrived at the top of this rise they saw nothing. Coleman was very uncertain. He was not sure that this picket had not carried with him a general alarm, and in that case there would soon occur a certain amount of shooting. However, as far as he understood the business, there was no way but forward. Inasmuch as he did not indicate to the Wainwright party that he wished them to do differently, they followed on doggedly after him and the dragoman. He knew now that the dragoman's heart had for the tenth time turned to dog-biscuit, so he kept abreast of him. And soon together they walked into a cavalry outpost, commanded by no less a person than the dashing young captain, who came laughing out to meet them.

Suddenly losing all colour of war, the condition was now such as might occur in a drawing room. Coleman felt the importance of establishing highly conventional relations between the captain and the Wainwright party. To compass this he first seized his dragoman, and the dragoman, enlightened immediately, spun a series of lies which must have led the captain to believe that the entire heart of the American republic had been taken out of that western continent and transported to Greece. Coleman was proud of the captain, The latter immediately went and bowed in the manner of the French school and asked everybody to have a cup of coffee, although acceptation would have proved his ruin and disgrace. Coleman refused in the name of courtesy. He called his party forward, and now they proceeded merely as one crowd. Marjory had dismounted in the meantime.

The moment was come. Coleman felt it. The first rush was from the students. Immediately he was buried in a thrashing mob of them. "Good boy! Good boy! Great man! Oh, isn't he a peach? How did he do it? He came in strong at the finish! Good boy, Coleman!" Through this mist of glowing youthful congratulatioin he saw the professor standing at the outskirts with direct formal thanks already moving on his lips, while near him his wife wept joyfully. Marjory was evidently enduring some inscrutable emotion.

After all, it did penetrate his mind that it was indecent to accept all this wild gratitude, but there was built within him no intention of positively declaring himself lacking in all credit, or at least, lacking in all credit in the way their praises defined it. In truth he had assisted them, but he had been at the time largely engaged in assisting himself, and their coming had been more of a boon to his loneliness than an addition to his care. However, he soon had no difficulty in making his conscience appropriate every line in these hymns sung in his honour. The students, curiously wise of men, thought his conduct quite perfect. "Oh, say, come off!" he protested. "Why, I didn't do anything. You fellows are crazy. You would have gotten in all right by yourselves. Don't act like asses -"

As soon as the professor had opportunity he came to Coleman. He was a changed little man, and his extraordinary bewilderment showed in his face. It was the disillusion and amazement of a stubborn mind that had gone implacably in its one direction and found in the end that the direction was all wrong, and that really a certain mental machine had not been infallible. Coleman remembered what the American minister in Athens had described of his protests against the starting of the professor's party on this journey, and of the complete refusal of the professor to recognise any value in the advice. And here now was the consequent defeat. It was mirrored in the professor's astonished eyes. Coleman went directly to his dazed old teacher. "Well, you're out of it now, professor," he said warmly. "I congratulate you on your escape, sir." The professor looked at him, helpless to express himself, but the correspondent was at that time suddenly enveloped in the hysterical gratitude of Mrs. Wainwright, who hurled herself upon him with extravagant manifestations. Coleman played his part with skill. To both the professor and Mrs. Wainwright his manner was a combination of modestly filial affection and a pretentious disavowal of his having done anything at all. It seemed to charm everybody but Marjory. It irritated him to see that she was apparently incapable of acknowledging that he was a grand man.

He was actually compelled to go to her and offer congratulations upon her escape, as he had congratulated the professor. If his manner to her parents had been filial, his manner to her was parental. "Well, Marjory," he said kindly, "you have been in considerable danger. I suppose you're glad to be through with it." She at that time made no reply, but by her casual turn he knew that he was expected to walk along by her side. The others knew it, too, and the rest of the party left them free to walk side by side in the rear.

"This is a beautiful country here-abouts if one gets a good chance to see it," he remarked. Then he added: "But I suppose you had a view of it when you were going out to Nikopolis?"

She answered in muffled tones. "Yes, we thought it very beautiful."

Did you note those streams from the mountains "That seemed to me the purest water I'd ever seen, but I bet it would make one ill to drink it. There is, you know, a prominent German chemist who has almost proven that really pure water is practical poison to the human stomach."

"Yes ?" she said.

There was a period of silence, during which he was perfectly comfortable because he knew that she was ill at ease. If the silence was awkward, she was suffering from it. As for himself, he had no inclination to break it. His position was, as far as the entire Wainwright party was concerned, a place where he could afford to wait. She turned to him at last. "Of course, I know how much you have done for us, and I want you to feel that we all appreciate it deeply-deeply." There was discernible to the ear a certain note of desperation.

"Oh, not at all," he said generously. " Not at all. I didn't do anything. It was quite an accident. Don't let that trouble you for a moment."

"Well, of course you would say that," she said more steadily. "But I-we-we know how good and how-brave it was in you to come for us, and I - we must never forget it."

As a matter of fact," replied Coleman, with an appearance of ingenuous candor, " I was sent out here by the Eclipse to find you people, and of course I worked rather hard to reach you, but the final meeting was purely accidental and does not redound to my credit in the least."

As he had anticipated, Marjory shot him a little glance of disbelief. "Of course you would say that," she repeated with gloomy but flattering conviction.

"Oh, if I had been a great hero," he said smiling, "no doubt I would have kept up this same manner which now sets so well upon me, but I am telling you the truth when I say that I had no part in your rescue at all."

She became slightly indignant. "Oh, if you care to tell us constantly that you were of no service to us, I don't see what we can do but continue to declare that you were."

Suddenly he felt vulgar. He spoke to her this time with real meaning. "I beg of 'you never to mention it again. That will be the best way."

But to this she would not accede. "No, we will often want to speak of it."

He replied "How do you like Greece? Don't you think that some of these ruins are rather out of shape in the popular mind? Now, for my part, I would rather look at a good strong finish at a horserace than to see ten thousand Parthenons in a bunch."

She was immediately in the position of defending him from himself. "You would rather see no such thing. You shouldn't talk in that utterly trivial way. I like the Parthenon, of course, but I can't think of it now because my head. is too full of my escape from where I was so-so frightened."

Coleman grinned. " Were you really frightened?"

"Naturally," she answered. "I suppose I was more frightened for mother and father, but I was frightened enough for myself. It was not-not a nice thing."

"No, it wasn't," said Coleman. "I could hardly believe my senses, when the minister at Athens told me that, you all had ventured into such a trap, and there is no doubt but what you can be glad that you are well out of it."

She seemed to have some struggle with herself and then she deliberately said: "Thanks to you."

Coleman embarked on what he intended to make a series of high-minded protests. "Not at all -" but at that moment the dragoman whirled back from the van-guard with a great collection of the difficulties which had been gathering upon him. Coleman was obliged to resign Marjory and again take up the active leadership. He disposed of the dragoman's difficulties mainly by declaring that they were not difficulties at all. He had learned that this was the way to deal with dragomen. The fog had already lifted from the valley and, as they passed along the wooded mountain-side the fragrance of leaves and earth came to them. Ahead, along the hooded road, they could see the blue clad figures of Greek infantrymen. Finally they passed an encampment of a battalion whose line was at a right angle to the highway. A hundred yards in advance was the bridge across the Louros river. And there a battery of artillery was encamped. The dragoman became involved in all sorts of discussions with other Greeks, but Coleman stuck to his elbow and stifled all aimless oration. The Wainwright party waited for them in the rear in an observant but patient group.

Across a plain, the hills directly behind Arta loomed up showing the straight yellow scar of a modern entrenchment. To the north of Arta were some grey mountains with a dimly marked road winding to the summit. On one side of this road were two shadows. It took a moment for the eye to find these shadows, but when this was accomplished it was plain that they were men. The captain of the battery explained to the dragoman that he did not know that they were not also Turks. In which case the road to Arta was a dangerous path. It was no good news to Coleman. He waited a moment in order to gain composure and then walked back to the Wainwright party. They must have known at once from his peculiar gravity that all was not well. Five of the students and the professor immediately asked: "What is it?"

He had at first some old-fashioned idea of concealing the ill tidings from the ladies, but he perceived what flagrant nonsense this would be in circumstances in which all were fairly likely to incur equal dangers, and at any rate he did not see his way clear to allow their imagination to run riot over a situation which might not turn out to be too bad. He said slowly: "You see those mountains over there? Well, troops have been seen there and the captain of this battery thinks they are Turks. If they are Turks the road to Arta is distinctly-er-unsafe."

This new blow first affected the Wainwright party as being too much to endure. "They thought they had gone through enough. This was a general sentiment. Afterward the emotion took colour according to the individual character. One student laughed and said: "Well, I see our finish."

Another student piped out: "How do they know they are Turks? What makes them think they are Turks "

Another student expressed himself with a sigh. "This is a long way from the Bowery."

The professor said nothing but looked annihilated; Mrs. Wainwright wept profoundly; Marjory looked expectantly toward Coleman.

As for the correspondent he was adamantine and reliable and stern, for he had not the slightest idea that those men on the distant hill were Turks at all.

CHAPTER XIV

"OH," said a student, "this game ought to quit. I feel like thirty cents. We didn't come out here to be pursued about the country by these Turks. Why don't they stop it?"

Coleman was remarking: "Really, the only sensible thing to do now is to have breakfast. There is no use in worrying ourselves silly over this thing until we've got to."

They spread the blankets on the ground and sat about a feast of bread, water cress and tinned beef. Coleman was the real host, but he contrived to make the professor appear as that honourable person. They ate, casting their eyes from time to time at the distant mountain with its two shadows. People began to fly down the road from Jannina, peasants hurriedly driving little flocks, women and children on donkeys and little horses which they clubbed unceasingly. One man rode at a gallop, shrieking and flailing his arms in the air. They were all Christian peasants of Turkey, but they were in flight now because they did not wish to be at home if the Turk was going to return and reap revenge for his mortification. The Wainwright party looked at Coleman in abrupt questioning.

"Oh, it's all right," he said, easily. "They are always

taking on that way."

Suddenly the dragoman gave a shout and dashed up the road to the scene of a melee where a little ratfaced groom was vociferously defending three horses from some Greek officers, who as vociferously were stating their right to requisition them. Coleman ran after his dragoman. There was a sickening pow-wow, but in the end Coleman, straight and easy in the saddle, came cantering back on a superb open-mouthed snorting bay horse. He did not mind if the half-wild animal plunged crazily. It was part of his role. "They were trying to steal my horses," he explained. He leaped to the ground, and holding the horse by the bridle, he addressed his admiring companions. "The groom - the man who has charge of the horses - says that he thinks that the people on the mountain-side are Turks, but I don't see how that is possible. You see -" he pointed wisely -" that road leads directly south to Arta, and it is hardly possible that the Greek army would come over here and leave that approach to Arta utterly unguarded. It would be too foolish. They must have left some men to cover it, and that is certainly what those troops are. If you are all ready and willing, I don't see anything to do but make a good, stout-hearted dash for Arta. It would be no more dangerous than to sit here." The professor was at last able to make his formal speech. "Mr. Coleman," he said distinctly, "we place ourselves entirely in your hands." It was some. how pitiful. This man who, for years and years had reigned in a little college town almost as a monarch, passing judgment with the air of one who words the law, dealing criticism upon the universe as one to whom all things are plain, publicly disdaining defeat as one to whom all things are easy - this man was now veritably appealing to Coleman to save his wife, his daughter and himself, and really declared himself de. pendent for safety upon the ingenuity and courage of the correspondent.

The attitude of the students was utterly indifferent. They did not consider themselves helpless at all. they were evidently quite ready to withstand anything but they looked frankly up to Coleman as their intelligent leader. If they suffered any, their only expression of it was in the simple grim slang of their period.

"I wish I was at Coney Island."

"This is not so bad as trigonometry, but it's worse than playing billiards for the beers."

And Coke said privately to Coleman: "Say, what in hell are these two damn peoples fighting for, anyhow?"

When he saw that all opinions were in favour of following him loyally, Coleman was impelled to feel a responsibility. He was now no errant rescuer, but a properly elected leader of fellow beings in distress. While one of the students held his horse, he took the dragoman for another consultation with the captain of the battery. The officer was sitting on a large stone, with his eyes fixed into his field glasses. When again questioned he could give no satisfaction as to the identity of the troops on the distant mountain. He merely shrugged his shoulders and said that if they were Greeks it was very good, but if they were Turks it was very bad. He seemed more occupied in trying to impress the correspondent that it was a matter of soldierly indifference to himself. Coleman, after loathing him sufficiently in silence, returned to the others and said: "Well, we'll chance it."

They looked to him to arrange the caravan. Speaking to the men of the party he said: "Of course, any one of you is welcome to my horse if you can ride it, but-if you're not too tired-I think I had myself better ride, so that I can go ahead at times."

His manner was so fine as he said this that the students seemed fairly to worship him. Of course it had been most improbable that any of them could have ridden that volcanic animal even if one of them had tried it.

He saw Mrs. Wainwright and Marjory upon the backs of their two little natives, and hoisted the professor into the saddle of the groom's horse, leaving instructions with the servant to lead the animal always and carefully. He and the dragoman then mounted at the head of the procession, and amid curious questionings from the soldiery they crossed the bridge and started on the trail to Arta. The rear was brought up by the little grey horse with the luggage, led by one student and flogged by another.

Coleman, checking with difficulty the battling disposition of his horse, was very uneasy in his mind because the last words of the captain of the battery had made him feel that perhaps on this ride he would be placed in a position where only the best courage would count, and he did not see his way clear to feeling very confident about his conduct in such a case. Looking back upon the caravan, he saw it as a most unwieldy thing, not even capable of running away. He hurried it with sudden, sharp contemptuous phrases.

On the. march there incidentally flashed upon him a new truth. More than half of that student band were deeply in love with Marjory. Of course, when he had been distant from her he had had an eternal jealous reflection to that effect. It was natural that he should have thought of the intimate camping relations between Marjory and these young students with a great deal of bitterness, grinding his teeth when picturing their opportunities to make Marjory fall in love with some one of them. He had raged particularly about Coke, whose father had millions of dollars. But he had forgotten all these jealousies in the general splendour of his exploits. Now, when he saw the truth, it seemed. to bring him back to his common life and he saw himself suddenly as not being frantically superior in any way to those other young men. The more closely he looked at this last fact, the more convinced he was of its truth. He seemed to see that he had been impropererly elated over his services to the Wainwrights, and that, in the end, the girl might fancy a man because the man had done her no service at all. He saw his proud position lower itself to be a pawn in the game. Looking back over the students, he wondered which one Marjory might love. This hideous Nikopolis had given eight men chance to win her. His scorn and his malice quite centered upon Coke, for he could never forget that the man's father had millions of dollars. The unfortunate Coke chose that moment to address him querulously: "Look here, Coleman, can't you tell us how far it is to Arta ?"

"Coke," said Coleman, "I don't suppose you take me for a tourist agency, but if you can only try to distinguish between me and a map with the scale of miles printed in the lower left-hand corner, you will not contribute so much to the sufferings of the party which you now adorn."

The students within hearing guffawed and Coke

retired, in confusion.

The march was not rapid. Coleman almost wore out his arms holding in check his impetuous horse. Often the caravan floundered through mud, while at the same time a hot, yellow dust came from the north.

They were perhaps half way to Arta when Coleman decided that a rest and luncheon were the things to be considered. He halted his troop then in the shade of some great trees, and privately he bade his dragoman prepare the best feast which could come out of those saddle-bags fresh from Athens. The result was rather gorgeous in the eyes of the poor wanderers. First of all there were three knives, three forks, three spoons, three tin cups and three tin plaies, which the entire party of twelve used on a most amiable socialistic principle. There were crisp, salty biscuits and olives, for which they speared in the bottle. There was potted turkey, and potted ham, and potted tongue, all tasting precisely alike. There were sardines and the ordinary tinned beef, disguised sometimes with onions, carrots and potatoes. Out of the saddle-bags came pepper and salt and even mustard. The dragoman made coffee over a little fire of sticks that blazed with a white light. The whole thing was prodigal, but any philanthropist would have approved of it if he could have seen the way in which the eight students laid into the spread. When there came a polite remonstrance - notably from Mrs. Wainwright-Coleman merely pointed to a large bundle strapped back of the groom's saddle. During the coffee he was considering how best to get the students one by one out of the sight of the Wainwrights where he could give them good drinks of whisky.

There was an agitation on the road toward Arta. Some

people were coming on horses. He paid small heed until he heard a thump of pausing hoofs near him, and a musical voice say: "Rufus! "

He looked up quickly, and then all present saw his eyes really bulge. There on a fat and glossy horse sat Nora Black, dressed in probably one of the most correct riding habits which had ever been seen in the East. She was smiling a radiant smile, which held the eight students simply spell-bound. They would have recognised her if it had not been for this apparitional coming in the wilds of southeastern Europe. Behind her were her people-some servants and an old lady on a very little pony. "Well, Rufus? " she said.

Coleman made the mistake of hesitating. For a fraction of a moment he had acted as if he were embarrassed, and was only going to nod and say: "How d'do ?"

He arose and came forward too late. She was looking at him with a menacing glance which meant difficulties for him if he was not skilful. Keen as an eagle, she swept her glance over the face and figure of Marjory. Without. further introduction, the girls seemed to understand that they were enemies.

Despite his feeling of awkwardness, Coleman's mind was mainly occupied by pure astonishment. "Nora Black?" he said, as if even then he could not believe his senses. "How in the world did you get down here" ?

She was not too amiable, evidently, over his reception, and she seemed to know perfectly that it was in her power to make him feel extremely unpleasant. "Oh, it's not so far," she answered. "I don't see where you come in to ask me what I'm doing here. What are you doing here? " She lifted her eyes and shot the half of a glance at Marjory. Into her last question she had interjected a spirit of ownership in which he saw future woe. It turned him cowardly. "Why, you know I was sent up here by the paper to rescue the Wainwright party, and I've got them. I'm taking them to Arta. But why are you here?"

"I am here," she said, giving him the most defiant of glances, " principally to look for you."

Even the horse she rode betrayed an intention of abiding upon that spot forever. She had made her communication with Coleman appear to the Wain-wright party as a sort of tender reunion.

Coleman looked at her with a steely eye. "Nora, you can certainly be a devil when you choose."

"Why don't you present me to your friends? Miss; Nora Black, special correspondent of the New York Daylighi, if you please. I belong to your opposition. I am your rival, Rufus, and I draw a bigger salary-see? Funny looking gang, that. Who is the old Johnnie in the white wig?"

"Er-where you goin' - you can't" - blundered Coleman miserably "Aw-the army is in retreat and you must go back to - don't you see?"

"Is it?" she agked. After a pause she added coolly: "Then I shall go back to Arta with you and your precious Wainwrights."

CHAPTER XV

GIVING Coleman another glance of subtle menace Nora repeated: "Why don't you present me to your friends?" Coleman had been swiftly searching the whole world for a way clear of this unhappiness, but he knew at last that he could only die at his guns. "Why, certainly," he said quickly, "if you wish it." He sauntered easily back to the luncheon blanket. "This is Miss Black of the New York Daylight and she says that those people on the mountain are Greeks." The students were gaping at him, and Marjory and her father sat in the same silence. But to the relief of Coleman and to the high edification of the students, Mrs. Wainwright cried out: "Why, is she an American woman?" And seeing Coleman's nod of assent she rustled to her feet and advanced hastily upon the complacent horsewoman. "I'm delighted to see you. Who would think of seeing an American woman way over here. Have you been here long? Are you going on further? Oh, we've had such a dreadful time." Coleman remained long enough to hear Nora say: "Thank you very much, but I shan't dismount. I am going to ride back to Arta presently."

Then he heard Mrs. Wainwright cry: "Oh, are you indeed? Why we, too, are going at once to Arta. We can all go together." Coleman fled then to the bosom of the students, who all looked at him with eyes of cynical penetration. He cast a glance at Marjory more than fearing a glare which denoted an implacable resolution never to forgive this thing. On the contrary he had never seen her so content and serene. "You have allowed your coffee to get chilled," she said considerately. "Won't you have the man warm you some more?"

"Thanks, no," he answered with gratitude.

Nora, changing her mind, had dismounted and was coming with Mrs. Wainwright. That worthy lady had long had a fund of information and anecdote the sound of which neither her husband nor her daughter would endure for a moment. Of course the rascally students were out of the question. Here, then, was really the first ear amiably and cheerfully open, and she was talking at what the students called her "thirty knot gait."

"Lost everything. Absolutely everything. Neither of us have even a brush and comb, or a cake of soap, or enough hairpins to hold up our hair. I'm going to take Marjory's away from her and let her braid her hair down her back. You can imagine how dreadful it is -"

From time to time the cool voice of Nora sounded without effort through this clamour. " Oh, it will be no trouble at all. I have more than enough of everything. We can divide very nicely."

Coleman broke somewhat imperiously into this feminine chat. "Well, we must be moving, you know," and his voice started the men into activity. When the traps were all packed again on the horse Coleman looked back surprised to see the three women engaged in the most friendly discussion. The combined parties now made a very respectable squadron. Coleman rode off at its head without glancing behind at all. He knew that they were following from the soft pounding of the horses hoofs on the sod and from the mellow hum of human voices.

For a long time he did not think to look upon himself as anything but a man much injured by circumstances. Among his friends he could count numbers who had lived long lives without having this peculiar class of misfortune come to them. In fact it was so unusual a misfortune that men of the world had not found it necessary to pass from mind to mind a perfect formula for dealing with it. But he soon began to consider himself an extraordinarily lucky person inasmuch as Nora Black had come upon him with her saddle bags packed with inflammable substances, so to speak, and there had been as yet only enough fire to boil coffee for luncheon. He laughed tenderly when he thought of the innocence of Mrs. Wainwright, but his face and back flushed with heat when lie thought of the canniness of the eight American college students.

He heard a horse cantering up on his left side and looking he saw Nora Black. She was beaming with satisfaction and good nature. "Well, Rufus," she cried flippantly, "how goes it with the gallant rescuer? You've made a hit, my boy. You are the success of the season."

Coleman reflected upon the probable result of a direct appeal to Nora. He knew of course that such appeals were usually idle, but he did not consider Nora an ordinary person. His decision was to venture it. He drew his horse close to hers. "Nora," he said, "do you know that you are raising the very devil?"

She lifted her finely penciled eyebrows and looked at him with the baby-stare. "How?" she enquired.

"You know well enough," he gritted out wrathfully.

"Raising the very devil?" she asked. "How do you mean?" She was palpably interested for his answer. She waited for his reply for an interval, and then she asked him outright. "Rufus Coleman do you mean that I am not a respectable woman?"

In reality he had meant nothing of the kind, but this direct throttling of a great question stupefied him utterly, for he saw now that she' would probably never understand him in the least and that she would at any rate always pretend not to understand him and that the more he said the more harm he manufactured. She studied him over carefully and then wheeled her horse towards the rear with some parting remarks. "I suppose you should attend more strictly to your own affairs, Rufus. Instead of raising the devil I am lending hairpins. I have seen you insult people, but I have never seen you insult anyone quite for the whim of the thing. Go soak your head."

Not considering it advisable to then indulge in such immersion Coleman rode moodily onward. The hot dust continued to sting the cheeks of the travellers and in some places great clouds of dead leaves roared in circles about them. All of the Wainwright party were utterly fagged. Coleman felt his skin crackle and his throat seemed to be coated with the white dust. He worried his dragoman as to the distance to Arta until the dragoman lied to the point where he always declared that Arta was only off some hundreds of yards.

At their places in the procession Mrs. Wainwright and Marjory were animatedly talking to Nora and the old lady on the little pony. They had at first suffered great amazement at the voluntary presence of the old lady, but she was there really because she knew no better. Her colossal ignorance took the form, mainly, of a most obstreperous patriotism, and indeed she always acted in a foreign country as if she were the special commissioner of the President, or perhaps as a special commissioner could not act at all. She was very aggressive, and when any of the travelling arrangements in Europe did not suit her ideas she was won't to shrilly exclaim: "Well ! New York is good enough for me." Nora, morbidly afraid that her expense bill to the Daylight would not be large enough, had dragged her bodily off to Greece as her companion, friend and protection. At Arta they had heard of the grand success of the Greek army. The Turks had not stood for a moment before that gallant and terrible advance; no; they had scampered howling with fear into the north. Jannina would fall-well, Jannina would fall as soon as the Greeks arrived. There was no doubt of it. The correspondent and her friend, deluded and hurried by the light-hearted confidence of the Greeks in Arta, had hastened out then on a regular tourist's excursion to see Jannina after its capture. Nora concealed from her friend the fact that the editor of the Daylight particularly wished her to see a battle so that she might write an article on actual warfare from a woman's point of view. With her name as a queen of comic opera, such an article from her pen would be a burning, sensation.

Coleman had been the first to point out to Nora that instead of going on a picnic to Jannina, she had better run back to Arta. When the old lady heard that they had not been entirely safe, she was furious with Nora. "The idea!" she exclaimed to Mrs. Wainwright. "They might have caught us! They might have caught us!"

"Well," said Mrs. Wainwright. "I verily believe they would have caught us if it had not been for Mr. Coleman."

"Is he the gentleman on the fine horse?"

"Yes; that's him. Oh, he has been sim-plee splendid. I confess I was a little bit-er-surprised. He was in college under my husband. I don't know that we thought very great things of him, but if ever a man won golden opinions he has done so from us"

"Oh, that must be the Coleman who is such a great friend of Nora's."

"Yes?" said Mrs. Wainwright insidiously. "Is he? I didn't know. Of course he knows so many people." Her mind had been suddenly illumined by the old lady and she thought extravagantly of the arrival of Nora upon the scene. She remained all sweetness to the old lady. "Did you know he was here? Did you expect to meet him? I seemed such a delightful coincidence." In truth she was being subterraneously clever.

"Oh, no; I don't think so. I didn't hear Nora mention it. Of course she would have told me. You know, our coming to Greece was such a surprise. Nora had an engagement in London at the Folly Theatre in Fly by Night, but the manager was insufferable, oh, insufferable. So, of course, Nora wouldn't stand it a minute, and then these newspaper people came along and asked her to go to Greece for them and she accepted. I am sure I never expected to find us-aw-fleeing from the Turks or I shouldn't have Come."

"Mrs. Wainwright was gasping. "You don't mean that she is - she is Nora Black, the actress."

"Of course she is," said the old lady jubilantly.

"Why, how strange," choked Mrs. Wainwrignt. Nothing she knew of Nora could account for her stupefaction and grief. What happened glaringly to her was the duplicity of man. Coleman was a ribald deceiver. He must have known and yet he had pretended throughout that the meeting was a pure accident She turned with a nervous impulse to sympathist with her daughter, but despite the lovely tranquillity of the girl's face there was something about her which forbade the mother to meddle. Anyhow Mrs. Wainwright was sorry that she had told nice things of Coleman's behaviour, so she said to the old lady: "Young men of these times get a false age so quickly. We have always thought it a great pity, about Mr. Coleman."

"Why, how so?" asked the old lady.

"Oh, really nothing. Only, to us he seemed rather - er - prematurely experienced or something of that kind. The old lady did not catch the meaning of the phrase. She seemed surprised. "Why, I've never seen any full-grown person in this world who got experience any too quick for his own good."

At the tail of the procession there was talk between the two students who had in charge the little grey horse-one to lead and one to flog. "Billie," said one, " it now becomes necessary to lose this hobby into the hands of some of the other fellows. Whereby we will gain opportunity to pay homage to the great Nora. Why, you egregious thick-head, this is the chance of a life-time. I'm damned if I'm going to tow this beast of burden much further."

"You wouldn't stand a show," said Billie pessimistically. " Look at Coleman."

"That's all right. Do you mean to say that you prefer to continue towing pack horses in the presence of this queen of song and the dance just because you think Coleman can throw out his chest a little more than you. Not so. Think of your bright and sparkling youth. There's Coke and Pete Tounley near Marjory. We'll call 'em." Whereupon he set up a cry. "Say, you people, we're not getting a, salary for this. Supposin' you try for a time. It'll do you good." When the two addressed bad halted to await the arrival of the little grey horse, they took on glum expressions. "You look like poisoned pups," said the student who led the horse. "Too strong for light work. Grab onto the halter, now, Peter, and tow. We are going ahead to talk to Nora Black."

"Good time you'll have," answered Peter Tounley.

"Coleman is cuttin' up scandalous. You won't stand a show."

"What do you think of him?" said Coke. "Seems curious, all 'round. Do you suppose he knew she would

Stephen Crane

show up? It was nervy to -"

"Nervy to what? " asked Billie.

"Well," said Coke, "seems to me he is playing both ends against the middle. I don't know anything about Nora Black, but -"

The three other students expressed themselves with conviction and in chorus. " Coleman's all right."

"Well, anyhow," continued Coke, " I don't see my way free to admiring him introducing Nora Black to the Wainwrights."

"He didn't," said the others, still in chorus.

"Queer game," said Peter Tounley. " He seems to know her pretty well."

"Pretty damn well," said Billie.

"Anyhow he's a brick," said Peter Tounley. "We mustn't forget that. Lo, I begin to feel that our Rufus is a fly guy of many different kinds. Any play that he is in commands my respect. He won't be hit by a chimney in the daytime, for unto him has come much wisdom, I don't think I'll worry."

"Is he stuck on Nora Black, do you know?" asked Billie.

"One thing is plain," replied Coke. "She has got him somehow by the short hair and she intends him to holler murder. Anybody can see that."

"Well, he won't holler murder," said one of them with conviction. "I'll bet you he won't. He'll hammer the war-post and beat the tom-tom until he drops, but he won't holler murder."

"Old Mother Wainwright will be in his wool presently," quoth Peter Tounley musingly, "I could see it coming in her eye. Somebody has given his snap away, or something." "Aw, he had no snap," said Billie. "Couldn't you see how rattled he was? He would have given a lac if dear Nora hadn't turned up."

"Of course," the others assented. "He was rattled."

"Looks queer. And nasty," said Coke.

"Nora herself had an axe ready for him."

They began to laugh. " If she had had an umbrella she would have basted him over the head with it. Oh, my! He was green."

"Nevertheless," said Peter Tounley, "I refuse to worry over our Rufus. When he can't take care of himself the rest of us want to hunt cover. He is a fly guy -"

Coleman in the meantime had become aware that the light of Mrs. Wainwright's countenance was turned from him. The party stopped at a well, and when he offered her a drink from his cup he thought she accepted it with scant thanks. Marjory was still gracious, always gracious, but this did not reassure him, because he felt there was much unfathomable deception in it. When he turned to seek consolation in the manner of the professor he found him as before, stunned with surprise, and the only idea he had was to be as tractable as a child.

When he returned to the head of the column, Nora again cantered forward to join him. "Well, me gay Lochinvar," she cried, "and has your disposition improved? "

"You are very fresh," he said.

She laughed loud enough to be heard the full length of the caravan. It was a beautiful laugh, but full of insolence and confidence. He flashed his eyes malignantly upon her, but then she only laughed more. She could see that he wished to strangle her. "What a disposition!" she said. "What a disposition! You are not. nearly so nice as your friends. Now, they are charming, but you-Rufus, I wish you would get that temper mended. Dear Rufus, do it to please me. You know you like to please me. Don't you now, dear?" He finally laughed. "Confound you, Nora. I would like to kill you."

But at his laugh she was all sunshine. It was as if she. had been trying to taunt him into good humour with her. "Aw, now, Rufus, don't be angry. I'll be good, Rufus. Really, I will. Listen. I want to tell you something. Do you know what I did? Well, you know, I never was cut out for this business, and, back there, when you told me about the Turks being near and all that sort of thing, I was frightened almost to death. Really, I was. So, when nobody was looking, I sneaked two or three little drinks out of my flask. Two or three little drinks -"

CHAPTER XVI

"GOOD God!" said Coleman. "You don't Mean -"

Nora smiled rosily at him. "Oh, I'm all right," she answered." Don't worry about your Aunt Nora, my precious boy. Not for a minute."

Coleman was horrified. "But you are not going to - you are not going to -"

"Not at all, me son. Not at all," she answered.

I'm not going to prance. I'm going to be as nice as pie, and just ride quietly along here with dear little Rufus. Only * * you know what I can do when I get started, so you had better be a very good boy. I might take it into my head to say some things, you know."

Bound hand and foot at his stake, he could not even chant his defiant torture song. It might precipitate - in fact, he was sure it would precipitate the grand smash. But to the very core of his soul, he for the time hated Nora Black. He did not dare to remind her that he would revenge himself; he dared only to dream of this revenge, but it fairly made his thoughts flame, and deep in his throat he was swearing an inflexible persecution of Nora Black. The old expression of his sex came to him, "Oh, if she were only a man!" she

Stephen Crane

had been a man, he would have fallen upon her tooth and nail. Her motives for all this impressed him not at all; she was simply a witch who bound him helpless with the pwer of her femininity, and made him eat cinders. He was so sure that his face betrayed him that he did not dare let her see it. "Well, what are you going to do about it ? " he asked, over his shoulder.

"O-o-oh," she drawled, impudently. "Nothing." He could see that she was determined not to be confessed. "I may do this or I may do that. It all depends upon your behaviour, my dear Rufus."

As they rode on, he deliberated as to the best means of dealing with this condition. Suddenly he resolved to go with the whole tale direct to Marjory, and to this end he half wheeled his horse. He would reiterate that he loved her and then explain - explain! He groaned when he came to the word, and ceased formulation.

The cavalcade reached at last the bank of the Aracthus river, with its lemon groves and lush grass. A battery wheeled before them over the ancient bridge - a flight of short, broad cobbled steps up as far as the centre of the stream and a similar flight down to the other bank. The returning aplomb of the travellers was well illustrated by the professor, who, upon sighting this bridge, murmured: "Byzantine."

This was the first indication that he had still within him a power to resume the normal.

The steep and narrow street was crowded with soldiers; the smoky little coffee shops were a-babble with people discussing the news from the front. None seemed to heed the remarkable procession that wended its way to the cable office. Here Coleman resolutely took precedence. He knew that there was no good in expecting intelligence out of the chaotic clerks, but he managed to get upon the wires this message :

"Eclipse, New York: Got Wainwright party; all well. Coleman." The students had struggled to send messages to their people in America, but they had only succeeded in deepening the tragic boredom of the clerks.

When Coleman returned to the street he thought that he had seldom looked upon a more moving spectacle than the Wainwright party presented at that moment. Most of the students were seated in a row, dejectedly, upon the kerb. The professor and Mrs. Wainwright looked like two old pictures, which, after an existence in a considerate gloom, had been brought out in their tawdriness to the clear light. Hot white dust covered everybody, and from out the grimy faces the eyes blinked, red-fringed with sleeplessness. Desolation sat upon all, save Marjory. She possessed some marvellous power of looking always fresh. This quality had indeed impressed the old lady on the little pony until she had said to Nora Black: "That girl would look well anywhere." Nora Black had not been amiable in her reply.

Coleman called the professor and the dragoman for a durbar. The dragoman said: "Well, I can get one carriage, and we can go immediate-lee."

"Carriage be blowed!" said Coleman. "What these people need is rest, sleep. You must find a place at once. These people can't remain in the street." He spoke in anger, as if he had previously told the dragoman and the latter had been inattentive. The man immediately departed.

Coleman remarked that there was no course but to remain in the street until his dragoman had found them a habitation. It was a mournful waiting. The students sat on the kerb. Once they whispered to Coleman, suggesting a drink, but he told them that he knew only one cafe, the entrance of which would be in plain sight of the rest of the party. The ladies talked together in a group of four. Nora Black was bursting with the fact that her servant had hired rooms in Arta on their outcoming journey, and she wished Mrs. Wainwright and Marjory to come to them, at least for a time, but she dared not risk a refusal, and she felt something in Mrs. Wainwright's manner which led her to be certain that such would be the answer to her invitation. Coleman and the professor strolled slowly up and down the walk.

"Well, my work is over, sir," said Coleman. "My paper told me to find you, and, through no virtue of my own, I found you. I am very glad of it. I don't know of anything in my life that has given me greater pleasure."

The professor was himself again in so far as he had lost all manner of dependence. But still he could not yet be bumptious. "Mr. Coleman," he said, "I am placed under life-long obligation to you. * * * I am not thinking of myself so much. * * * My wife and daughter -" His gratitude was so genuine that he could not finish its expression.

"Oh, don't speak of it," said Coleman. "I really didn't do anything at all."

The dragoman finally returned and led them all to a house which he had rented for gold. In the great, bare, upper chamber the students dropped wearily to the floor, while the woman of the house took the Wainwrights to a more secluded apartment., As the door closed on them, Coleman turned like a flash.

"Have a drink," he said. The students arose around him like the wave of a flood. "You bet." In the absence of changes of clothing, ordinary food, the possibility of a bath, and in the presence of great weariness and dust, Coleman's whisky seemed to them a glistening luxury. Afterward they laid down as if to sleep, but in reality they were too dirty and too fagged to sleep. They simply lay murmuring Peter Tounley even developed a small fever.

It was at this time that Coleman. suddenly discovered his acute interest in the progressive troubles of his affair of the heart had placed the business of his newspaper in the rear of his mind. The greater part of the next hour he spent in getting off to New York that dispatch which created so much excitement for him later. Afterward he was free to reflect moodily upon the ability of Nora Black to distress him. She, with her retinue, had disappeared toward her own rooms. At dusk he went into the street, and was edified to see Nora's dragoman dodging along in his wake. He thought that this was simply another manifestation of Nora's interest in his movements, and so he turned a corner, and there pausing, waited until the dragoman spun around directly into his arms. But it seemed that the man had a note to deliver, and this was only his Oriental way of doing it.

The note read: "Come and dine with me to-night." It

was, not a request. It was peremptory. "All right," he said, scowling at the man.

He did not go at once, for he wished to reflect for a time and find if he could not evolve some weapons of his own. It seemed to him that all the others were liberally supplied with weapons.

A clear, cold night had come upon the earth when he signified to the lurking dragoman that he was in readiness to depart with him to Nora's abode. They passed finally into a dark court-yard, up a winding staircase, across an embowered balcony, and Coleman entered alone a room where there were lights.

His, feet were scarcely over the threshold before he had concluded that the tigress was now going to try some velvet purring. He noted that the arts of the stage had not been thought too cheaply obvious for use. Nora sat facing the door. A bit of yellow silk had been twisted about the crude shape of the lamp, and it made the play of light, amber-like, shadowy and yet perfectly clear, the light which women love. She was arrayed in a puzzling gown of that kind of Grecian silk which is so docile that one can pull yards of it through a ring. It was of the colour of new straw. Her chin was leaned pensively upon her palm and the light fell on a pearly rounded forearm. She was looking at him with a pair of famous eyes, azure, perhaps-certainly purple at times - and it may be, black at odd moments-a pair of eyes that had made many an honest man's heart jump if he thought they were looking at him. It was a vision, yes, but Coleman's cynical knowledge of drama overpowered his sense of its beauty. He broke out brutally, in the phrases of the American street. "Your dragoman is a rubber-neck. If he keeps darking me I will simply have to kick the stuffing out of him."

She was alone in the room. Her old lady had been instructed to have a headache and send apologies. She was not disturbed by Coleman's words. "Sit down, Rufus, and have a cigarette, and don't be cross, because I won't stand it."

He obeyed her glumly. She had placed his chair where not a charm of her could be lost upon an observant man. Evidently she did not purpose to allow him to irritate her away from her original plan. Purring was now her method, and none of his insolence could achieve a growl from the tigress. She arose, saying softly: "You look tired, almost ill, poor boy. I will give you some brandy. I have almost everything that I could think to make those Daylight people buy." With a sweep of her hand she indicated the astonishing opulence of the possessions in different parts of the room.

As she stood over him with the brandy there came through the smoke of his cigarette the perfume of orris-root and violet.

A servant began to arrange the little cold dinner on a camp table, and Coleman saw with an enthusiasm which he could not fully master, four quart bottles of a notable brand of champagne placed in a rank on the floor.

At dinner Nora was sisterly. She watched him, waited upon him, treated him to an affectionate inti. macy for which he knew a thousand men who would have hated him. The champagne was cold.

Slowly he melted. By the time that the boy came with little cups of Turkish coffee he was at least amiable. Nora talked dreamily. "The dragoman says this room used to be part of the harem long ago." She shot him a watchful glance, as if she had expected the fact to affect him. "Seems curious, doesn't it? A harem. Fancy that." He smoked one cigar and then discarded tobacco, for the perfume of orris-root and violet was making him meditate. Nora talked on in a low voice. She knew that, through half-closed lids, he was looking at her in steady speculation. She knew that she was conquering, but no movement of hers betrayed an elation. With the most exquisite art she aided his contemplation, baring to him, for instance, the glories of a statuesque neck, doing it all with the manner of a splendid and fabulous virgin who knew not that there was such a thing as shame. Her stockings were of black silk.

Coleman presently answered her only in monosyllable, making small distinction between yes and no. He simply sat watching her with eyes in which there were two little covetous steel-coloured flames.

He was thinking, "To go to the devil-to go to the devil-to go to the devil with this girl is not a bad fate-not a bad fate-not a bad fate."

CHAPTER XVII

"Come out on the balcony," cooed Nora. "There are some funny old storks on top of some chimneys near here and they clatter like mad all day and night."

They moved together out to the balcony, but Nora retreated with a little cry when she felt the coldness of the night. She said that she would get a cloak. Coleman was not unlike a man in a dream. He walked to the rail of the balcony where a great vine climbed toward the roof. He noted that it was dotted with. blossoms, which in the deep purple of the Oriental night were coloured in strange shades of maroon. This truth penetrated his abstraction until when Nora came she found him staring at them as if their colour was a revelation which affected him vitally. She moved to his side without sound and he first knew of her presence from the damning fragrance. She spoke just above her breath. "It's a beautiful evening." "Yes," he answered. She was at his shoulder. If he moved two inches he must come in contact. They remained in silence leaning upon the rail. Finally he began to mutter some commonplaces which meant nothing particularly, but into his tone as he mouthed them was the note of a forlorn and passionate lover. Then as if by accident he traversed the two inches and his shoulder was against the soft and yet firm shoulder of Nora Black. There was something in his throat at this time which changed his voice into a mere choking noise. She did not move. He could see her eyes glowing innocently out of the pallour which the darkness gave to her face. If he was touching her, she did not seem to know it.

"I am awfully tired," said Coleman, thickly. "I think I will go home and turn in."

"You must be, poor boy," said Nora tenderly.

"Wouldn't you like a little more of that champagne?"

"Well, I don't mind another glass."

She left him again and his galloping thought pounded to the old refrain. "To go to the devil-to go to the devil-to go to the devil with this girl is not a bad fate-not a bad fate-not a bad fate." When she returned he drank his glass of champagne. Then he mumbled: "You must be cold. Let me put your cape around you better. It won't do to catch cold here, you know."

She made a sweet pretence of rendering herself to his care. "Oh, thanks * * * I am not really cold * * * There that's better."

Of course all his manipulation of the cloak had been a fervid caress, and although her acting up to this point had remained in the role of the splendid and fabulous virgin she now turned her liquid eyes to his with a look that expressed knowledge, triumph and delight. She was sure of her victory. And she said: "Sweetheart * * * don't you think I am as nice as Marjory?" The impulse had been airily confident. It was as if the silken cords had been parted by the sweep of a sword. Coleman's face had instantly stiffened and he looked like a man suddenly recalled to the ways of light. It may easily have been that in a moment he would have lapsed again to his luxurious dreaming. But in his face the girl had read a fatal character to her blunder and her resentment against him took precedence of any other emotion. She wheeled abruptly from him and said with great contempt: "Rufus, you had better go home. You're tired and sleepy, and more or less drunk."

He knew that the grand tumble of all their little embowered incident could be neither stayed or mended. "Yes," he answered, sulkily, "I think so too." They shook hands huffily and he went away.

When he arrived among the students he found that they had appropriated everything of his which would conduce to their comfort. He was furious over it. But to his bitter speeches they replied in jibes.

"Rufus is himself again. Admire his angelic disposition. See him smile. Gentle soul."

A sleepy voice said from a comer: "I know what pinches him."

"What ? " asked several.

"He's been to see Nora and she flung him out bodily."

"Yes?" sneered Coleman. "At times I seem to see in you, Coke, the fermentation of some primeval form of sensation, as if it were possible for you to develop a mind in two or three thousand years, and then at other times you appear * * * much as you are now."

As soon as they had well measured Coleman's temper all of the students save Coke kept their mouths tightly closed. Coke either did not understand or his mood was too vindictive for silence. " Well, I know you got a throw-down all right," he muttered.

"And how would you know when I got a throw down? You pimply, milk-fed sophomore."

The others perked up their ears in mirthful appreciation of this language.

"Of course," continued Coleman, "no one would protest against your continued existence, Coke, unless you insist on recalling yourself violently to people's attention in this way. The mere fact of your living would not usually be offensive to people if you weren't eternally turning a sort of calcium light on your prehensile attributes." Coke was suddenly angry, angry much like a peasant, and his anger first evinced itself in a mere sputtering and spluttering. Finally he got out a rather long speech, full of grumbling noises, but he was understood by all to declare that his prehensile attributes had not led him to cart a notorious woman about the world with him. When they quickly looked at Coleman they saw that he was livid. " You -"

But, of course, there immediately arose all sorts of protesting cries from the seven non-combatants. Coleman, as he took two strides toward Coke's corner, looked fully able to break him across his knee, but for this Coke did not seem to care at all. He was on his feet with a challenge in his eye. Upon each cheek burned a sudden hectic spot. The others were clamouring, "Oh, say, this won't do. Quit it. Oh, we mustn't have a fight. He didn't mean it, Coleman."

Peter Tounley pressed Coke to the wall saying: "You damned young jackass, be quiet."

They were in the midst of these. festivities when a door opened and disclosed the professor. He might. have been coming into the middle of a row in one of the corridors of the college at home only this time he carried a candle. His speech, however, was a Washurst speech: "Gentlemen, gentlemen, what does this mean?" All seemed to expect Coleman to make the answer. He was suddenly very cool. "Nothing, professor," he said, "only that this-only that Coke has insulted me. I suppose that it was only the irresponsibility of a boy, and I beg that you will not trouble over it."

"Mr. Coke," said the professor, indignantly, "what have you to say to this?" Evidently he could not clearly see Coke, and he peered around his candle at where the virtuous Peter Tounley was expostulating with the young man. The figures of all the excited group moving in the candle light caused vast and uncouth shadows to have conflicts in the end of the room.

Peter Tounley's task was not light, and beyond that he had the conviction that his struggle with Coke was making him also to appear as a rowdy. This conviction was proven to be true by a sudden thunder from the old professor, "Mr. Tounley, desist!"

In wrath he desisted and Coke flung himself forward. He paid less attention to the professor than if the latter had been a jack-rabbit. "You say I insulted you? he shouted crazily in Coleman's face.

"Well * * * I meant to, do you see?"

Coleman was glacial and lofty beyond everything. "I am glad to have you admit the truth of what I have said."

Coke was, still suffocating with his peasant rage, which would not allow him to meet the clear, calm expressions of Coleman. "Yes * * * I insulted you * * * I insulted you because what I said was correct * * my prehensile attributes * * yes but I have never -"

He was interrupted by a chorus from the other students. "Oh, no, that won't do. Don't say that. Don't repeat that, Coke."

Coleman remembered the weak bewilderment of the little professor in hours that had not long passed, and it was with something of an impersonal satisfaction that he said to himself: " The old boy's got his war-paint on again." The professor had stepped sharply up to Coke and looked at him with eyes that seemed to throw out flame and heat. There was a moment's pause, and then the old scholar spoke, biting his words as if they were each a short section of steel wire. "Mr. Coke, your behaviour will end your college career abruptly and in gloom, I promise you. You have been drinking."

Coke, his head simply floating in a sea of universal defiance, at once blurted out: "Yes, sir."

"You have been drinking?" cried the professor, ferociously. "Retire to your-retire to your - retire -" And then in a voice of thunder he shouted: "Retire."

Whereupon seven hoodlum students waited a decent moment, then shrieked with laughter. But the old professor would have none of their nonsense. He quelled them all with force and finish.

Coleman now spoke a few words." Professor, I can't tell you how sorry I am that I should be concerned in any such riot as this, and since we are doomed to be bound so closely into each other's society I offer myself without reservation as being willing to repair the damage as well as may be, done. I don t see how I can forget at once that Coke's conduct was insolently unwarranted, but * * * if he has anything to sayof a nature that might heal the breach I would be willing to to meet him in the openest manner." As he made these remarks Coleman's dignity was something grand, and, Morever, there was now upon his face that curious look of temperance and purity which had been noted in New York as a singular physical characteristic. If he. was guilty of anything in this affair at all - in fact, if he had ever at any time been guilty of anything-no mark had come to stain that bloom of innocence. The professor nodded in the fullest appreciation and sympathy. "Of course * * * really there is no other sleeping placeI suppose it would be better -" Then he again attacked Coke. "Young man, you have chosen an unfortunate moment to fill us with a suspicion that you may not be a gentleman. For the time there is nothing to be done with you." He addressed the other students. "There is nothing for me to do, young gentleman, but to leave Mr. Coke in your care. Good-night, sirs. Good-night, Coleman." He left the room with his candle.

When Coke was bade to "Retire" he had, of course, simply retreated fuming to a corner of the room where he remained looking with yellow eyes like an animal from a cave. When the others were able to see through the haze of mental confusion they found that Coleman was with deliberation taking off his boots. "Afterward, when he removed his waist-coat, he took great care to wind his large gold watch.

The students, much subdued, lay again in their places, and when there was any talking it was of an extremely local nature, referring principally to the floor As being unsuitable for beds and also referring from time to time to a real or an alleged selfishness on the part of some one of the recumbent men. Soon there was only the sound of heavy breathing.

When the professor had returned to what he called the Wainwright part of the house he was greeted instantly with the question: "What was it?" His wife and daughter were up in alarm. "What was it" they repeated, wildly.

He was peevish. "Oh, nothing, nothing. But that young Coke is a regular ruffian. He had gotten him. self into some tremendous uproar with Coleman. When I arrived he seemed actually trying to assault him. Revolting! He had been drinking. Coleman's behaviour, I must say, was splendid. Recognised at once the delicacy of my position-he not being a student. If I had found him in the wrong it would have been simpler than finding him in the right. Confound that rascal of a Coke." Then, as he began a partial disrobing, he treated them to grunted scrap of information. "Coke was quite insane * * * I feared that I couldn't control him * * * Coleman was like ice * * * and as much as I have seen to admire in him during the last few days, this quiet beat it all. If he had not recognised my helplessness as far as he was concerned the whole thing might have been a most miserable business. He is a very fine young man." The dissenting voice to this last tribute was the voice of Mrs. Wainwright. She said: " Well, Coleman drinks, too - everybody knows that."

"I know," responded the professor, rather bashfully, but I am confident that he had not touched a drop." Marjory said nothing.

The earlier artillery battles had frightened most of the furniture out of the houses of Arta, and there was left in this room only a few old red cushions, and the Wainwrights were camping upon the floor. Marjory was enwrapped in Coleman's macintosh, and while the professor and his wife maintained some low talk of the recent incident she in silence had turned her cheek into the yellow velvet collar of the coat. She felt something against her bosom, and putting her hand carefully into the top pocket of the coat she found three cigars. These she took in the darkness and laid aside, telling herself to remember their position in the morning. She had no doubt that Coleman: would rejoice over them, before he could get back to, Athens where there were other good cigars.

CHAPTER XVIII

THE ladies of the Wainwright party had not complained at all when deprived of even such civilised advantages as a shelter and a knife and fork and soap and water, but Mrs. Wainwright complained bitterly amid the half-civilisation of Arta. She could see here no excuse for the absence of several hundred things which she had always regarded as essential to life. She began at 8.30 A. M. to make both the professor and Marjory woeful with an endless dissertation upon the beds in the hotel at Athens. Of course she had not regarded them at the time as being exceptional beds * * * that was quite true, * * * but then one really never knew what one was really missing until one really missed it * * * She would never have thought that she would come to consider those Athenian beds as excellent * * * but experience is a great teacher * * * makes - one reflect upon the people who year in and year out have no beds at all, poor things. * * * Well, it made one glad if one did have a good bed, even if it was at the time on the other side of the world. If she ever reached it she did not know what could ever induce her to leave it again. * * * She would never be induced -

"'Induced!'" snarled the professor. The word represented to him a practiced feminine misusage of truth, and at such his white warlock always arose."

"Induced!' Out of four American women I have seen lately, you seem to be the only one who would say that you had endured this thing because you had been 'induced' by others to come over here. How absurd!"

Mrs. Wainwright fixed her husband with a steely eye. She saw opportunity for a shattering retort. "You don't mean, Harrison, to include Marjory and I in the same breath with those two women? "

The professor saw no danger ahead for himself. He merely answered: "I had no thought either way. It did not seem important."

"Well, it is important," snapped Mrs. Wainwright.

"Do you know that you are speaking in the same breath of Marjory and Nora Black, the actress? "

"No," said the professor. "Is that so?" He was astonished, but he was not aghast at all. "Do you mean to say that is Nora Black, the comic opera star?"

"That's exactly who she is," said Mrs. Wainwright, dramatically. "And I consider that - I consider that Rufus Coleman has done no less than - misled us."

This last declaration seemed to have no effect upon the professor's pure astonishment, but Marjory looked at her mother suddenly. However, she said no word, exhibiting again that strange and, inscrutable counte-nance which masked even the tiniest of her maidenly emotions.

Mrs. Wainwright was triumphant, and she immediately set about celebrating her victory. "Men never see those things," she said to her husband. " Men never see those things. You would have gone on forever without finding out that your-your-hospitality was, being abused by that Rufus Coleman."

The professor woke up." Hospitality ?" he said, indignantly. "Hospitality? I have not had any hospitality to be abused. Why don't you talk sense? It is not that, but-it might-" He hesitated and then spoke slowly. "It might be very awkward. Of course one never knows anything definite about such people, but I suppose * * * Anyhow, it was strange in Coleman to allow her to meet us."

"It Was all a pre-arranged plan," announced the triumphant Mrs. Wainwright. "She came here on putpose to meet Rufus Coleman, and he knew it, and I should not wonder if they had not the exact spot picked out where they were going to meet."

"I can hardly believe that," said the professor, in distress. "I can, hardly believe that. It does, not seem to me that Coleman -"

"Oh yes. Your dear Rufus Coleman," cried Mrs. Wainwright. " You think he is very fine now. But I can remember when you didn't think -"

And the parents turned together an abashed look at their daughter. The professor actually flushed with shame. It seemed to him that he had just committed an atrocity upon the heart of his child. The instinct of each of them was to go to her and console her in their arms. She noted it immediately, and seemed to fear it. She spoke in a clear and even voice. "I don't think, father, that you should distress me by supposing that I am concerned at all if Mr. Coleman cares to get Nora Black over here."

"Not at all," stuttered the professor. "I -"

Mrs. Wainwright's consternation turned suddenly to, anger. "He is a scapegrace. A rascal. A - a -"

"Oh," said Marjory, coolly, "I don't see why it isn't his own affair. He didn't really present her to you, mother, you remember? She seemed quite to force her way at first, and then you-you did the rest. It should be very easy to avoid her, now that we are out of the wilderness. And then it becomes a private matter of Mr. Coleman's. For my part, I rather liked her. I don't see such a dreadful calamity."

"Marjory!" screamed her mother. "How dreadful. Liked her! Don't let me hear you say such shocking things."

"I fail to see anything shocking," answered Marjory, stolidly.

The professor was looking helplessly from his daughter to his wife, and from his wife to his daughter, like a man who was convinced that his troubles would never end. This new catastrophe created a different kind of difficulty, but he considered that the difficulties were as robust as had been the preceding ones. He put on his hat and went out of the room. He felt an impossibility of saying anything to Coleman, but he felt that he must look upon him. He must look upon this man and try to know from his manner the measure of guilt. And incidentally he longed for the machinery of a finished society which prevents its parts from clashing, prevents it with its great series of I law upon law, easily operative but relentless. Here he felt as a man flung into the jungle with his wife and daughter, where they could become the victims of any sort of savagery. His thought referred once more to what he considered the invaluable services of Coleman, and as he observed them in conjunction with the present accusation, he was simply dazed. It was then possible that one man could play two such divergent parts. He had not learned this at Washurst. But no; the world was not such a bed of putrefaction. He would not believe it; he would not believe it.

After adventures which require great nervous en. durance, it is only upon the second or third night that the common man sleeps hard. The students had expected to slumber like dogs on the first night after their trials. but none slept long, And few slept.

Coleman was the first man to arise. When he left the room the students were just beginning to blink. He took his dragoman among the shops and he bought there all the little odds and ends which might go to make up the best breakfast in Arta. If he had had news of certain talk he probably would not have been buying breakfast for eleven people. Instead, he would have been buying breakfast for one. During his absence the students arose and performed their frugal toilets. Considerable attention was paid to Coke by the others. "He made a monkey of you," said Peter Tounley with unction. "He twisted you until you looked like a wet, grey rag. You had better leave this wise guy alone."

It was not the night nor was it meditation that had taught Coke anything, but he seemed to have learned something from the mere lapse of time. In appearance he was subdued, but he managed to make a temporary jauntiness as he said: "Oh, I don't know."

"Well, you ought to know," said he who was called Billie. "You ought to know. You made an egregious snark of yourself. Indeed, you sometimes resembled a boojum. Anyhow, you were a plain chump. You exploded your face about something of which you knew nothing, and I'm damned if I believe you'd make even a good retriever."

"You're a half-bred water-spaniel," blurted Peter Tounley. "And," he added, musingly, "that is a pretty low animal."

Coke was argumentative. "Why am I? "he asked, turning his head from side to side. "I don't see where I was so wrong."

"Oh, dances, balloons, picnics, parades and ascensions," they retorted, profanely. "You swam voluntarily into water that was too deep for you. Swim out. Get dry. Here's a towel."

Coke, smitten in the face with a wet cloth rolled into a ball, grabbed it and flung it futilely at a well-dodging companion "No," he cried, "I don't see it. Now look here. I don't see why we shouldn't all resent this Nora Black business."

One student said: "Well, what's the matter with Nora B lack, anyhow?"

Another student said "I don't see how you've been issued any license to say things about Nora Black."

Another student said dubiously: "Well, he knows her well."

And then three or four spoke at once. "He was very badly rattled when she appeared upon the scene."

Peter Tounley asked: "Well, which of you people know anything wrong about Nora Black? "

There was a pause, and then Coke said: " Oh, of course - I don't know-but-"

He who was called Billie then addressed his companions. "It wouldn't be right to repeat any old lie about Nora Black, and by the same token it wouldn't be right to see old Mother Wainwright chummin' with her. There is no wisdom in going further than that. Old Mother Wainwright don't know that her fair companion of yesterday is the famous comic opera star. For my part, I believe that Coleman is simply afraid to tell her. I don't think he wished to see Nora Black yesterday any more than he wished to see the devil. The discussion, as I understand itconcerned itself only with what Coleman had to do with the thing, and yesterday anybody could see that he was in a panic."

They heard a step on the stair, and directly Coleman entered, followed by his dragoman. They were laden with the raw material for breakfast. The correspondent looked keenly among the students, for it was plain that they had been talking of him. It, filled him with rage, and for a stifling moment he could not think why he failed to immediately decamp in chagrin and leave eleven orphans to whatever fate. their general incompetence might lead them. It struck him as a deep shame that even then he and his paid man were carrying in the breakfast. He wanted to fling it all on the floor and walk out. Then he remembered Marjory. She was the reason. She was the reason for everything.

But he could not repress certain, of his thoughts. "Say, you people," he said, icily, "you had better soon learn to hustle for yourselves. I may be a dragoman, and a butler, and a cook, and a housemaid, but I'm blowed if I'm a wet nurse." In reality, he had taken the most generous pleasure in working for the others before their eyes had even been opened from sleep, but it was now all turned to wormwood. It is certain that even this could not have deviated this executive man from labour and management. because these were his life. But he felt that he was about to walk out of the room, consigning them all to Hades. His glance of angry, reproach fastened itself mainly upon Peter Tounley, because he knew that of all, Peter was the most innocent.

Peter, Tounley was abashed by this glance. So you've brought us something to eat, old man. That is tremendously nice of you - we - appreciate it like everything."

Coleman was mollified by Peter's tone. Peter had had that emotion which is equivalent to a sense of guilt, although in reality he was speckless. Two or three of the other students bobbed up to a sense of the situation. They ran to Coleman, and with polite cries took his provisions from him. One dropped a bunch of lettuce on the floor, and others reproached him with scholastic curses. Coke was seated near the window, half militant, half conciliatory. It was impossible for him to keep up a manner of deadly enmity while Coleman was bringing in his breakfast. He would have much preferred that Coleman had not brought in his breakfast. He would have much preferred to have foregone breakfast altogether. He would have much preferred anything. There seemed to be a conspiracy of circumstance to put him in the wrong and make him appear as a ridiculous young peasant. He was the victim of a benefaction, and he hated Coleman harder now than at any previous time. He saw that if he stalked out and took his breakfast alone in a cafe, the others would consider him still more of an outsider. Coleman had expressed himself like a man of the world and a gentleman, and Coke was convinced that he was a superior man of the world and a superior gentleman, but that he simply had not had words to express his position at the proper time. Coleman was glib. Therefore, Coke had been the victim of an attitude as well as of a benefaction. And so he deeply hated Coleman.

The others were talking cheerfully. "What the deuce are these, Coleman? Sausages? Oh, my. And look at these burlesque fishes. Say, these Greeks don't care what they eat. Them thar things am sardines in the crude state. No? Great God, look at those things. Look. What? Yes, they are. Radishes. Greek synonym for radishes."

The professor entered. "Oh," he said apologetically, as if he were intruding in a boudoir. All his serious desire to probe Coleman to the bottom ended in embarrassment. Mayhap it was not a law of feeling, but it happened at any rate. "He had come in a puzzled frame of mind, even an accusative frame of mind, and almost immediately he found himself suffer. ing like a culprit before his judge. It is a phenomenon of what we call guilt and innocence.

"Coleman welcomed him cordially. "Well, professor, good-morning. I've rounded up some things that at least may be eaten."

"You are very good " very considerate, Mr. Coleman, "answered the professor, hastily. "I'am sure we are much indebted to you." He had scanned the correspondent's face, land it had been so devoid of guile that he was fearful that his suspicion, a base suspicion, of this noble soul would be detected. "No, no, we can never thank you enough."

Some of the students began to caper with a sort of decorous hilarity before their teacher. "Look at the sausage, professor. Did you ever see such sausage" Isn't it salubrious "And see these other things, sir. Aren't they curious" I shouldn't wonder if they were alive. Turnips, sir? No, sir. I think they are Pharisees. I have seen a Pharisee look like a pelican, but I have never seen a Pharisee look like a turnip, so I think these turnips must be Pharisees, sir, Yes, they may be walrus. We're not sure. Anyhow, their angles are geometrically all wrong. Peter, look out." Some green stuff was flung across the room. The professor laughed; Coleman laughed. Despite Coke, dark-browed, sulking. and yet desirous of reinstating himself, the room had waxed warm with the old college feeling, the feeling of lads who seemed never to treat anything respectfully and yet at the same time managed to treat the real things with respect. The professor himself contributed to their wild carouse over the strange Greek viands. It was a vivacious moment common to this class in times of relaxation, and it was understood perfectly.

Coke arose. "I don't see that I have any friends here,"

he said, hoarsely, " and in consequence I don't see why I should remain here."

All looked at him. At the same moment Mrs. Wainwright and Marjory entered the room.

CHAPTER XIX

"Good-morning," said Mrs. Wainwright jovially to the students and then she stared at Coleman as if he were a sweep at a wedding.

"Good-morning," said Marjory.

Coleman and the students made reply. "Good-morning. Good-morning. Good-morning. Good-morning -"

It was curious to see this greeting, this common phrase, this bit of old ware, this antique, come upon a dramatic scene and pulverise it. Nothing remained but a ridiculous dust. Coke, glowering, with his lips still trembling from heroic speech, was an angry clown, a pantaloon in rage. Nothing was to be done to keep him from looking like an ass. He, strode toward the door mumbling about a walk before breakfast.

Mrs. Wainwright beamed upon him. "Why, Mr. Coke, not before breakfast? You surely won't have time." It was grim punishment. He appeared to go blind, and he fairly staggered out of the door mumbling again, mumbling thanks or apologies or explanations. About the mouth of Coleman played a sinister smile. The professor cast. upon his wife a glance expressing weariness. It was as if he said "There you go again. You can't keep your foot out of it." She understood the glance, and so she asked blankly: "Why, What's the matter? Oh." Her belated mind grasped that it waw an aftermath of the quarrel of Coleman and Coke. Marjory looked as if she was distressed in the belief that her mother had been stupid. Coleman was outwardly serene. It was Peter Tounley who finally laughed a cheery, healthy laugh and they all looked at him with gratitude as if his sudden mirth had been a real statement or reconciliation and consequent peace.

The dragoman and others disported themselves until a breakfast was laid upon the floor. The adventurers squatted upon the floor. They made a large company. The professor and Coleman discussed the means of getting to Athens. Peter Tounley sat next to Marjory. "Peter," she said, privately, "what was all this trouble between Coleman and Coke?"

Peter answered blandly: "Oh, nothing at Nothing at all."

"Well, but -" she persisted, "what was the cause of it?"

He looked at her quaintly. He was not one of those in love with her, but be was interested in the affair. "Don't you know?" he asked.

She understood from his manner that she had been some kind of an issue in the quarrel. "No," she answered, hastily. "I don't."

"Oh, I don't mean that," said Peter. "I only meant - I only meant - oh, well, it was nothing-really."

"It must have been about something," continued Marjory. She continued, because Peter had denied that she was concerned in it. "Whose fault?"

"I really don't know. It was all rather confusing," lied Peter, tranquilly.

Coleman and the professor decided to accept a plan of the correspondent's dragoman to start soon on the first stage of the journey to Athens. The dragoman had said that he had found two large carriages rentable.

Coke, the outcast, walked alone in the narrow streets. The flight of the crown prince's army from Larissa had just been announced in Arta, but Coke was probably the most woebegone object on the Greek peninsula.

He encountered a strange sight on the streets. A woman garbed in the style for walking of an afternoon on upper Broadway was approaching him through a mass of kilted mountaineers and soldiers in soiled overcoats. Of course he recognised Nora Black.

In his conviction that everybody in the world was at this time considering him a mere worm, he was sure that she would not heed him. Beyond that he had been presented to her notice in but a transient and cursory fashion. But contrary to his conviction, she turned a radiant smile upon him. "Oh," she said, brusquely, "you are one of the students. Good morning." In her manner was all the confidence of an old warrior, a veteran, who addresses the universe with assurance because of his past battles.

Coke grinned at this strange greeting. "Yes, Miss Black," he answered, " I am one of the students."

She did not seem to quite know how to formulate her

next speech. Er - I suppose you're going to Athens at once "You must be glad after your horrid experiences."

"I believe they are going to start for Athens today," said Coke.

Nora was all attention. "'They ?'" she repeated. "Aren't you going with them? "

"Well," he said, " * * Well -"

She saw of course that there had been some kind of trouble. She laughed. "You look as if somebody had kicked you down stairs," she said, candidly. She at once assumed an intimate manner toward him which was like a temporary motherhood. "Come, walk with me and tell me all about it." There was in her tone a most artistic suggestion that whatever had happened she was on his side. He was not loath. The street was full of soldiers whose tongues clattered so loudly that the two foreigners might have been wandering in a great cave of the winds. "Well, what was the row about ?" asked Nora. "And who was in it? "

It would have been no solace to Coke to pour out his tale even if it had been a story that he could have told Nora. He was not stopped by the fact that he had gotten himself in the quarrel because he had insulted the name of the girt at his side. He did not think of it at that time. The whole thing was now extremely vague in outline to him and he only had a dull feeling of misery and loneliness. He wanted her to cheer him.

Nora laughed again. "Why, you're a regular little kid. Do you mean to say you've come out here sulking alone because of some nursery quarrel?" He was ruffled by her manner. It did not contain the cheering he required. "Oh, I don't know that I'm such a regular little kid," he said, sullenly. "The quarrel was not a nursery quarrel."

"Why don't you challenge him to a duel?" asked Nora, suddenly. She was watching him closely.

"Who?" said Coke.

"Coleman, you stupid," answered Nora.

They stared at each other, Coke paying her first the tribute of astonishment and then the tribute of admiration. "Why, how did you guess that?" he demanded.

"Oh," said Nora., "I've known Rufus Coleman for years, and he is always rowing with people."

"That is just it," cried Coke eagerly. "That is just it. I fairly hate the man. Almost all of the other fellows will stand his abuse, but it riles me, I tell you. I think he is a beast. And, of course, if you seriously meant what you said about challenging him to a duel - I mean if there is any sense in that sort of thing - I would challenge Coleman. I swear I would. I think he's a great bluffer, anyhow. Shouldn't wonder if he would back out. Really, I shouldn't.

Nora smiled humourously at a house on her side of the narrow way. "I wouldn't wonder if he did either" she answered. After a time she said " Well, do you mean to say that you have definitely shaken them? Aren't you going back to Athens with them or anything? "

"I - I don't see how I can," he said, morosely.

"Oh," she said. She reflected for a time. At last she turned to him archly and asked: "Some words over a lady?"

Coke looked at her blankly. He suddenly remembered the horrible facts. " No-no-not over a lady."

"My dear boy, you are a liar," said Nora, freely. "You are a little unskilful liar. It was some words over a lady, and the lady's name is Marjory Wainwright."

Coke felt as though he had suddenly been let out of a cell, but he continued a mechanical denial. "No, no * * It wasn't truly * * upon my word * * "

"Nonsense," said Nora. "I know better. Don't you think you can fool me, you little cub. I know you're in love with Marjory Wainwright, and you think Coleman is your rival. What a blockhead you are. Can't you understand that people see these things?"

"Well -" stammered Coke.

"Nonsense," said Nora again. "Don't try to fool me, you may as well understand that it's useless. I am too wise."

"Well -" stammered Coke.

"Go ahead," urged Nora. "Tell me about it. Have it out."

He began with great importance and solemnity. "Now, to tell you the truth * * that is why I hate him * * I hate him like anything. * * I can't see why everybody admires him so. I don't see anything to him myself. I don't believe he's got any more principle than a wolf. I wouldn't trust him with two dollars. Why, I know stories about him that would make your hair curl. When I think of a girl like Marjory - "

His speech had become a torrent. But here Nora raised her hand. "Oh! Oh! Oh! That will do. That will do. Don't lose your senses. I don't see why this girl Marjory is any too good. She is no chicken, I'll bet. Don't let yourself get fooled with that sort of thing."

Coke was unaware of his incautious expressions. He floundered on. while Nora looked at him as if she wanted to wring his neck. " No - she's too fine and too good - for him or anybody like him - she's too fine and too good -"

"Aw, rats," interrupted Nora, furiously. "You make me tired."

Coke had a wooden-headed conviction that he must make Nora understand Marjory's infinite superiority to all others of her sex, and so he passed into a pariegyric, each word of which was a hot coal to the girl addressed. Nothing would stop him, apparently. He even made the most stupid repetitions. Nora finally stamped her foot formidably. "Will you stop? Will you stop?" she said through her clenched teeth. "Do you think I want to listen to your everlasting twaddle about her? Why, she's - she's no better than other people, you ignorant little mamma's boy. She's no better than other people, you swab!"

Coke looked at her with the eyes of a fish. He did not understand. "But she is better than other people," he persisted.

Nora seemed to decide suddenly that there would be no accomplishment in flying desperately against this rock-walled conviction. "Oh, well," she said, with marvellous good nature, "perhaps you are right, numbskull. But, look here; do you think she cares for him?"

In his heart, his jealous heart, he believed that Marjory loved Coleman, but he reiterated eternally to himself that it was not true. As for speaking it to,another, that was out of the question. "No," he said, stoutly, "she doesn't care a snap for him." If he had admitted it, it would have seemed to him that. he was somehow advancing Coleman's chances.

"'Oh, she doesn't, eh?" said Nora enigmatically.

"She doesn't?" He studied her face with an abrupt, miserable suspicion, but he repeated doggedly: "No, she doesn't."

"Ahem," replied Nora. "Why, she's set her cap for him all right. She's after him for certain. It's as plain as day. Can't you see that, stupidity ?"

"No," he said hoarsely.

"You are a fool," said Nora. "It isn't Coleman that's after her. It is she that is after Coleman."

Coke was mulish. "No such thing. Coleman's crazy about her. Everybody has known it ever since he was in college. You ask any of the other fellows."

Nora was now very serious, almost doleful. She remained still for a time, casting at Coke little glances of hatred. "I don't see my way clear to ask any of the other fellows," she said at last, with considerable bitterness. "I'm not in the habit of conducting such enquiries."

Coke felt now that he disliked her, and he read plainly her dislike of him. If they were the two villains of the play, they were not having fun together at all. Each had some kind of a deep knowledge that their aspirations, far from colliding, were of such character that the success of one would mean at least assistance to the other, but neither could see how to confess if. Pethapt it was from shame, perhaps it was because Nora thought Coke to have little wit; perhaps it was because Coke thought Nora to have little conscience. Their talk was mainly rudderless. From time to time Nora had an inspiration to come boldly at the point, but this inspiration was commonly defeated by, some extraordinary manifestation of Coke's incapacity. To her mind, then, it seemed like a proposition to ally herself to a butcher-boy in a matter purely sentimental. She Wondered indignantly how she was going to conspire With this lad, who puffed out his infantile cheeks in order to conceitedly demonstrate that he did not understand the game at all. She hated Marjory for it. Evidently it was only the weaklings who fell in love with that girl. Coleman was an exception, but then, Coleman was misled, by extraordinary artifices. She meditatecf for a moment if she should tell Coke to go home and not bother her. What at last decided the question was his unhappiness. Shd clung to this unhappiness for its value as it stood alone, and because its reason for existence was related to her own unhappiness. "You Say you are not going back toAthens with your party. I don't suppose you're going to stay here. I'm going back to Athens to-day. I came up here to see a battle, but it doesn't seem that there are to be any more battles., The fighting will now all be on the other side of the mountains." Apparent she had learned in some haphazard way that the Greek peninsula was divided by a spine of almost inaccessible mountains, and the war was thus split into two simultaneous campaigns. The Arta campaign was known to be ended. "If you want to go back to Athens without consorting with your friends, you had better go back with me. I can take you in my carriage as far as the beginning of the railroad. Don't you worry. You've got money enough, haven't you ? The professor isn't keeping your money ?"

"Yes," he said slowly, "I've got money enough." He was apparently dubious over the proposal. In their abstracted walk they had arrived in front of the house occupied by Coleman and the Wainwright party. Two carriages, forlorn in dusty age, stood before the door. Men were carrying out new leather luggage and flinging it into the traps amid a great deal of talk which seemed to refer to nothing. Nora and Coke stood looking at the scene without either thinking of the importance of running away, when out tumbled seven students, followed immediately but in more decorous fashion by the Wainwrights and Coleman.

Some student set up a whoop. "Oh, there he is. There's Coke. Hey, Coke, where you been? Here he is, professor." For a moment after the hoodlum had subsided, the two camps stared at each other in silence.

CHAPTER XX

NORA and Coke were an odd looking pair at the time. They stood indeed as if rooted to the spot, staring vacuously, like two villagers, at the surprising travellers. It was not an eternity before the practiced girl of the stage recovered her poise, but to the end of the incident the green youth looked like a culprit and a fool. Mrs. Wainwright's glower of offensive incredulity was a masterpiece. Marjory nodded pleasantly; the professor nodded. The seven students clambered boisterously into the forward carriage making it clang with noise like a rook's nest. They shouted to Coke. "Come on; all aboard; come on, Coke; - we're off. Hey, there, Cokey, hurry up." The professor, as soon as he had seated himself on the forward seat of' the second carriage, turned in Coke's general direction and asked formally: "Mr. Coke, you are coming with us?" He felt seemingly much in doubt as to the propriety of abandoning the headstrong young man, and this doubt was not at all decreased by Coke's appearance with Nora Black. As far as he could tell, any assertion of authority on his part would end only in a scene in which Coke would probably insult him with some gross violation of collegiate conduct. As at first the young man made no reply, the professor after waiting spoke again. "You understand, Mr. Coke, that if you separate yourself from the party you encounter my strongest disapproval, and if I did not feel responsible to the college and your father for your safe journey to New York I-I don't know but what I would have you expelled by cable if that were possible."

Although Coke had been silent, and Nora Black had had the appearance of being silent, in reality she had lowered her chin and whispered sideways and swiftly. She had said: "Now, here's your time. Decide quickly, and don't look such a wooden Indian." Coke pulled himself together with a visible effort, and spoke to the professor from an inspiration in which he had no faith. "I understand my duties to you, sir, perfectly. I also understand my duty to the college. But I fail to see where either of these obligations require me to accept the introduction of objectionable people into the party. If I owe a duty to the college and to you, I don't owe any to Coleman, and, as I understand it, Coleman was not in the original plan of this expedition. If such had been the case, I would not have been here. I can't tell what the college may see fit to do, but as for my father I I have no doubt of how he will view it."

The first one to be electrified by the speech was Coke himself. He saw with a kind of sub-conscious amazement this volley of bird-shot take effect upon the face of the old professor. The face of Marjory flushed crimson as if her mind had sprung to a fear that if Coke could develop ability in this singular fashion he might succeed in humiliating her father in the street in the presence of the seven students, her mother, Coleman and-herself. She had felt the birdshot sting her father.

When Coke had launched forth, Coleman with his legs stretched far apart had just struck a match on the wall of the house and was about to light a cigar. His groom was leading up his horse. He saw the value of Coke's argument more appreciatively and sooner perhaps than did Coke. The match dropped from his fingers, and in the white sunshine and still air it burnt on the pavement orange coloured and with langour. Coleman held his cigar with all five fingers - in a manner out of all the laws of smoking. He turned toward Coke. There was danger in the moment, but then in a flash it came upon him that his role was not of squabbling with Coke, far less of punching him. On the contrary, he was to act the part of a cool and instructed man who refused to be waylaid into foolishness by the outcries of this pouting youngster and who placed himself in complete deference to the wishes of the professor. Before the professor had time to embark upon any reply to Coke, Coleman was at the side of the carriage and, with a fine assumption of distress, was saying: "Professor, I could very easily ride back to Agrinion alone. It would be all right. I don't want to -"

To his surprise the professor waved at him to be silent as if he were a mere child. The old man's face was set with the resolution of exactly what he was going to say to Coke. He began in measured tone, speaking with feeling, but with no trace of anger.

"Mr. Coke, it has probably escaped your attention that Mr. Coleman, at what I consider a great deal of peril to himself, came out to rescue this party-you and others-and although he studiously disclaims all merit in his finding us and bringing us in, I do not regard it in that way, and I am surprised that any member of this party should conduct himself in this manner toward a man who has been most devotedly and generously at our service." It was at this time that the professor raised himself and shook his finger at Coke, his voice now ringing with scorn. In such moments words came to him and formed themselves into sentences almost too rapidly for him to speak them. "You are one of the most remarkable products of our civilisation which I have yet come upon. What do you mean, sir? Where are your senses? Do you think that all this pulling and pucking is manhood? I will tell you what I will do with you. I thought I brought out eight students to Greece, but when I find that I brought out, seven students and - er - an - ourang-outang - don't get angry, sir - I don't care for your anger - I say when I discover this I am naturally puzzled for a moment. I will leave you to the judgment of your peers. Young gentlemen!" Of the seven heads of the forward carriage none had to be turned. All had been turned since the beginning of the talk. If the professor's speech had been delivered in one of the class-rooms of Washurst they would have glowed with delight over the butchery of Coke, but they felt its portentous aspect. Butchery here in Greece thousands of miles from home presented to them more of the emphasis of downright death and destruction. The professor called out "Young gentlemen, I have done all that I can do without using force, which, much to my regret, is impracticable. If you will persuade your fellow student to accompany you I think our consciences will be the better for not having left a weak minded brother alone among the by-paths." The valuable aggregation of intelligence and refinement which decorated the interior of the first carriage did not hesitate over answering this appeal. In fact, his fellow students had worried among themselves over Coke, and their desire to see him come out of his troubles in fair condition was intensified by the fact that they had lately concentrated much thought upon him. There was a somewhat comic pretense of speaking so that only Coke could hear. Their chorus was law sung. "Oh, cheese it, Coke. Let up on your-self, you blind ass.

Wait till you get to Athens and then go and act like a monkey. All this is no good -"

The advice which came from the carriage was all in one direction, and there was so much of it that the hum of voices sounded like a wind blowing through a forest.

Coke spun suddenly and said something to Nora Black. Nora laughed rather loudly, and then the two turned squarely and the Wainwright party contemplated what were surely at that time the two most insolent backs in the world.

The professor looked as if he might be going to have a fit. Mrs. Wainwright lifted her eyes toward heaven, and flinging out her trembling hands, cried: "Oh, what an outrage. What an outrage! That minx -" The concensus of opinion in the first carriage was perfectly expressed by Peter Tounley, who with a deep drawn breath, said: "Well, I'm damned!" Marjory had moaned and lowered her head as from a sense of complete personal shame. Coleman lit his cigar and mounted his horse. "Well, I suppose there is nothing for it but to be off, professor? "His tone was full of regret, with sort of poetic regret. For a moment the professor looked at him blankly, and then gradually recovered part of his usual manner. "Yes," he said sadly, "there is nothing for it but to go on." At a word from the dragoman, the two impatient drivers spoke gutturally to their horses and the carriages whirled out of Arta. Coleman, his dragoman and the groom trotted in the dust from the wheels of the Wainwright carriage. The correspondent always found his reflective faculties improved by the constant pounding of a horse on the trot, and he was not sorry to have now a period for reflection, as well as this artificial stimulant. As he viewed the game he had in his hand about all the cards that were valuable. In fact, he considered that the only ace against him was Mrs.Wainwright. He had always regarded her as a stupid person, concealing herself behind a mass of trivialities which were all conventional, but he thought now that the more stupid she was and the more conventional in her triviality the more she approached to being the very ace of trumps itself. She was just the sort of a card that would come upon the table mid the neat play of experts and by some inexplicable arrangement of circumstance, lose a whole game for the wrong man. After Mrs. Wainwright he worried over the students. He believed them to be reasonable enough; in fact, he honoured them distinctly in regard to their powers of reason, but he knew that people generally hated a row. It, put them off their balance, made them sweat over a lot of pros and cons, and prevented them from thinking for a time at least only of themselves. Then they came to resent the principals in a row. Of course the principal, who was thought to be in the wrong, was the most resented, but Coleman believed that, after all, people always came to resent the other principal, or at least be impatient and suspicious of him. If he was a correct person, why was he in a row at all? The principal who had been in the right often brought this impatience and suspicion upon himself, no doubt, by never letting the matter end, continuing to yawp about his virtuous suffering, and not allowing people to return to the steady contemplation of their own affairs. As a precautionary measure he decided to say nothing at all about the late trouble, unless some one addressed him upon it. Even then he would be serenely laconic. He felt that he must be popular with the seven students. In the first place, it was nice that in the presence of Marjory they should like him, and in the second place he feared to displease them as a body because he believed that he had some dignity. Hoodlums are seldom dangerous to other hoodlums, but if they catch pomposity alone in the field, pomposity is their prey. They tear him to mere bloody ribbons, amid heartless shrieks. When Coleman put himself on the same basis with the students, he could cope with them easily, but he did not want the wild pack after him when Marjory could see the chase. And so be reasoned that his best attitude was to be one of rather taciturn serenity.

On the hard military road the hoofs of the horses made such clatter that it was practically impossible to hold talk between the carriages and the horsemen without all parties bellowing. The professor, however, strove to overcome the difficulties. He was apparently under-going a great amiability toward Coleman. Frequently he turned with a bright face, and pointing to some object in the landscape, obviously tried to convey something entertaining to Coleman's mind. Coleman could see his lips mouth the words. He always nodded cheerily in answer and yelled.

The road ultimately became that straight lance-handle which Coleman - it seemed as if many years had passed - had traversed with his dragoman and the funny little carriers. He was fixing in his mind a possible story to the Wainwrights about the snake and his first dead Turk. But suddenly the carriages left this road and began a circuit of the Gulf of Arta, winding about an endless series of promontories. The journey developed into an excess of dust whirling from a road, which half circled the waist of cape after cape. All dramatics were lost in the rumble of wheels and in the click of hoofs. They passed a little soldier leading a prisoner by a string. They passed more frightened peasants, who seemed resolved to flee down into the very boots of Greece. And people looked at them with scowls, envying them their speed. At the little town from which Coleman embarked at one stage of the upward journey, they found crowds in the streets. There was no longer any laughter, any confidence, any vim. All the spirit of the visible Greek nation seemed to have been knocked out of it in two blows. But still they talked and never ceased talking. Coleman noticed that the most curious changes had come upon them since his journey to the frontier. They no longer approved of foreigners. They seemed to blame the travellers for something which had transpired in the past few days. It was not that they really blamed the travellers for the nation's calamity: It was simply that their minds were half stunned by the news of defeats, and, not thinking for a moment to blame themselves, or even not thinking to attribute the defeats to mere numbers and skill, they were savagely eager to fasten it upon something near enough at hand for the operation of vengeance.

Coleman perceived that the dragoman, all his former plumage gone, was whining and snivelling as he argued to a dark-browed crowd that was running beside the cavalcade. The groom, who always had been a miraculously laconic man, was suddenly launched forth garrulously. The, drivers, from their high seats, palavered like mad men, driving with oat hand and gesturing with the other, explaining evidently their own great innocence.

Coleman saw that there was trouble, but he only sat more stiffly in his saddle. The eternal gabble moved him to despise the situation. At any rate, the travellers would soon be out of this town and on to a more sensible region.

However he saw the driver of the first carriage suddenly pull up boforg a little blackened coffee shop and inn. The dragman spurred forward and began wild expostulation. The second carriage pulled close behind the other. The crowd, murmuring like a Roman mob in Nero's time, closed around them.

.

CHAPTER XXI

COLEMAN pushed his horse coolly through to the dragoman;s side. "What is it?" he demanded. The dragoman was broken-voiced. "These peoples, they say you are Germans, all Germans, and they are angry," he wailed. "I can do nossing-nossing."

"Well, tell these men to drive on," said Coleman, "tell them theymust drive on."

"They will not drive on," wailed the dragoman, still more loudly. " I can do nossing. They say here is place for feed the horse. It is the custom and they will note drive on."

"Make them drive on."

"They will note," shrieked the agonised servitor. Coleman looked from the men waving their arms and chattering on the box-seats to the men of the crowd who also waved their arms and chattered. In this throng far to the rear of the fighting armies there did not seem to be a single man who was not ablebodied, who had not been free to enlist as a soldier. They were of that scurvy behind-the-rear-guard which every nation has in degree proportionate to its worth. The manhood of Greece had gone to the frontier, leaving at home this rabble of talkers, most of whom were armed with rifles for mere pretention. Coleman loathed them to the end of his soul. He thought them a lot of infants who would like to prove their courage upon eleven innocent travellers, all but unarmed, and in this fact he was quick to see a great danger to the Wainwright party. One could deal with soldiers; soldiers would have been ashamed to bait helpless people; but this rabble -

The fighting blood of the correspondent began to boil, and he really longed for the privilege to run amuck through the multitude. But a look at the Wainwrights kept him in his senses. The professor had turned pale as a dead man. He sat very stiff and still while his wife clung to him, hysterically beseeching him to do something, do something, although what he was to do she could not have even imagined.

Coleman took the dilemma by its beard. He dismounted from his horse into the depths of the crowd and addressed the Wainwrights. "I suppose we had better go into this place and have some coffee while the men feed their horses. There is no use in trying to make them go on." His manner was fairly casual, but they looked at him in glazed horror. "It is the only thing to do. This crowd is not nearly so bad as they think they are. But we've got to look as if we felt confident." He himself had no confidence with this angry buzz in his ears, but be felt certain that the only correct move was to get everybody as quickly as possible within the shelter of the inn. It might not be much of a shelter for them, but it was better than the carriages in the street.

The professor and Mrs. Wainwright seemed to be considering their carriage as a castle, and they looked as if their terror had made them physically incapable of leaving it. Coleman stood waiting. Behind him the clapper-tongued crowd was moving ominously. Marjory arose and stepped calmly down to him. He thrilled to the end of every nerve. It was as if she had said: " I don't think there is great danger, but if there is great danger, why * * here I am * ready * with you." It conceded everything, admitted everything. It was a surrender without a blush, and it was only possible in the shadow of the crisis when they did not know what the next moments might contain for them. As he took her hand and she stepped past him he whispered swiftly and fiercely in her ear, "I love you." She did not look up, but he felt that in this quick incident they had claimed each other, accepted each other with a far deeper meaning and understanding than could be possible in a mere drawing-room. She laid her hand on his arm, and with the strength of four men he twisted his horse into the making of furious prancing side-steps toward the door of the inn, clanking side-steps which mowed a wide lane through the crowd for Marjory, his Marjory. He was as haughty as a new German lieutenant, and although he held the fuming horse with only his left hand, he seemed perfectly capable of hurling the animal over a house without calling into service the arm which was devoted to Marjory.

It was not an exhibition of coolness such as wins applause on the stage when the hero placidly lights a cigarette before the mob which is clamouring for his death. It was, on the contrary, an exhibition of down-right classic disdain, a disdain which with the highest arrogance declared itself in every glance of his eye into the faces about him. "Very good * * attack me if you like * * there is nothing to prevent it * * you mongrels." Every step of his progress was made a renewed insult to them. The very air was charged with what this lone man was thinking of this threatening crowd.

His audacity was invincible. They actually made way for it as quickly as children would flee from a ghost. The horse, dancing; with ringing steps, with his glistening neck arched toward the iron hand at his bit, this powerful, quivering animal was a regular engine of destruction, and they gave room until Coleman halted him - at an exclamation from Marjory.

"My mother and father." But they were coming close behind and Coleman resumed this contemptuous journey to the door of the inn. The groom, with his new-born tongue, was clattering there to the populace. Coleman gave him the horse and passed after the Wainwrights into the public room of the inn. He was smiling. What simpletons!

A new actor suddenly appeared in the person of the keeper of the inn. He too had a rifle and a prodigious belt of cartridges, but it was plain at once that he had elected to be a friend of the worried travellers. A large part of the crowd were thinking it necessary to enter the inn and pow-wow more. But the innkeeper stayed at the door with the dragoman, and together they vociferously held back the tide. The spirit of the mob had subsided to a more reasonable feeling. They no longer wished to tear the strangers limb from limb on the suspicion that they were Germans. They now were frantic to talk as if some inexorable law had kept them silent for ten years and this was the very moment of their release. Whereas, their simultaneous and interpolating orations had throughout made noise much like a coal-breaker. Coleman led the Wainwrights to a table in a far part of the room. They took chairs as if he had commanded them. "What an outrage," he said jubilantly. "The apes." He was keeping more than half an eye upon the door, because he knew that the quick coming of the students was important.

Then suddenly the storm broke in wrath. Something had happened in the street. The jabbering crowd at the door had turned and were hurrying upon some central tumult. The dragoman screamed to Coleman. Coleman jumped and grabbed the dragoman. "Tell this man to take them somewhere up stairs," he cried, indicating the Wainwrights with a sweep of his arm. The innkeeper seemed to understand sooner than the dragoman, and he nodded eagerly. The professor was crying: "What is it, Mr. Coleman? What is it ?" An instant later, the correspondent was out in the street, buffeting toward a scuffle. Of course it was the students. It appeared, afterward, that those seven young men, with their feelings much ruffled, had been making the best of their way toward the door of the inn, when a large man in the crowd, during a speech which was surely most offensive, had laid an arresting hand on the shoulder of Peter Tounley. Whereupon the excellent Peter Tounley had hit the large man on the jaw in such a swift and skilful manner that the large man had gone spinning through a group of his countrymen to the hard earth, where he lay holding his face together and howling. Instantly, of course, there had been a riot. It might well be said that even then the affair could have ended in a lot of talking, but in the first place the students did not talk modern Greek, and in the second place they were now past all thought of talking. They regarded this affair seriously as a fight, and now that they at last were in it, they were in it for every pint of blood in their bodies. Such a pack of famished wolves had never before been let loose upon men armed with Gras rifles.

They all had been expecting the row, and when Peter Tounley had found it expedient to knock over the man, they had counted it a signal: their arms immediately begun to swing out as if they had been wound up. It was at this time that Coleman swam brutally through the Greeks and joined his countrymen. He was more frightened than any of those novices. When he saw Peter Tounley overthrow a dreadful looking brigand whose belt was full of knives, and who crashed to the ground amid a clang of cartridges, he was appalled by the utter simplicity with which the lads were treating the crisis. It was to them no common scrimmage at Washurst, of course, but it flashed through Coleman's mind that they had not the slightegt sense of the size of the thing. He expected every instant to see the flash of knives or to hear the deafening intonation of a rifle fired against hst ear. It seemed to him miraculous that the tragedy was so long delayed.

In the meantirne he was in the affray. He jilted one man under the chin with his elbow in a way that reeled him off from Peter Tounley's back; a little person in thecked clothes he smote between the eyes; he recieved a gun-butt emphatically on the aide of the neck; he felt hands tearing at him; he kicked the pins out from under three men in rapid succession. He was always yelling. "Try to get to the inn, boys, try to get to the inn. Look out, Peter. Take care for his knife, Peter -" Suddenly he whipped a rifle out of the hands of a man and swung it, whistling. He had gone stark mad with the others.

The boy Billy, drunk from some blows and bleeding, was already. staggering toward the inn over the clearage which the wild Coleman made with the clubbed rifle. Tho others follewed as well as they might while beating off a discouraged enemy. The remarkable innkeeper had barred his windows with strong wood shutters. He held the door by the crack for them, and they stumbled one by on through the portal. Coleman did not know why they were not all dead, nor did he understand the intrepid and generous behaviour of the innkeeper, but at any rate he felt that the fighting was suspended, and he wanted to see Marjory. The innkeeper was, doing a great pantomime in the middle of the darkened room, pointing to the outer door and then aiming his rifle at it to explain his intention of defending them at all costs. Some of the students moved to a billiard table and spread themselves wearily upon it. Others sank down where they stood. Outside the crowd was beginning to roar. Coleman's groom crept out from under the little Coffee bar and comically saluted his master. The dragoman was not present. Coleman felt that he must see Marjory, and he made signs to the innkeeper. The latter understood quickly, and motioned that Coleman should follow him. They passed together through a dark hall and up a darker stairway, where after Coleman stepped out into a sun-lit room, saying loudly: "Oh, it's all right. It's all over. Don't worry."

Three wild people were instantly upon him. "Oh, what was it? What did happen? Is anybody hurt? Oh, tell us, quick!" It seemed at the time that it was an avalanche of three of them, and it was not until later that he recognised that Mrs. Wainwright had tumbled the largest number of questions upon him. As for Marjory, she had said nothing until the time when she cried:

"Oh-he is bleeding - he is bleeding. Oh, come, quick!"
She fairly dragged him out of one room into another
room, where there was a jug of water. She wet her
handkerchief and softly smote his wounds. "Bruises,"
she said, piteously, tearfully. "Bruises. Oh, dear! How
they must hurt you.' The handkerchief was soon
stained crimson.

When Coleman spoke his voice quavered. "It isn't
anything. Really, it isn't anything." He had not known
of these wonderful wounds, but he almost choked in
the joy of Marjory's ministry and her half coherent
exclamations. This proud and beautiful girl, this
superlative creature, was reddening her handkerchief
with his blood, and no word of his could have
prevented her from thus attending him. He could hear
the professor and Mrs. Wainwright fussing near him,
trying to be of use. He would have liked to have been
able to order them out of the room. Marjory's cool
fingers on his face and neck had conjured within him a
vision at an intimacy tnat was even sweeter than
anything which he had imagined, and he longed to
pour out to her the bubbling, impassioned speech
which came to his lips. But, always doddering behind
him, were the two old people, strenuous to be of help
to him.

Suddenly a door opened and a youth appeared, simply
red with blood. It was Peter Tounley. His first remark
was cheerful. "Well, I don't suppose those people will
be any too quick to look for more trouble."

Coleman felt a swift pang because he had forgotten to
announce the dilapidated state of all the students. He
had been so submerged by Marjory's tenderness that all
else had been drowned from his mind. His heart beat

quickly as he waited for Marjory to leave him and rush to Peter Tounley.

But she did nothing of the sort. "Oh, Peter," she cried in distress, and then she turned back to Coleman. It was the professor and Mrs. Wainwright who, at last finding a field for their kindly ambitions, flung them. selves upon Tounley and carried him off to another place. Peter was removed, crying: " Oh, now, look here, professor, I'm not dying or anything of the sort Coleman and Marjory were left alone. He suddenly and forcibly took one of her hands and the blood stained hankerchief dropped to the floor.

CHAPTER XXII

From below they could hear the thunder of weapons and fits upon the door of the inn amid a great clamour of. tongues. Sometimes there arose the argumtntative howl of the innkeeper. Above this roar, Coleman's quick words sounded in Marjory's ear.

"I've got to go. I've got to go back to the boys, but - I love you."

"Yes go, go," she whispered hastily. "You should be there, but-come back."

He held her close to him. "But you are mine, remember," he said fiercely and sternly. "You are mine-forever-As I am yours-remember." Her eyes half closed. She made intensely solemn answer. "Yes." He released her and vphs gone. In the glooming coffee room of the inn he found the students, the dragoman, the groom and the innkeeper armed with a motley collection of weapons which ranged from the rifle of the innkeeper to the table leg in the hands of Peter-Tounley. The last named young student of archeology was in a position of temporary leadefship and holding a great pow-bow with the innkeeper through the medium of peircing outcries by the dragoman. Coleman had not yet undestood why none of them had been either stabbed or shot in the fight in the steeet, but

Stephen Crane

it seemed to him now that affairs were leading toward a crisis of tragedy. He thought of the possibilities of having the dragoman go to an upper window and harangue the people, but he saw no chance of success in such a plan. He saw that the crowd would merely howl at the dragoman while the dragoman howled at the crowd. He then asked if there was any other exit from the inn by which they could secretly escape. He learned that the door into the coffee room was the only door which pierced the four great walls. All he could then do was to find out from the innkeeper how much of a siege the place could stand, and to this the innkeeper answered volubly and with smiles that this hostelry would easily endure until the mercurial temper of the crowd had darted off in a new direction. It may be curious to note here that all of Peter Tounley's impassioned communication with the innkeeper had been devoted to an endeavour to learn what in the devil was the matter with these people, as a man about to be bitten by poisonous snakes should, first of all, furiously insist upon learning their exact species before deciding upon either his route, if he intended to run away, or his weapon if he intended to fight them.

The innkeeper was evidently convinced that this house would withstand the rage of the populace, and he was such an unaccountably gallant little chap that Coleman trusted entirely to his word. His only fear or suspicion was an occasional one as to the purity of the dragoman's translation.

Suddenly there was half a silence on the mob without the door. It is inconceivable that it could become altogether silent, but it was as near to a rational stillness of tongues as it was able. Then there was a loud knocking by a single fist and a new voice began to spin Greek, a voice that was somewhat like the rattle of pebbles in a tin box. Then a startling voice called out in English. "Are you in there, Rufus? "

Answers came from every English speaking person in the room in one great outburst. "Yes."

"Well, let us in," called Nora Black. "It is all right. We've got an officer with us."

"Open the door," said Coleman with speed. The little innkeeper labouriously unfastened the great bars, and when the door finally opened there appeared on the threshold Nora Black with Coke and an officer of infantry, Nora's little old companion, and Nora's dragoman.

"We saw your carriage in the street," cried the queen of comic opera as she swept into the room. She was beaming with delight. "What is all the row, anyway? O-o-oh, look at that student's nose. Who hit him? And look at Rufus. What have you boys been doing?"

Her little Greek officer of infantry had stopped the mob from flowing into the room. Coleman looked toward the door at times with some anxiety. Nora, noting it, waved her hand in careless reassurance; "Oh, it's, all right. Don't worry about them any more. He is perfectly devoted to me. He would die there on the threshold if I told him it would please me. Speaks splendid French. I found him limping along the road and gave him a lift. And now do hurry up and tell me exactly what happened." They all told what had happened, while Nora and Coke listened agape. Coke, by the way, had quite floated back to his old position with the students. It had been easy in the stress of excitement and wonder. Nobody had any titne to think of the excessively remote incidents of the early morning. All minor interests were lost in the marvel of the present situation.

"Who landed you in the eye, Billie?" asked the awed Coke. "That was a bad one." "Oh, I don't know," said Billie. "You really couldn't tell who hit you, you know. It was a football rush. They had guns and knives, but they didn't use 'em. I don't know why Jinks! I'm getting pretty stiff. My face feels as if it were made of tin. Did they give you people a row, too?"

"No; only talk. That little officer managed them. Out-talked them, I suppose. Hear him buzz, now." The Wainwrights came down stairs. Nora Black went confidently forward to meet them. "You've added one more to your list of rescuers," She cried, with her glowing, triumphant smile. "Miss Black of the New York Daylight-at your service. How in the world do you manage to get yourselves into such dreadful Scrapes? You are the most remarkable people. You need a guardian. Why, you might have all been killed. How exciting it must seem to be regularly of your party." She had shaken cordiaily one of Mrs. Wainwright's hands without that lady indicating assent to the proceeding but Mrs. Wainwright had not felt repulsion. In fact she had had no emotion springing directly from it. Here again the marvel of the situation came to deny Mrs. Wainwright the right to resume a state of mind which had been so painfully interesting to her a few hours earlier.

The professor, Coleman and all the students were talking together. Coke had addressed Coleman civilly and Coleman had made a civil reply. Peace was upon them.

Nora slipped her arm lovingly through Marjbry's arm. "That Rufus! Oh, that Rufus," she cried joyously. "I'll give him a good scolding as soon as I see him alone. I might have foreseen that he would get you all into trouble. The old stupid!"

Marjory did not appear to resent anything. "Oh, I don't think it was Mr. Coleman's fault at ail," she answered calmly. "I think it was more the fault of Peter Tounley, poor boy."

"Well, I'd be glad to believe it, I'd be glad to believe it," said Nora. "I want Rufus to keep out of that sort of thing, but he is so hot-headed and foolish." If she had pointed out her proprietary stamp on Coleman's cheek she could not have conveyed what she wanted with more clearness.

"Oh," said the impassive Marjory, "I don't think you need have any doubt as to whose fault it was, if there were any of our boys at fault. Mr. Coleman was inside when the fighting commenced, and only ran out to help the boys. He had just brought us safely through the mob, and, far from being hot-headed and foolish, he was utterly cool in manner, impressively cool, I thought. I am glad to be able to reassure you on these points, for I see that they worry you."

"Yes, they do worry me," said Nora, densely. They worry me night and day when he is away from me."

"Oh," responded Marjory, "I have never thought of Mr. Coleman as a man that one would worry about much. We consider him very self-reliant, able to take care of himself under almost any conditions, but then, of course, we do not know him at all in the way that you

Stephen Crane

know him. I should think that you would find that he came off rather better than you expected from most of his difficulties. But then, of course, as. I said, you know him so much better than we do." Her easy indifference was a tacit dismissal of Coleman as a topic.

Nora, now thoroughly alert, glanced keenly into the other girl's face, but it was inscrutable. The actress had intended to go careering through a whole circle of daring illusions to an intimacy with,Coleman, but here, before she had really developed her attack, Marjory, with a few conventional and indifferent sentences, almost expressive of boredom, had made the subject of Coleman impossible. An effect was left upon Nora's mind that Marjory had been extremely polite in listening to much nervous talk about a person in whom she had no interest.

The actress was dazed. She did not know how it had all been done. Where was the head of this thing? And where Was the tail? A fog had mysteriously come upon all her brilliant prospects of seeing Marjory Wainwright suffer, and this fog was the product of a kind of magic with which she was not familiar. She could not think how to fight it. After being simply dubious throughout a long pause, she in the end went into a great rage. She glared furiously at Marjory, dropped her arm as if it had burned her and moved down upon Coleman. She must have reflected that at any rate she could make him wriggle. When she was come near to him, she called out: "Rufus!" In her tone was all the old insolent statement of ownership. Coleman might have been a poodle. She knew how to call his same in a way that was anything less than a public scandal. On this occasion everybody looked at him and then went silent, as people awaiting the startling denouement of a drama. "Rufus!" She was baring his shoulder to show the fieur-de-lis of the criminal. The students gaped.

Coleman's temper was, if one may be allowed to speak in that way, broken loose inside of him. He could hardly beeathe; he felt that his body was about to explode into a thousand fragments. He simply snarled out "What?" Almost at once he saw that she had at last goaded him into making a serious tactical mistake. It must be admitted that it is only when the relations between a man and a woman are the relations of wedlock, or at least an intimate resemblance to it, that the man snarls out "What?" to the woman. Mere lovers say "I beg your pardon?" It is only Cupid's finished product that spits like a cat. Nora Black had called him like a wife, and he had answered like a husband. For his cause, his manner could not possibly have been worse. He saw the professor stare at him in surprise and alarm, and felt the excitement of the eight students. These latter were diabolic in the celerity with which they picked out meanings. It was as plain to them as if Nora Black had said: "He is my property."

Coleman would have given his nose to have been able to recall that single reverberating word. But he saw that the scene was spelling downfall for him, and he went still more blind and desperate of it. His despair made him burn to make matters Worse. He did not want to improve anything at all. "What?" he demanded. "What do ye' want?"

Nora was sweetly reproachful. "I left my jacket in the carriage, and I want you to get it for me."

"Well, get it for yourself, do you see? Get it for yourself."

Now it is plainly to be seen that no one of the people listening there had ever heard a man speak thus to a woman who was not his wife. Whenever they had heard that form of spirited repartee it had come from the lips of a husband. Coleman's rude speech was to their ears a flat announcement of an extraordinary intimacy between Nora Black and thecorrespondent. Any other interpretation would not have occurred to them. It was so palpable that it greatly distressed them with its arrogance and boldness. The professor had blushed. The very milkiest word in his mind at the time was the word vulgarity.

Nora Black had won a great battle. It was her Agincourt. She had beaten the clever Coleman in a way that had left little of him but rags. However, she could have lost it all again if she had shown her feeling of elation. At Coleman's rudeness her manner indicated a mixture of sadness and embarrassment. Her suffering was so plain to the eye that Peter Tounley was instantly moved. "Can't I get your jacket for you, Miss Black?" he asked hastily, and at her grateful nod he was off at once.

Coleman was resolved to improve nothing. His overthrow seemed to him to be so complete that he could not in any way mend it without a sacrifice of his dearest prides. He turned away from them all and walked to an isolated corner of the room. He would abide no longer with them. He had been made an outcast by Nora Black, and he intended to be an outcast. There was no sense in attempting to stem this extraordinary deluge. It was better to acquiesce. Then suddenly he was angry with Marjory. He did not exactly see why he was angry at Marjory, but he was angry at her nevertheless. He thought of how he could revenge himself upon her. He decided to take horse with his groom and dragoman and proceed forthwith on the road, leaving the jumble as it stood. This would pain Marjory, anyhow, he hoped. She would feel it deeply, he hoped. Acting upon this plan, he went to the professor. Well, of course you are all right now, professor, and if you don't mind, I would like to leave you-go on ahead. I've got a considerable pressure of business on my mind, and I think I should hurry on to Athens, if you don't mind."

The professor did not seem to know what to say. "Of course, if you wish it-sorry, I'm sure - of course it is as you please-but you have been such a power in our favour-it seems too bad to lose you-but-if you wish it-if you insist -"

"Oh, yes, I quite insist," said Coleman, calmly. "I quite insist. Make your mind easy on that score, professor. I insist."

"Well, Mr. Coleman," stammered the old man. "Well, it seems a great pity to lose you-you have been such a power in our favour -"

"Oh, you are now only eight hours from the railway. It is very easy. You would not need my assistance, even if it were a benefit!

"But -" said the professor.

Coleman's dragoman came to him then and said: "There is one man here who says you made to take one rifle in the fight and was break his head. He was say he wants sunthing for you was break his head. He says hurt."

"How much does he want?" asked Coleman, impatiently.

The dragoman wrestled then evidently with a desire to protect this mine from outside fingers. "I - I think two gold piece plenty." "Take them," said Coleman. It seemed to him preposterous that this idiot with a broken head should interpolate upon his tragedy. "Afterward you and the groom get the three horses and we will start for Athens at once."

"For Athens? At once?" said Marjory's voice in his ear.

CHAPTER XXIII

"Om," said Coleman, "I was thinking of starting."

"Why?" asked Marjory, unconcernedly.

Coleman shot her a quick glance. "I believe my period of usefulness is quite ended," he said. with just a small betrayal of bitter feeling.

"It is certainly true that you have had a remarkable period of usefulness to us," said Marjory with a slow smile, "but if it is ended, you should not run away from us."

Coleman looked at her to see what she could mean. From many women, these words would have been equal, under the circumstances, to a command to stay, but he felt that none might know what impulses moved the mind behind that beautiful mask. In his misery he thought to hurt her into an expression of feeling by a rough speech. "I'm so in love with Nora Black, you know, that I have to be very careful of myself."

"Oh," said Marjory, never thought of that. I should think you would have to be careful of yourself." She did not seem moved in any way. Coleman despaired of finding her weak spot. She was a'damantine, this girl. He searched his mind for something to say which would be still more gross than his last outbreak, but when he felt that he was about to hit upon it, the professor interrupted with an agitated speech to Marjory. "You had better go to your mother, my child, and see that you are all ready to leave here as soon as the carriages come up."

"We have absolutely nothing to make ready," said Marjory, laughing. "But I'll go and see if mother needs anything before we start that I can get for her." She went away without bidding good-bye to Coleman. The sole maddening impression to him was that the matter of his going had not been of sufficient importance to remain longer than a moment upon her mind. At the same time he decided that he would go, irretrievably go.

Even then the dragoman entered the room. "We will pack everything - upon the horse?"

"Everything - yes."

Peter Tounley came afterward. "You are not going to bolt?"

"Yes, I'm off," answered Coleman recovering himself for Peter's benefit. "See you in Athens, probably."

Presently the dragoman announced the readiness of the horses. Coleman shook hands with the students and the Professor amid cries of surprise and polite regret. "What? Going, oldman? Really? What for? Oh, wait for us. We're off in a few minutes. Sorry as the devil, old boy, to' see you go."He accepted their protestations with a somewhat sour face. He knew perfectly well that they were thinking of his departure as something that related to Nora Black. At the last, he bowed to the ladies as a collection. Marjory's answering bow was affable; the bow of Mrs. Wainwright spoke a resentment for something; and Nora's bow was triumphant mockery. As he swung into the saddle an idea struck him with over whelming force. The idea was that he was a fool. He was a colossal imbecile. He touched the spur to his horse and the animal leaped superbly, making the Greeks hasten for safety in all directions. He was off; he could no more return to retract his devious idiocy than he could make his horse fly to Athens. What was done was done. He could not mend it. And he felt like a man that had broken his own heart; perversely, childishly, stupidly broken his own heart. He was sure that Marjory was lost to him. No man could be degraded so publicly and resent it so crudely and still retain a Marjory. In his abasement from his defeat at the hands of Nora Black he had performed every imaginable block-headish act and had finally climaxed it all by a departure which left the tongue of Nora to speak unmolested into the ear of Marjory. Nora's victory had been a serious blow to his fortunes, but it had not been so serious as his own subsequent folly. He had generously muddled his own affairs until he could read nothing out of them but despair.

He was in the mood for hatred. He hated many people. Nora Black was the principal item, but he did not hesitate to detest the professor, Mrs. Wainwright, Coke and all the students. As for Marjory, he would revenge himself upon her. She had done nothing that he defined clearly but, at any rate, he would take revenge for it. As much as was possible, he would make her suffer. He would convince her that he was a tremendous and inexorable person. But it came upon his mind that he was powerless in all ways. If he hated many people they probably would not be even interested in his emotion and, as for his revenge upon Marjory, it was beyond his strength. He was nothing but the complaining victim of Nora Black and himself.

He felt that he would never again see Marjory, and while feeling it he began to plan his attitude when next they met. He would be very cold and reserved. At Agrinion he found that there would be no train until the next daybreak. The dragoman was excessively annoyed over it, but Coleman did not scold at all. As a matter of fact his heart had given a great joyus bound. He could not now prevent his being overtaken. They were only a few leagues away, and while he was waiting for the train they would easily cover the distance. If anybody expressed surprise at seeing him he could exhibit the logical reasons. If there had been a train starting at once he would have taken it. His pride would have put up with no subterfuge. If the Wainwrights overtook him it was because he could not help it. But he was delighted that he could not help it. There had been an interposition by some specially beneficent fate. He felt like whistling. He spent the early half of the night in blissful smoke, striding the room which the dragoman had found for him. His head was full of plans and detached impressive scenes in which he figured before Marjory. The simple fact that there was no train away from Agrinion until the next daybreak had wrought a stupendous change in his outlook. He unhesitatingly considered it an omen of a good future. He was up before the darkness even contained presage of coming light, but near the railway station was a little hut where coffee was being served to several prospective travellers who had come even earlier to the rendezvous. There was no evidence of the Wainwrights.

Coleman sat in the hut and listened for the rumble of wheels. He was suddenly appalled that the Wainwrights were going to miss the train. Perhaps they had decided against travelling during the night. Perbaps this thing, and perhaps that thing. The morning was very cold. Closely muffled in his cloak, he went to the door and stared at where the road was whitening out of night. At the station stood a little spectral train, and the engine at intervals emitted a long, piercing scream which informed the echoing land that, in all probability, it was going to start after a time for the south. The Greeks in the coffee room were, of course, talking.

At last Coleman did hear the sound of hoofs and wheels. The three carriages swept up in grand procession. The first was laden with students; in the second was the professor, the Greek officer, Nora Black's old lady and other persons, all looking marvellously unimportant and shelved. It was the third carriage at which Coleman stared. At first be thought the dim light deceived his vision, but in a moment he knew that his first leaping conception of the arrangement of the people in this vehicle had been perfectly correct. Nora Black and Mrs. Wainwright sat side by side on the back seat, while facing them were Coke and Marjory.

They looked cold but intimate.

The oddity of the grouping stupefied Coleman. It was anarchy, naked and unashamed. He could not imagine how such changes could have been consummated in the short time he had been away from them, but he laid it all to some startling necromancy on the part of Nora Black, some wondrous play which had captured them all because of its surpassing skill and because they were, in the main, rather gullible people. He was wrong. The magic had been wrought by the unaided foolishness of Mrs. Wainwfight. As soon as Nora Black had succeeded in creating an effect of intimacy and dependence between herself and Coleman, the professor had flatly stated to his wife that the presence of Nora Black in the party, in the inn, in the world, was a thiag that did not meet his approval in any way. She should be abolished. As for Coleman, he would not defend him. He preferred not to talk to him. It made him sad. Coleman at least had been very indiscreet, very indiscreet. It was a great pity. But as for this blatant woman, the sooner they rid themselves of her, the sooner he would feel that all the world was not evil.

Whereupon Mrs. Wainwright had changed front with the speed of light and attacked with horse, foot and guns. She failed to see, she had declared, where this poor, lone girt was in great fault. Of course it was probable that she had listened to this snaky. tongued Rufus Coleman, but that was ever the mistake that women made. Oh, certainly; the professor would like to let Rufus Coleman off scot-free. That was the way with men. They defended each other in all cases. If wrong were done it was the woman who suffered. Now, since this poor girl was alone far off here in Greece, Mrs. Wainwright announced that she had such full sense of her duty to her sex that her conscience would not allow her to scorn and desert a sister, even if that sister was, approximately, the victim of a creature like Rufus Coleman. Perhaps the poor thing loved this wretched man, although it was hard to imagine any woman giving her heart to such. a monster.

The professor had then asked with considerable spirit for the proofs upon which Mrs. Wainwright named Coleman a monster, and had made a wry face over her completely conventional reply. He had told her categorically his opinion of her erudition in such matters.

But Mrs. Wainwright was not to be deterred from an exciting espousal of the cause of her sex. Upon the instant that the professor strenuously opposed her she becamean apostle, an enlightened, uplifted apostle to the world on the wrongs of her sex. She had come down with this thing as if it were a disease. Nothing could stop her. Her husband, her daughter, all influences in other directions, had been overturned with a roar, and the first thing fully clear to the professor's mind had been that his wife was riding affably in the carriage with Nora Black. Coleman aroused when he heard one of the students cry out: "Why, there is Rufus Coleman's dragoman. He must be here." A moment later they thronged upon him. "Hi, old man, caught you again! Where did you break to? Glad to catch you, old boy. How are you making it? Where's your horse?"

"Sent the horses on to, Athens," said Coleman. He had not yet recovered his composure, and he was glad to find available this commonplace return to their exuberant greetings and questions. "Sent them on to Athens with the groom."

In the mean time the engine of the little train was screaming to heaven that its intention of starting was most serious. The diligencia careered to the station platform and unburdened. Coleman had had his dragoman place his luggage in a little first-class carriage and he defiantly entered it and closed the door.

He had a sudden return to the old sense of downfall, and with it came the original rebellious desires. However, he hoped that somebody would intrude upon him. It was Peter Tounley. The student flung open the door and then yelled to the distance: "Here's an empty one." He clattered into the compartment. "Hello, Coleman! Didn't know you were in here!" At his heels came Nora Black, Coke and Marjory. "Oh!" they said, when they saw the occupant of the carriage. "Oh!" Coleman was furious. He could have distributed some of his traps in a way to create more room, but he did not move.

CHAPTER XXIV

THERE was a demonstration of the unequalled facilities of a European railway carriage for rendering unpleasant things almost intolerable. These people could find no way to alleviate the poignancy of their position. Coleman did not know where to look. Every personal mannerism becomes accentuated in a European railway carriage. If you glance at a man, your glance defines itself as a stare. If you carefully look at nothing, you create for yourself a resemblance to all wooden-headed things. A newspaper is, then, in the nature of a preservative, and Coleman longed for a newspaper.

It was this abominable railway carriage which exacted the first display of agitation from Marjory. She flushed rosily, and her eyes wavered over the cornpartment. Nora Black laughed in a way that was a shock to the nerves. Coke seemed very angry, indeed, and Peter Tounley was in pitiful distress. Everything was acutely, painfully vivid, bald, painted as glaringly as a grocer's new wagon. It fulfilled those traditions which the artists deplore when they use their pet phrase on a picture, "It hurts." The damnable power of accentuation of the European railway carriage seemed, to Coleman's amazed mind, to be redoubled and redoubled.

It was Peter Tounley who seemed to be in the greatest agony. He looked at the correspondent beseechingly and said: "It's a very cold morning, Coleman." This was an actual appeal in the name of humanity.

Coleman came squarely. to the front and even grinned a little at poor Peter Tounley's misery. "Yes, it is a cold morning, Peter. I should say it to one of the coldest mornings in my recollection."

Peter Tounley had not intended a typical American emphasis on the polar conditions which obtained in the compartment at this time, but Coleman had given the word this meaning. Spontaneously every body smiled, and at once the tension was relieved. But of course the satanic powers of the railway carriage could not be altogether set at naught. Of course it fell to the lot of Coke to get the seat directly in front of Coleman, and thus, face to face, they were doomed to stare at each other.

Peter Tounley was inspired to begin conventional babble, in which he took great care to make an appear. ance of talking to all in the carriage. "Funny thing I never knew these mornings in Greece were so cold. I thought the climate here was quite tropical. It must have been inconvenient in the ancient times, when, I am told, people didn't wear near so manyer-clothes. Really, I don't see how they stood it. For my part, I would like nothing so much as a buffalo robe. I suppose when those great sculptors were doing their masterpieces, they had to wear gloves. Ever think of that? Funny, isn't it? Aren't you cold, Marjory ? I am. jingo! Imagine the Spartans in ulsters, going out to meet an enemy in cape-overcoats, and being desired by their mothers to return with their ulsters or wrapped in them."

It was rather hard work for Peter Tounley. Both Marjory and Coleman tried to display an interest in his labours, and they laughed not at what he said, but because they believed it assisted him. The little train, meanwhile, wandered up a great green slope, and the day rapidly coloured the land.

At first Nora Black did not display a militant mood, but as time passed Coleman saw clearly that she was considering the advisability of a new attack. She had Coleman and Marjory in conjunction and where they were unable to escape from her. The opportunities were great. To Coleman, she seemed to be gloating over the possibilities of making more mischief. She was looking at him speculatively, as if considering the best place to hit him first. Presently she drawled: "Rufus, I wish you would fix my rug about me a little better." Coleman saw that this was a beginning. Peter Tounley sprang to his feet with speed and enthusiasm. "Oh, let me do it for you." He had her well muffled in the rug before she could protest, even if a protest had been rational. The young man had no idea of defending Coleman. He had no knowledge of the necessity for it. It had been merely the exercise of his habit of amiability, his chronic desire to see everybody comfortable. His passion in this direction was well known in Washurst, where the students had borrowed a phrase from the photographers in order to describe him fully in a nickname. They called him "Look-pleasant Tounley." This did not in any way antagonise his perfect willingness to fight on occasions with a singular desperation, which usually has a small stool in every mind where good nature has a throne.

"Oh, thank you very much, Mr. Tounley," said Nora Black, without gratitude. "Rufus is always so lax in these matters."

"I don't know how you know it," said Coleman boldly, and he looked her fearlessly in the eye. The battle had begun.

"Oh," responded Nora, airily, " I have had opportunity enough to know it, I should think, by this time."

"No," said Coleman, "since I have never paid you particular and direct attention, you cannot possibly know what I am lax in and what I am not lax in. I would be obliged to be of service at any time, Nora, but surely you do not consider that you have a right to my services superior to any other right."

Nora Black simply went mad, but fortunately part of her madness was in the form of speechlessness. Otherwise there might have been heard something approaching to billingsgate.

Marjory and Peter Tounley turned first hot and then cold, and looked as if they wanted to fly away; and even Coke, penned helplessly in with this unpleasant incident, seemed to have a sudden attack of distress. The only frigid person was Coleman. He had made his declaration of independence, and he saw with glee that the victory was complete. Nora Black might storm and rage, but he had announced his position in an unconventional blunt way which nobody in the carriage could fail to understand. He felt somewhat like smiling with confidence and defiance in Nora's face, but he still had the fear for Marjory.

Unexpectedly, the fight was all out of Nora Black. She had the fury of a woman scorned, but evidently she had perceived that all was over and lost. The remainder of her wrath dispensed itself in glares which Coleman withstood with great composure.

A strained silence fell upon the group which lasted until they arrived at the little port of Mesalonghi, whence they were to take ship for Patras. Coleman found himself wondering why he had not gone flatly at the great question at a much earlier period, indeed at the first moment when the great question began to make life exciting for him. He thought that if he had charged Nora's guns in the beginning they would have turned out to be the same incapable artillery. Instead of that he had run away and continued to run away until he was actually cornered and made to fight, and his easy victory had defined him as a person who had, earlier, indulged in much stupidity and cowardice. Everything had worked out so simply, his terrors had been dispelled so easily, that he probably was led to overestimate his success. And it occurred suddenly to him. He foresaw a fine occasion to talk privately to Marjory when all had boarded the steamer for Patras and he resolved to make use of it. This he believed would end the strife and conclusively laurel him.

The train finally drew up on a little stone pier and some boatmen began to scream like gulls. The steamer lay at anchor in the placid blue cove. The embarkation was chaotic in the Oriental fashion and there was the customary misery which was only relieved when the travellers had set foot on the deck of the steamer. Coleman did not devote any premature attention to finding Marjory, but when the steamer was fairly out on the calm waters of the Gulf of Corinth, he saw her pacing to and fro with Peter Tounley. At first he lurked in the distance waiting for an opportunity, but ultimately he decided to make his own opportunity. He approached them. "Marjory,would you let me speak to you alone for a few moments? You won't mind, will you, Peter? "

"Oh, no, certainly not," said Peter Tounley.

"Of course. It is not some dreadful revelation, is it?" said Marjory, bantering him coolly.

"No," answered Coleman, abstractedly. He was thinking of what he was going to say. Peter Tounley vanished around the corner of a deck-house and Marjory and Coleman began to pace to and fro even as Marjory and Peter Tounley had done. Coleman had thought to speak his mind frankly and once for all, and on the train he had invented many clear expressions of his feeling. It did not appear that he had forgotten them. It seemed, more, that they had become entangled in his mind in such a way that he could not unravel the end of his discourse.

In the pause, Marjory began to speak in admiration of the scenery. "I never imagined that Greece was so full of mountains. One reads so much of the Attic Plains, but aren't these mountains royal? They look so rugged and cold, whereas the bay is absolutely as blue as the old descriptions of a summer sea."

"I wanted to speak to you about Nora Black," said Coleman.

"Nora Black? Why?" said Marjory, lifting her eyebrows.

You know well enough," said Coleman, in a head. long fashion. " You must know, you must have seen it. She knows I care for you and she wants to stop it. And she has no right to-to interfere. She is a fiend, a perfect fiend. She is trying to make you feel that I care for her."

"And don't you care for her ?" asked Marjory.

"No," said Coleman, vehemently. "I don't care for her at all."

"Very well," answered Marjory, simply. "I believe you." She managed to give the words the effect of a mere announcement that she believed him and it was in no way plain that she was glad or that she esteemed the matter as being of consequence.

He scowled at her in dark resentment. "You mean by that, I suppose, that you don't believe me ?"

"Oh," answered Marjory, wearily, "I believe you. I said so. Don't talk about it any more."

"Then," said Coleman, slowly, "you mean that you do not care whether I'm telling the truth or not?"

"Why, of course I care," she said. "Lying is not nice."

He did not know, apparently, exactly how to deal with her manner, which was actually so pliable that-it was marble, if one may speak in that way. He looked ruefully at the sea. He had expected a far easier time. "Well -" he began.

"Really," interrupted Marjory, "this is something

which I do not care to discuss. I would rather you would not speak to me at all about it. It seems too-too-bad. I can readily give you my word that I believe you, but I would prefer you not to try to talk to me about it or - anything of that sort. Mother!"

Mrs. Wainwright was hovering anxiously in the vicinity, and she now bore down rapidly upon the pair. "You are very nearly to Patras," she said reproachfully to her daughter, as if the fact had some fault of Marjory's concealed in it. She in no way acknowledged the presence of Coleman.

"Oh, are we ?" cried Marjory.

"Yes," said Mrs. Wainwright. "We are."

She stood waiting as if she expected Marjory to instantly quit Coleman. The girl wavered a moment and then followed her mother. "Good-bye." she said. "I hope we may see you again in Athens." It was a command to him to travel alone with his servant on the long railway journey from Patras to Athens. It was a dismissal of a casual acquaintance given so graciously that it stung him to the depths of his pride. He bowed his adieu and his thanks. When the yelling boatmen came again, he and his man proceeded to the shore in an early boat without looking in any way after the welfare of the others.

At the train, the party split into three sections. Coleman and his man had one compartment, Nora Black and her squad had another, and the Wainwrights and students occupied two more.

The little officer was still in tow of Nora Black. He

was very enthusiastic. In French she directed him to remain silent, but he did not appear to understand. "You tell him," she then said to her dragoman, "to sit in a corner and not to speak until I tell him to, or I won't have him in here." She seemed anxious to unburden herself to the old lady companion. "Do you know," she said, " that girl has a nerve like steel. I tried to break it there in that inn, but I couldn't budge her. If I am going to have her beaten I must prove myself to be a very, very artful person."

"Why did you try to break her nerve?" asked the old lady, yawning. "Why do you want to have her beaten?"

"Because I do, old stupid," answered Nora. "You should have heard the things I said to her."

"About what?"

"About Coleman. Can't you understand anything at all?"

"And why should you say anything about Coleman to her?" queried the old lady, still hopelessly befogged.

"Because," cried Nora, darting a look of wrath at her companion, "I want to prevent that marriage." She had been betrayed into this avowal by the singularly opaque mind of the old lady. The latter at once sat erect. - "Oh, ho," she said, as if a ray of light had been let into her head. "Oh, ho. So that's it, is it?"

"Yes, that's it, rejoined Nora, shortly.

The old lady was amazed into a long period of meditation. At last she spoke depressingly. "Well, how are you going to prevent it? Those things can't be done in these days at all. If they care for each other -"

Nora burst out furiously. "Don't venture opinions until you know what you are talking about, please. They don't care for each other, do you see? She cares for him, but he don't give a snap of his fingers for her."

"But," cried the bewildered lady, "if he don't care for her, there will be nothing to prevent. If he don't care for her, he won't ask her to marry him, and so there won't be anything to prevent."

Nora made a broad gesture of impatience. "Oh, can't you get anything through your head ? Haven't you seen that the girl has been the only young woman in that whole party lost up there in the mountains, and that naturally more than half of the men still think they are in love with her? That's what it is. Can't you see? It always happens that way. Then Coleman comes along and makes a fool of himself with the others."

The old lady spoke up brightly as if at last feeling able to contribute something intelligent to the talk. "Oh, then, he does care for her."

Nora's eyes looked as if their glance might shrivel the old lady's hair. "Don't I keep telling you that it is no such thing? Can't you understand? It is all glamour! Fascination! Way up there in the wilderness! Only one even passable woman in sight."

"I don't say that I am so very keen," said the old lady, somewhat offended, "but I fail to see where I could improve when first you tell me he don't care for her, and then you tell me that he does care for her."

"Glamour,' 'Fascination,'" quoted Nora. "Don't you understand the meaning of the words?"

"Well," asked the other, didn't he know her, then, before he came over here?"

Nora was silent for a time, while a gloom upon her face deepened. It had struck her that the theories for which she protested so energetically might not be of such great value. Spoken aloud, they had a sudden new flimsiness. Perhaps she had reiterated to herself that Coleman was the victim of glamour only because she wished it to be true. One theory, however, remained unshaken. Marjory was an artful rninx, with no truth in her.

She presently felt the necessity of replying to the question of her companion. "Oh," she said, carelessly, " I suppose they were acquainted-in a way."

The old lady was giving the best of her mind to the subject. "If that's the case -" she observed, musingly, "if that's the case, you can't tell what is between 'em."

The talk had so slackened that Nora's unfortunate Greek admirer felt that here was a good opportunity to present himself again to the notice of the actress. The means was a smile and a French sentence, but his reception would have frightened a man in armour. His face blanched with horror at the storm, he had invoked, and he dropped limply back as if some one had shot him. "You tell this little snipe to let me alone!" cried Nora, to the dragoman. "If he dares to come around me with any more of those Parisian dude speeches, I - I don't know what I'll do! I won't have it, I say." The impression upon the dragoman was hardly less in effect. He looked with bulging eyes at Nora, and then began to stammer at the officer. The latter's voice could sometimes be heard in awed whispers for the more elaborate explanation of some detail of the tragedy. Afterward, he remained meek and silent in his corner, barely more than a shadow, like the proverbial husband of imperious beauty.

"Well," said the old lady, after a long and thoughtful pause, "I don't know, I'm sure, but it seems to me that if Rufus Coleman really cares for that girl, there isn't much use in trying to stop him from getting her. He isn't that kind of a man."

"For heaven's sake, will you stop assuming that he does care for her?" demanded Nora, breathlessly.

"And I don't see," continued the old lady, "what you want to prevent him for, anyhow."

CHAPTER XXV

"I FEEL in this radiant atmosphere that there could be no such thing as war-men striving together in black and passionate hatred." The professor's words were for the benefit of his wife and daughter. He was viewing the sky-blue waters of the Gulf of Corinth with its background of mountains that in the sunshine were touched here and there with a copperish glare. The train was slowly sweeping along the southern shore. "It is strange to think of those men fighting up there in the north. And it is strange to think that we ourselves are but just returning from it."

"I cannot begin to realise it yet," said Mrs. Wainwright, in a high voice.

"Quite so," responded the professor, reflectively.

"I do not suppose any of us will realise it fully for some time. It is altogether too odd, too very odd."

"To think of it!" cried Mrs. WainWright. "To think of it! Supposing those dreadful Albanians or those awful men from the Greek mountains had caught us! Why, years from now I'll wake up in the night and think of it! "

The professor mused. "Strange that we cannot feel it

Stephen Crane

strongly now. My logic tells me to be aghast that we ever got into such a place, but my nerves at present refuse to thrill. I am very much afraid that this singular apathy of ours has led us to be unjust to poor Coleman." Here Mrs. Wainwright objected. Poor Coleman! I don't see why you call him poor Coleman.

"Well," answered the professor, slowly, "I am in doubt about our behaviour. It -"

"Oh," cried the wife, gleefully," in doubt about our behaviour! I'm in doubt about his behaviour."

"So, then, you do have a doubt. of his behaviour?" "Oh, no," responded Mrs. Wainwright, hastily, "not about its badness. What I meant to say was that in the face of his outrageous conduct with that - that woman, it is curious that you should worry about our behaviour. It surprises me, Harrison."

The professor was wagging his head sadly. "I don't know I don't know It seems hard to judge * * I hesitate to -"

Mrs. Wainwright treated this attitude with disdain. "It is not hard to judge," she scoffed, "and I fail to see why you have any reason for hesitation at all. Here he brings this woman -"

The professor got angry. "Nonsense! Nonsense! I do not believe that he brought her. If I ever saw a spectacle of a woman bringing herself, it was then. You keep chanting that thing like an outright parrot."

"Well," retorted Mrs. Wainwright, bridling, "I suppose you imagine that you understand such things, Men usually think that, but I want to tell you that you seem to me utterly blind."

"Blind or not, do stop the everlasting reiteration of that sentence."

Mrs. Wainwright passed into an offended silence, and the professor, also silent, looked with a gradually dwindling indignation at the scenery.

Night was suggested in the sky before the train was near to Athens. " My trunks," sighed Mrs. Wainwright. "How glad I will be to get back to my trunks! Oh, the dust! Oh, the misery! Do find out when we will get there, Harrison. Maybe the train is late."

But, at last, they arrived in Athens, amid a darkness which was confusing, and, after no more than the common amount of trouble, they procured carriages and were taken to the hotel. Mrs. Wainwright's impulses now dominated the others in the family. She had one passion after another. The majority of the servants in the hotel pretended that they spoke English, but, in three minutes, she drove them distracted with the abundance and violence of her requests. It came to pass that in the excitement the old couple quite forgot Marjory. It was not until Mrs. Wainwright, then feeling splendidly, was dressed for dinner, that she thought to open Marjory's door and go to render a usual motherly supervision of the girl's toilet.

There was no light: there did not seem to be any-body in the room. "Marjory!" called the mother, in alarm. She listened for a moment and then ran hastily out again. "Harrison!" she cried. "I can't find Marjory!" The professor had been tying his cravat. He let the loose ends fly. "What?" he ejaculated, opening his mouth wide. Then they both rushed into Marjory's room. "Marjory!" beseeched the old man in a voice which would have invoked the grave.

The answer was from the bed. "Yes?" It was low, weary, tearful. It was not like Marjory. It was dangerously the voice of a hcart-broken woman. They hurried forward with outcries. "Why, Marjory! Are you ill, child? How long have you been lying in the dark? Why didn't you call us? Are you ill?"

"No," answered this changed voice, "I am not ill. I only thought I'd rest for a time. Don't bother."

The professor hastily lit the gas and then father and mother turned hurriedly to the bed. In the first of the illumination they saw that tears were flowing unchecked down Marjory's face.

The effect.of this grief upon the professor was, in part, an effect of fear. He seemed afraid to touch it, to go near it. He could, evidently, only remain in the outskirts, a horrified spectator. The mother, how. ever, flung her arms about her daughter. "Oh, Marjory!" She, too, was weeping.

The girl turned her face to the pillow and held out a hand of protest. " Don't, mother! Don't!"

"Oh, Marjory! Oh, Marjory!"

"Don't, mother. Please go away. Please go away. Don't speak at all, I beg of you."

"Oh, Marjory! Oh, Marjory!"

"Don't." The girl lifted a face which appalled them. It had something entirely new in it. "Please go away, mother. I will speak to father, but I won't - I can't - I can't be pitied."

Mrs. Wainwright looked at her husband. "Yes," said the old man, trembling. "Go!" She threw up her hands in a sorrowing gesture that was not without its suggestion that her exclusion would be a mistake. She left the room.

The professor dropped on his knees at the bedside and took one of Marjory's hands. His voice dropped to its tenderest note. "Well, my Marjory?"

She had turned her face again to the pillow. At last she answered in muffled tones, "You know." Thereafter came a long silence full of sharpened pain. It was Marjory who spoke first. "I have saved my pride, daddy, but - I have-lost-everything - else." Even her sudden resumption of the old epithet of her childhood was an additional misery to the old man. He still said no word. He knelt, gripping her fingers and staring at the wall.

"Yes, I have lost everything - else."

The father gave a low groan. He was thinking deeply, bitterly. Since one was only a human being, how was one going to protect beloved hearts assailed with sinister fury from the inexplicable zenith? In this tragedy he felt as helpless as an old grey ape. He did not see a possible weapon with which he could defend his child from the calamity which was upon her. There was no wall, no shield which could turn this sorrow from the heart of his child. If one of his hands loss could have spared her, there would have been a sacrifice of his hand, but he was potent for nothing. He could only groan and stare at the wall. He reviewed the past half in fear that he would suddenly come upon his error which was now the cause of Marjory's tears. He dwelt long upon the fact that in Washurst he had refused his consent to Marjory's marriage with Coleman, but even now he could not say that his judgment was not correct. It was simply that the doom of woman's woe was upon Marjory, this ancient woe of the silent tongue and the governed will, and he could only kneel at the bedside and stare at the wall.

Marjory raised her voice in a laugh. "Did I betray myself? Did I become the maiden all forlorn ? Did I giggle to show people that I did not care? No - I did not - I did not. And it was such a long time, daddy! Oh, such a long time! I thought we would never get here. I thought I would never get where I could be alone like this, where I could-cry-if I wanted to. I am not much of - a crier, am I, daddy? But this time-this-time -"

She suddenly drew herself over near to her father and looked at him. "Oh, daddy, I want to tell you one thing. just one simple little thing." She waited then, and while she waited her father's head went lower and lower. "Of course, you know - I told you once. I love him! I love him! Yes, probably he is a rascal, but, do you know, I don't think I would mind if he was a-an assassin. This morning I sent him away, but, daddy, he didn't want to go at all. I know he didn't. This Nora Black is nothing to him. I know she is not. I am sure of it. Yes - I am sure of it. * * * I never expected to talk this way to any living creature, but - you are so good, daddy. Dear old daddy -"

She ceased, for she saw that her father was praying.

The sight brought to her a new outburst of sobbing, for her sorrow now had dignity and solemnity from thebowed white head of her old father, and she felt that her heart was dying amid the pomp of the church. It was the last rites being performed at the death-bed. Into her ears came some imagining of the low melan. choly chant of monks in a gloom.

Finally her father arose. He kissed her on the brow. "Try to sleep, dear," he said. He turned out the gas and left the room. His thought was full of chastened emotion.

But if his thought was full of chastened emotion, it received some degree of shock when he arrived in the presence of Mrs. Wainwright. "Well, what is all this about ?" she demanded, irascibly. "Do you mean to say that Marjory is breaking her heart over that man Coleman? It is all your fault -" She was apparently still ruffled over her exclusion.

When the professor interrupted her he did not speak with his accustomed spirit, but from something novel in his manner she recognised a danger signal. "Please do not burst out at it in that way."

"Then it Is true?" she asked. Her voice was a mere awed whisper.

"It is true," answered the professor.

"Well," she said, after reflection, "I knew it. I alway's knew it. If you hadn't been so blind! You turned like a weather-cock in your opinions of Coleman. You never could keep your opinion about him for more than an hour. Nobody could imagine what you might think next. And now you see the result of it! I warned you! I told you what this Coleman was, and if Marjory is suffering now, you have only yourself to blame for it. I warned you!"

"If it is my fault," said the professor, drearily, "I hope God may forgive me, for here is a great wrong to my daughter."

Well, if you had done as I told you -" she began.

Here the professor revolted. "Oh, now, do not begin on that," he snarled, peevishly. Do not begin on that."

"Anyhow," said Mrs. Wainwright, it is time that we should be going down to dinner. Is Marjory coming?"

"No, she is not," answered the professor, "and I do not know as I shall go myself."

"But you must go. Think how it would look! All the students down there dining without us, and cutting up capers! You must come."

"Yes," he said, dubiously, "but who will look after Marjory?"

"She wants to be left alone," announced Mrs. Wainwright, as if she was the particular herald of this news. " She wants to be left alone."

"Well, I suppose we may as well go down." Before they went, the professor tiptoed into his daughter's room. In the darkness he could only see her waxen face on the pillow, and her two eyes gazing fixedly at the ceiling. He did not speak, but immediately withdrew, closing the door noiselessly behind him.

CHAPTER XXVI

IF the professor and Mrs. Wainwright had descended sooner to a lower floor of the hotel, they would have found reigning there a form of anarchy. The students were in a smoking room which was also an entrance hall to the dining room, and because there was in the middle of this apartment a fountain containing gold fish, they had been moved to license and sin. They had all been tubbed and polished and brushed and dressed until they were exuberantly beyond themselves. The proprietor of the hotel brought in his dignity and showed it to them, but they minded it no more than if he had been only a common man. He drew himself to his height and looked gravely at them and they jovially said: "Hello, Whiskers." American college students are notorious in their country for their inclination to scoff at robed and crowned authority, and, far from being awed by the dignity of the hotel-keeper, they were delighted with it. It was something with which to sport. With immeasurable impudence, they copied his attitude, and, standing before him, made comic speeches, always alluding with blinding vividness to his beard. His exit disappointed them. He had not remained long under fire. They felt that they could have interested themselves with him an entire evening. "Come back, Whiskers! Oh, come back!" Out in the main hall he made a ges. ture of despair to some of his gaping minions and then fled to seclusion.

A formidable majority then decided that Coke was a gold fish, and that therefore his proper place was in the fountain. They carried him to it while he strug. gled madly. This quiet room with its crimson rugs and gilded mirrors seemed suddenly to have become an important apartment in hell. There being as yet no traffic in the dining room, the waiters were all at liberty to come to the open doors, where they stood as men turned to stone. To them, it was no less than incendiarism.

Coke, standing with one foot on the floor and the other on the bottom of the shallow fountain, blasphemed his comrades in a low tone, but with intention. He was certainly desirous of lifting his foot out of the water, but it seemed that all movement to that end would have to wait until he had successfully expressed his opinions. In the meantime, there was heard slow footsteps and the rustle of skirts, and then some people entered the smoking room on their way to dine. Coke took his foot hastily out of the fountain.

The faces of the men of the arriving party went blank, and they turned their cold and pebbly eyes straight to the front, while the ladies, after little expressions of alarm, looked As if they wanted to run. In fact, the whole crowd rather bolted from this extraordinary scene.

"There, now," said Coke bitterly to his companions. "You see? We looked like little schoolboys -"

"Oh, never mind, old man," said Peter Tounley. "We'll forgive you, although you did embarrass us. But, above everything, don't drip. Whatever you do, don't drip."

The students took this question of dripping and played upon it until they would have made quite insane anybody but another student. They worked it into all manner of forms, and hacked and haggled at Coke until he was driven to his room to seek other apparel. "Be sure and change both legs," they told him. "Remember you can't change one leg without changing both legs."

After Coke's departure, the United States minister entered the room, and instantly they were subdued. It was not his lofty station-that affected them. There are probably few stations that would have at all affected them. They became subdued because they unfeignedly liked the United States minister. They, were suddenly a group of well-bred, correctly attired young men who had not put Coke's foot in the fountain. Nor had they desecrated the majesty of the hotelkeeper.

"Well, I am delighted," said the minister, laughing as he shook hands with them all. " I was not sure I would ever see you again. You are not to be trusted, and, good boys as you are, I'll be glad to see you once and forever over the boundary of my jurisdiction. Leave Greece, you vagabonds. However, I am truly delighted to see you all safe."

"Thank you, sir," they said.

"How in the world did you get out of it? You must be remarkable chaps. I thought you were in a hopeless position. I wired and cabled everywhere I could, but I could find out nothing."

"A correspondent," said Peter Tounley. "I don't know if you have met him. His name is Coleman. He found us."

"Coleman ?" asked the minister, quickly.

"Yes, sir. He found us and brought us out safely."

"Well, glory be to Coleman," exclaimed the minister, after a long sigh of surprise. " Glory be to Coleman! I never thought he could do it."

The students were alert immediately. "Why, did you know about it, sir? Did he tell you he was coming after us ? "

"Of course. He came tome here in Athens. And asked where you were. I told him you were in a peck of trouble. He acted quietly and somewhat queerly,. and said that he would try to look you up. He said you were friends of his. I warned him against trying it. Yes, I said it was impossible, I   had no idea that he would really carry the thing out. But didn't he tell you anything about this himself?"

"No, sir'" answered Peter Tounley. "He never said much about it. I think he usually contended that it was mainly an accident."

"It was no accident," said the minister, sharply. "When a man starts out to do a thing and does it, you can't say it is an accident."

"I didn't say so, sir," said Peter Tounley diffidently.

"Quite true, quite true ! You didn't, but - this Coleman must be a man! "

"We think so, sir," said be who was called Billie. "He certainly brought us through in style."

"But how did he manage it?" cried the minister, keenly interested. "How did he do it ?"

"It is hard to say, sir. But he did it. He met us in the dead of night out near Nikopolis -"

"Near Nikopolis?"

"Yes, sir. And he hid us in a forest while a fight was going on, and then in the morning he brought us inside the Greek lines. Oh, there is a lot to tell -"

Whereupon they told it, or as much as they could of it. In the end, the minister said: "Well, where are the professor and Mrs. Wainwright? I want you all to dine with me to-night. I am dining in the public room, but you won't mind that after Epirus." "They should be down now, sir," answered a Student.

People were now coming rapidly to dinner and presently the professor and Mrs. Wainwright appeared. The old man looked haggard and white. He accepted the minister's warm greeting with a strained pathetic smile. "Thank you. We are glad to return safely."

Once at dinner the minister launched immediately into the subject of Coleman. "He must be altogether a most remarkable man. When he told me, very quietly, that he was going to try to rescue you, I frankly warned him against any such attempt. I thought he would merely add one more to a party of suffering people. But the. boys tell - me that he did actually rescue you."

"Yes, he did," said the professor. "It was a very gallant performance, and we are very grateful."

"Of course," spoke Mrs. Wainwright, "we might have rescued ourselves. We were on the right road, and all we had to do was to keep going on."

"Yes, but I understand -" said the minister. "I understand he took you into a wood to protect you from that fight, and generally protected you from all, kinds of trouble. It seems wonderful to me, not so much because it was done as because it was done by the man who, some time ago, calmy announced to me that he was going to do it. Extraordinary."

"Of course," said Mrs. Wainwright. "Oh, of course."

"And where is he now?" asked the minister suddenly. "Has he now left you to the mercies of civilisation?"

There was a moment's curious stillness, and then Mrs. Wainwright used that high voice which - the students believed-could only come to her when she was about to say something peculiarly destructive to the sensibilities. "Oh, of course, Mr. Coleman rendered us a great service, but in his private character he is not a man whom we exactly care to associate with."

"Indeed" said the minister staring. Then he hastily addressed the students. "Well, isn't this a comic war? Did you ever imagine war could be like this?" The professor remained looking at his wife with an air of stupefaction, as if she had opened up to him visions of imbecility of which he had not even dreamed. The students loyally began to chatter at the minister. "Yes, sir, it is a queer war. After all their bragging, it is funny to hear that they are running away with such agility. We thought, of course, of the old Greek wars."

Later, the minister asked them all to his rooms for coffee and cigarettes, but the professor and Mrs. Wainwright apologetically retired to their own quarters. The minister and the students made clouds of smoke, through which sang the eloquent descriptions of late adventures.

The minister had spent days of listening to questions from the State Department at Washington as to the whereabouts of the Wainwright party. "I suppose you know that you,are very prominent people in, the United States just now? Your pictures must have been in all the papers, and there must have been columns printed about you. My life here was made almost insupportable by your friends, who consist, I should think, of about half the population of the country. Of course they laid regular siege to the department. I am angry at Coleman for only one thing. When he cabled the news of your rescue to his news. paper from Arta, he should have also wired me, if only to relieve my failing mind. My first news of your escape was from Washington-think of that."

"Coleman had us all on his hands at Arta," said Peter Tounley. "He was a fairly busy man."

"I suppose so," said the minister. "By the way," he asked bluntly, "what is wrong with him? What did Mrs. Wainwright mean?"

They were silent for a time, but it seemed plain to him that it was not evidence that his question had demoralised them. They seemed to be deliberating upon the form of answer. Ultimately Peter Tounley coughed behind his hand. "You see, sir," he began, "there is-well, there is a woman in the case. Not that anybody would care to speak of it excepting to you. But that is what is the cause of things, and then, you see, Mrs. Wainwright is-well -" He hesitated a moment and then completed his sentence in the ingenuous profanity of his age and condition. "She is rather an extraordinary old bird."

"But who is the woman?

"Why, it is Nora Blaick, the actress." "Oh," cried the minister, enlightened. "Her Why, I saw her here. She was very beautiful, but she seemed harmless enough. She was somewhat-er-confident, perhaps, but she did not alarm me. She called upon me, and I confess I-why, she seemed charming." "She's sweet on little Rufus. That's the point," said an oracular voice.

"Oh," cried the host, suddenly. "I remember. She asked me where he was. She said she had heard he was in Greece, and I told her he had gone knight-erranting off after you people. I remember now. I suppose she posted after him up to Arta, eh ?"

"That's it. And so she asked you where he was?

"Yes."

"Why, that old flamingo - Mrs. Wainwright insists that it was a rendezvous."

Every one exchanged glances and laughed a little. "And did you see any actual fighting?" asked the minister.

"No. We only beard it -"

Afterward, as they were trooping up to their rooms, Peter Tounley spoke musingly. "Well, it looks to me now as if Old Mother Wainwright was just a bad-minded old hen."

"Oh, I don't know. How is one going to tell what the truth is?"

"At any rate, we are sure now that Coleman had nothing to do with Nora's debut in Epirus."

They had talked much of Coleman, but in their tones there always had been a note of indifference or carelessness. This matter, which to some people was as vital and fundamental as existence, remained to others who knew of it only a harmless detail of life, with no terrible powers, and its significance had faded greatly when had ended the close associat.ions of the late adventure.

After dinner the professor had gone directly to his daughter's room. Apparently she had not moved. He knelt by the bedside again and took one of her hands. She was not weeping. She looked at him and smiled through the darkness. "Daddy, I would like to die," she said. " I think-yes-I would like to die."

For a long time the old man was silent, but he arose at last with a definite abruptness and said hoarsely "Wait!"

Mrs. Wainwright was standing before her mirror with her elbows thrust out at angles above her head, while her fingers moved in a disarrangement of 'her hair. In the glass she saw a reflection of her husband coming from Marjory's room, and his face was set with some kind of alarming purpose. She turned to watch him actually, but he walked toward the door into the corridor and did not in any wise heed her.

"Harrison!" she called. "Where are you going?"

He turned a troubled face upon her, and, as if she had hailed him in his sleep, he vacantly said: "What ?"

"Where are you going?" she demanded with increasing trepidation.

He dropped heavily into a chair. "Going?" he repeated.

She was angry. "Yes! Going? Where are you going?"

"I am going -" he answered, "I am going to see Rufus Coleman."

Mrs. Wainwright gave voice to a muffled scream. "Not about Marjory ?"

"Yes," he said, "about Marjory."

It was now Mrs. Wainwright's turn to look at her husband with an air of stupefaction as if he had opened up to her visions of imbecility of which she had not even dreamed. "About Marjory!" she gurgled. Then suddenly her wrath flamed out. "Well, upon my word, Harrison Wainwright, you are, of all men in the world, the most silly and stupid. You are absolutely beyond belief. Of all projects! And what do you think Marjory would have to say of it if she knew it? I suppose you think she would like it? Why, I tell you she would keep her right hand in the fire until it was burned off before she would allow you to do such a thing."

"She must never know it," responded the professor, in dull misery.

"Then think of yourself! Think of the shame of it! The shame of it!"

The professor raised his eyes for an ironical glance at his wife. " Oh I have thought of the shame of it!"

"And you'll accomplish nothing," cried Mrs. Wainwright. "You'll accomplish nothing. He'll only laugh at you."

"If he laughs at me, he will laugh at nothing but a poor, weak, unworldly old man. It is my duty to go."

Mrs. Wainwright opened her mouth as if she was about to shriek. After choking a moment she said: "Your duty? Your duty to go and bend the knee to that man? Your duty?"

"'It is my duty to go,'" he repeated humbly. "If I can find even one chance for my daughter's happiness in a personal sacrifice. He can do no more than he can do no more than make me a little sadder."

His wife evidently understood his humility as a tribute to her arguments and a clear indication that she had fatally undermined his original intention. "Oh, he would have made you sadder," she quoth grimly. "No fear! Why, it was the most insane idea I ever heard of."

The professor arose wearily. "Well, I must be going to this work. It is a thing to have ended quickly." There was something almost biblical in his manner.

"Harrison!" burst out his wife in amazed lamentation. You are not really going to do it? Not really!"

"I am going to do it," he answered.

"Well, there!" ejaculated Mrs. Wainwright to the heavens. She was, so to speak, prostrate. "Well, there!"

As the professor passed out of the door she cried beseechingly but futilely after him. "Harrison." In a mechanical way she turned then back to the mirror and resumed the disarrangement of her hair. She addressed her image. "Well, of all stupid creatures under the sun, men are the very worst!" And her image said this to her even as she informed it, and afterward they stared at each other in a profound and tragic reception and acceptance of this great truth. Presently she began to consider the advisability of going to Marjdry with the whole story. Really, Harrison must not be allowed to go on blundering until the whole world heard that Marjory was trying to break her heart over that common scamp of a Coleman. It seemed to be about time for her, Mrs. Wainwright, to come into the situation and mend matters.

CHAPTER XXVIL

WHEN the professor arrived before Coleman's door, he paused a moment and looked at it. Previously, he could not have imagined that a simple door would ever so affect him. Every line of it seemed to express cold superiority and disdain. It was only the door of a former student, one of his old boys, whom, as the need arrived, he had whipped with his satire in the class rooms at Washurst until the mental blood had come, and all without a conception of his ultimately arriving before the door of this boy in the attitude of a supplicant. Hewould not say it; Coleman probably would not say it; but-they would both know it. A single thought of it, made him feel like running away. He would never dare to knock on that door. It would be too monstrous. And even as he decided that he was afraid to knock, he knocked.

Coleman's voice said; "Come in." The professor opened the door. The correspondent, without a coat, was seated at a paper-littered table. Near his elbow, upon another table, was a tray from which he had evidently dined and also a brandy bottle with several recumbent bottles of soda. Although he had so lately arrived at the hotel he had contrived to diffuse his traps over the room in an organised disarray which represented a long and careless occupation if it did not represent t'le scene of a scuffle. His pipe was in his mouth.

After a first murmur of surprise, he arose and reached in some haste for his coat. "Come in, professor, come in," he cried, wriggling deeper into his jacket as he held out his hand. He had laid aside his pipe and had also been very successful in flinging a newspaper so that it hid the brandy and soda. This act was a feat of deference to the professor's well known principles.

"Won't you sit down, sir?" said Coleman cordially. His quick glance of surprise had been immediately suppressed and his manner was now as if the professor's call was a common matter.

"Thank you, Mr. Coleman, I - yes, I will sit down." replied the old man. His hand shook as he laid it on the back of the chair and steadied himself down into it. "Thank you!" -

Coleman looked at him with a great deal of expectation.

"Mr. Coleman!"

"Yes, sir."

"I -"

He halted then and passed his hand over his face. His eyes did not seem to rest once upon Coleman, but they occupied themselves in furtive and frightened glances over the room. Coleman could make neither head nor tail of the affair. He would not have believed any man's statement that the professor could act in such an extraordinary fashion. "Yes, sir," he said again suggestively. The simple strategy resulted in a silence that was actually awkward. Coleman, despite his bewilderment, hastened into a preserving gossip. "I've had a great many cables waiting for me for heaven knows - how long and others have been arriving in flocks to-night. You have no idea of the row in America, professor. Why, everybody must have gone wild over the lost sheep. My paper has cabled some things that are evidently for you. For instance, here is one that says a new puzzle-game called Find the Wainwright Party has had a big success. Think of that, would you." Coleman grinned at the professor. "Find the Wainwright Party, a new puzzle-game."

The professor had seemed grateful for Coleman's tangent off into matters of a light vein. "Yes?" he said, almost eagerly. "Are they selling a game really called that?"

"Yes, really," replied Coleman. "And of course you know that-er-well, all the Sunday papers would of course have big illustrated articles - full pages - with your photographs and general private histories pertaining mostly to things which are none of their business." "Yes, I suppose they would do that," admitted the professor. "But I dare say it may not be as bad as you suggest."

"Very like not," said Coleman. " I put it to you forcibly so that in the future the blow will not be too cruel. They are often a weird lot."

"Perhaps they can't find anything very bad about us."

"Oh, no. And besides the whole episode will probably be forgotten by the time you return to the United States."

They talked onin this way slowly, strainedly, until they each found that the situation would soon become insupportable. The professor had come for a distinct purpose and Coleman knew it; they could not sit there lying at each other forever. Yet when he saw the pain deepening in the professor's eyes, the correspondent again ordered up his trivialities. "Funny thing. My paper has been congratulating me, you know, sir, in a wholesale fashion, and I think - I feel sure - that they have been exploiting my name all over the country as the Heroic Rescuer. There is no sense in trying to stop them, because they don't care whether it is true or not true. All they want is the privilege of howling out that their correspondent rescued you, and they would take that privilege without in any ways worrying if I refused my consent. You see, sir? I wouldn't like you to feel that I was such a strident idiot as I doubtless am appearing now before the public."

"No," said the professor absently. It was plain that he had been a very slack listener. "I - Mr. Coleman -" he began.

"Yes, sir," answered Coleman promptly and gently.

It was obviously only a recognition of the futility of further dallying that was driving the old man onward. He knew, of course, that if he was resolved to take this step, a longer delay would simply make it harder for him. The correspondent, leaning forward, was watching him almost breathlessly.

"Mr. Coleman, I understand - or at least I am led to believe - that you - at one time, proposed marriage to my daughter?"

The faltering words did not sound as if either man had aught to do with them. They were an expression by the tragic muse herself. Coleman's jaw fell and he looked glassily at the professor. He said: "Yes!" But already his blood was leaping as his mind flashed everywhere in speculation.

"I refused my consent to that marriage," said the old man more easily. "I do not know if the matter has remained important to you, but at any rate, I - I retract my refusal."

Suddenly the blank expression left Coleman's face and he smiled with sudden intelligence, as if information of what the professor had been saying had just reached him. In this smile there was a sudden be. trayal, too, of something keen and bitter which had lain hidden in the man's mind. He arose and made a step towards the professor and held out his hand. "Sir, I thank yod from the bottom of my heart!" And they both seemed to note with surprise that Coleman's voice had broken.

The professor had arisen to receive Coleman's hand. His nerve was now of iron and he was very formal. "I judge from your tone that I have not made a mistake - somcthing which I feared."

Coleman did not seem to mind the professor's formality. "Don't fear anything. Won't you sit down again? Will you have a cigar. * * No, I couldn't tell you how glad I am. How glad I am. I feel like a fool. It -"

But the professor fixed him with an Arctic eye and bluntly said: "You love her?"

The question steadied Coleman at once. He looked undauntedly straight into the professor's face. He simply said: "I love her!"

"You love her?" repeated the professor.

"I love her," repeated Coleman.

After some seconds of pregnant silence, the professor arose. " Well, if she cares to give her life to you I will allow it, but I must say that I do not consider you nearly good enough. Good-night." He smiled faintly as he held out his hand.

"Good-night, sir," said Coleman. "And I can't tell, you, now -"

Mrs. Wainwright, in her room was languishing in a chair and applying to her brow a handkerchief wet with cologne water. She, kept her feverish glarice upon the door. Remembering well the manner of her husband when he went out she could hardly identify him when he came in. Serenity, composure, even self-satisfaction, was written upon him. He, paid no attention to her, but going to a chair sat down with a groan of contentment.

"Well?" cried Mrs. Wainwright, starting up. "Well?"

"Well - what?" he asked.

She waved her hand impatiently. "Harrison, don't be absurd. You know perfectly well what I mean. It is a pity you couldn't think of the anxiety I have been in." She was going to weep.

"Oh, I'll tell you after awhile," he said stretching out his legs with the complacency of a rich merchant after a successful day.

"No! Tell me now," she implored him. "Can't you see I've worried myself nearly to death?" She was not going to weep, she was going to wax angry.

"Well, to tell the truth," said the professor with considerable pomposity, " I've arranged it. Didn't think I could do it at first, but it turned out "

"I Arranged it,"' wailed Mrs. Wainwright. "Arranged what?"

It here seemed to strike the professor suddenly that he was not such a flaming example for diplomatists as he might have imagined. "Arranged," he stammered. "Arranged."

"Arranged what?"

"Why, I fixed - I fixed it up."

"Fixed what up?"

"It - it -" began the professor. Then he swelled with indignation. " Why, can't you understand anything at all? I - I fixed it."

"Fixed what?"

"Fixed it. Fixed it with Coleman."

"Fixed what with Coleman?

The professor's wrath now took control of him. "Thunder and lightenin'! You seem to jump at the conclusion that I've made some horrible mistake. For goodness' sake, give me credit for a particle of sense."

"What did you do?" she asked in a sepulchral voice.

"Well," said the professor, in a burning defiance, " I'll tell you what I did. I went to Coleman and told him that once - as he of course knew - I had refused his marriage with my daughter, but that now -"

"Grrr," said Mrs. Wainwright.

"But that now -" continued the professor, "I retracted that refusal."

"Mercy on us!" cried Mrs. Wainwright, throwing herself back in the chair. "Mercy on us! What fools men are!"

"Now, wait a minute -" But Mrs. Wainwright began to croon: "Oh, if Marjory should hear of this! Oh, if she should hear of it! just let her. Hear -"

"But she must not," cried the professor, tigerishly. just you dare!" And the woman saw before her a man whose eyes were lit with a flame which almost expressed a temporary hatred.

The professor had left Coleman so abruptly that the correspondent found himself murmuring half coherent gratitude to the closed door of his room. Amazement soon began to be mastered by exultation. He flung himself upon the brandy and soda and negotiated a strong glass. Pacing. the room with nervous steps, he caught a vision of himself in a tall mirror. He halted before it. "Well, well," he said. " Rufus, you're a grand man. There is not your equal anywhere. You are a great, bold, strong player, fit to sit down to a game with the - best."

A moment later it struck him that he had appropriated too much. If the professor had paid him a visit and made a wonderful announcement, he, Coleman, had not been the engine of it. And then he enunciated clearly something in his mind which, even in a vague form, had been responsible for much of his early elation. Marjory herself had compassed this thing. With shame he rejected a first wild and preposterous idea that she had sent her father to him. He reflected that a man who for an instant could conceive such a thing was a natural-born idiot. With an equal feeling, he rejected also an idea that she could have known anything of her father's purpose. If she had known of his purpose, there would have been no visit.

What, then, was the cause? Coleman soon decided that the professor had witnessed some demonstration of Marjory's emotion which had been sufficiently severe in its character to force him to the extraordinary visit. But then this also was wild and preposterous. That coldly beautiful goddess would not have given a demonstration of emotion over Rufus Coleman sufficiently alarming to have forced her father on such an errand. That was impossible. No, he was wrong; Marjory even indirectly, could not be connected with the visit. As he arrived at this decision, the enthusiasm passed out of him and he wore a doleful, monkish face.

"Well, what, then, was the cause?" After eliminating Marjory from the discussion waging in his mind, he found it hard to hit upon anything rational. The only remaining theory was to the effect that the professor, having a very high sense of the correspond. ent's help in the escape of the Wainwright party, had decided that the only way to express his gratitude was to revoke a certain decision which he now could see had been unfair. The retort to this theory seemed to be that if the professor had had such a fine conception of the services rendered by Coleman, he had had ample time to display his appreciation on the road to Arta and on the road down from Arta. There was no necessity for his waiting until their arrival in Athens. It was impossible to concede that the professor's emotion could be anew one; if he had it now, he must have had it in far stronger measure directly after he had been hauled out of danger.

So, it may be seen that after Coleman had eliminated Marjory from the discussion that was waging in his mind, he had practically succeeded in eliminating the professor as well. This, he thought, mournfully, was eliminating with a vengeance. If he dissolved all the factors he could hardly proceed.

The mind of a lover moves in a circle, or at least on a more circular course than other minds, some of which at times even seem to move almost in a straight line. Presently, Coleman was at the point where he bad started, and he did not pause until he reached that theory which asserted that the professor had been inspired to his visit by some sight or knowledge of Marjory in distress. Of course, Coleman was wistfully desirous of proving to himself the truth of this theory.

The palpable agitation of the professor during the interview seemed to support it. If he had come on a mere journey of conscience, he would have hardly appeared as a white and trembling old, man. But then, said Coleman, he himself probably exaggerated this idea of the professor's appearance. It might have been that he was only sour and distressed over the performance of a very disagreeable duty.

The correspondent paced his room and smoked. Sometimes he halted at the little table where was the brandy and soda. He thought so hard that sometimes it seemed that Marjory had been to him to propose marriage, and at other times it seemed that there had been no visit from any one at all.

A desire to talk to somebody was upon him. He strolled down stairs and into the smoking and reading rooms, hoping to see a man he knew, even if it were Coke. But the only occupants were two strangers, furiously debating the war. Passing the minister's room, Coleman saw that there was a light within, and he could not forbear knocking. He was bidden to enter, and opened the door upon the minister, carefully reading his Spectator fresh from London. He looked up and seemed very glad. "How are you?" he cried. "I was tremendously anxious to see you, do you know! I looked for you to dine with me to-night, but you were not down?" "No; I had a great deal of work."

"Over the Wainwright affair? By the way, I want you to accept my personal thanks for that work. In a week more I would have gone demented and spent the rest of my life in some kind of a cage, shaking the bars and howling out State Department messages about the Wainwrights. You see, in my territory there are no missionaries to get into trouble, and I was living a life of undisturbed and innocent calm, ridiculing the sentiments of men from Smyrna and other interesting towns who maintained that the diplomatic service was exciting. However, when the Wainwright party got lost, my life at once became active. I was all but helpless, too; which was the worst of it. I suppose Terry at Constantinople must have got grandly stirred up, also. Pity he can't see you to thank you for saving him from probably going mad. By the way," he added, while looking keenly at Coleman, "the Wainwrights don't seem to be smothering you with gratitude?"

"Oh, as much as I deserve-sometimes more," answered Coleman. " My exploit was more or less of a fake, you know. I was between the lines by accident, or through the efforts of that blockhead of a dragoman. I didn't intend it. And then, in the night, when we were waiting in the road because of a fight, they almost bunked into us. That's all."

"They tell it better," said the minister, severely. "Especially the youngsters."

"Those kids got into a high old fight at a town up there beyond Agrinion. Tell you about that, did they? I thought not. Clever kids. You have noted that there are signs of a few bruises and scratches?" "Yes, but I didn't ask -" "Well, they are from the fight. It seems the people took us for Germans, and there was an awful palaver, which ended in a proper and handsome shindig. It raised the town, I tell you."

The minister sighed in mock despair. "Take these people home, will you ? Or at any rate, conduct them out of the field of my responsibility. Now, they would like Italy immensely, I am sure."

Coleman laughed, and they smoked for a time.

"That's a charming girl-Miss Wainwright," said the minister, musingly. "And what a beauty! It does my exiled eyes good to see her. I suppose all those youngsters are madly in love with her ? I don't see how they could help it."

"Yes," said Coleman, glumly. " More than half of them."

The minister seemed struck with a sudden thought. "You ought to try to win that splendid prize yourself. The rescuer ! Perseus! What more fitting?"

Coleman answered calmly: "Well * * * I think I'll take your advice."

CHAPTER XXVIII

THE next morning Coleman awoke with a sign of a resolute decision on his face, as if it had been a development of his sleep. He would see Marjory as soon as possible, see her despite any barbed-wire entanglements which might be placed in the way by her mother, whom he regarded as his strenuous enemy. And he would ask Marjory's hand in the presence of all Athens if it became necessary.

He sat a long time at his breakfast in order to see the Wainwrights enter the dining room, and as he was about to surrender to the will of time, they came in, the professor placid and self-satisfied, Mrs. Wainwright worried and injured and Marjory cool, beautiful, serene. If there had been any kind of a storm there was no trace of it on the white brow of the girl. Coleman studied her closely but furtively while his mind spun around his circle of speculation. Finally he noted the waiter who was observing him with a pained air as if it was on the tip of his tongue to ask this guest if he was going to remain at breakfast forever. Coleman passed out to the reading room where upon the table a multitude of great red guide books were crushing the fragile magazines of London and Paris. On the walls were various depressing maps with the name of a tourist agency luridly upon them, and there were also some pictures of hotels with their rates - in francs-printed beneath. The room was cold, dark, empty, with the trail of the tourist upon it.

Coleman went to the picture of a hotel in Corfu and stared at it precisely as if he was interested. He was standing before it when he heard Marjory's voice just without the door. "All right! I'll wait." He did not move for the reason that the hunter moves not when the unsuspecting deer approaches his hiding place. She entered rather quickly and was well toward the centre of the room before she perceived Coleman. "Oh," she said and stopped. Then she spoke the immortal sentence, a sentence which, curiously enough is common to the drama, to the novel, and to life. "I thought no one was here." She looked as if she was going to retreat, but it would have been hard to make such retreat graceful, and probably for this reason she stood her ground.

Coleman immediately moved to a point between her and the door. "You are not going to run away from me, Marjory Wainwright," he cried, angrily. "You at least owe it to me to tell me definitely that you don't love me - that you can't love me -"

She did not face him with all of her old spirit, but she faced him, and in her answer there was the old Marjory. "A most common question. Do you ask all your feminine acquaintances that? "

"I mean -" he said. "I mean that I love you and -"

"Yesterday-no. To-day-yes. To-morrow - who knows. Really, you ought to take some steps to know your own mind."

"Know my own mind," he retorted in a burst of indignation. "You mean you ought to take steps to know your own mind."

"My own mind! You -" Then she halted in acute confusion and all her face went pink. She had been far quicker than the man to define the scene. She lowered her head. Let me past, please -"

But Coleman sturdily blocked the way and even took one of her struggling hands. "Marjory -" And then his brain must have roared with a thousand quick sentences for they came tumbling out, one over the other. * * Her resistance to the grip of his fingers grew somewhat feeble. Once she raised her eyes in a quick glance at him. * * Then suddenly she wilted. She surrendered, she confessed without words. "Oh, Marjory, thank God, thank God -" Peter Tounley made a dramatic entrance on the gallop. He stopped, petrified. "Whoo!" he cried. "My stars!" He turned and fled. But Coleman called after him in a low voice, intense with agitation.

"Come back here, you young scoundrel! Come baok here I"

Peter returned, looking very sheepish. "I hadn't the slightest idea you -"

"Never mind that now. But look here, if you tell a single soul - particularly those other young scoundrels - I'll break -"

"I won't, Coleman. Honest, I won't." He was far more embarrassed than Coleman and almost equally so with Marjory. He was like a horse tugging at a tether. "I won't, Coleman! Honest!"

"Well, all right, then." Peter escaped.

The professor and his wife were in their sitting room writing letters. The cablegrams had all been answered, but as the professor intended to prolong his journey homeward into a month of Paris and London, there remained the arduous duty of telling their friends at length exactly what had happened. There was considerable of the lore of olden Greece in the professor's descriptions of their escape, and in those of Mrs. Wainwright there was much about the lack of hair-pins and soap.

Their heads were lowered over their writing when the door into the corridor opened and shut quickly, and upon looking up they saw in the room a radiant girl, a new Marjory. She dropped to her knees by her father's chair and reached her arms to his neck. "Oh, daddy! I'm happy I I'm so happy! "

"Why - what -" began the professor stupidly.

"Oh, I am so happy, daddy!

Of course he could not be long in making his conclusion. The one who could give such joy to Marjory was the one who, last night, gave her such grief. The professor was only a moment in under-standing. He laid his hand tenderly upon her head "Bless my soul," he murmured. "And so - and so - he -"

At the personal pronoun, Mrs. Wainwright lumbered frantically to her feet. "What?" she shouted. Coleman?"

"Yes," answered Marjory. "Coleman." As she spoke the name her eyes were shot with soft yet tropic flashes of light.

Mrs. Wainwright dropped suddenly back into her chair. "Well-of-all-things!" The professor was stroking his daughter's hair and although for a time after Mrs. Wainwright's outbreak there was little said, the old man and the girl seemed in gentle communion, she making him feel her happiness, he making her feel his appreciation. Providentially Mrs. Wainwright had been so stunned by the first blow that she was evidently rendered incapable of speech.

"And are you sure you will be happy with him? asked her father gently.

"All my life long," she answered.

"I am glad! I am glad!" said the father, but even as he spoke a great sadness came to blend with his joy. The hour when he was to give this beautiful and beloved life into the keeping of another had been heralded by the god of the sexes, the ruthless god that devotes itself to the tearing of children from the parental arms and casting them amid the mysteries of an irretrievable wedlock. The thought filled him with solemnity.

But in the dewy eyes of the girl there was no question. The world to her was a land of glowing promise.

"I am glad," repeated the professor.

The girl arose from her knees. "I must go away and- think all about it," she said, smiling. When the door of her room closed upon her, the mother arose in majesty.

"Harrison Wainwright," she declaimed, "you are not going to allow this monstrous thing!"

The professor was aroused from a reverie by these words. "What monstrous thing?" he growled.

"Why, this between Coleman and Marjory."

"Yes," he answered boldly.

"Harrison! That man who -"

The professor crashed his hand down on the table. "Mary! I will not hear another word of it! "

"Well," said Mrs. Wainwright, sullen and ominous, "time will tell! Time will tell!"

When Coleman bad turned from the fleeing Peter Tounley again to Marjory, he found her making the preliminary movements of a flight. "What's the matter?" he demanded anxiously.

"Oh, it's too dreadful"

"Nonsense," lie retorted stoutly. "Only Peter Tounley! He don't count. What of that?"

'Oh, dear! "She pressed her palm to a burning cheek. She gave him a star-like, beseeching glance. Let me go now-please."

"Well," he answered, somewhat affronted, "if you like -"

At the door she turned to look at him, and this glance

expressed in its elusive way a score of things which she had not yet been able to speak. It explained that she was loth to leave him, that she asked forgiveness for leaving him, that even for a short absence she wished to take his image in her eyes, that he must not bully her, that there was something now in her heart which frightened her, that she loved him, that she was happy -

When she had gone, Coleman went to the rooms of the American minister. A Greek was there who talked wildly as he waved his cigarette. Coleman waited in well-concealed impatience for the dvaporation of this man. Once the minister, regarding the correspondent hurriedly, interpolated a comment. "You look very cheerful?"

"Yes," answered Coleman, "I've been taking your advice."

"Oh, ho! " said the minister.

The Greek with the cigarette jawed endlessly. Coleman began to marvel at the enduring good manners of the minister, who continued to nod and nod in polite appreciation of the Greek's harangue, which, Coleman firmly believed, had no point of interest whatever. But at last the man, after an effusive farewell, went his way.

"Now," said the minister, wheeling in his chair tell me all about it."

Coleman arose, and thrusting his hands deep in his trousers' pockets, began to pace the room with long strides. He, said nothing, but kept his eyes on the floor.

"Can I have a drink?" he asked, abruptly pausing.

"What would you like? " asked the minister, bene-
volently, as he touched the bell.

"A brandy and soda. I'd like it very much. You see," he
said, as he resumed his walk, "I have no kind of right
to burden you with my affairs, but, to tell the truth, if I
don't get this news off my mind and into somebody's
ear, I'll die. It's this - I asked Marjory Wainwright to
marry me, and - she accepted, and - that's all."

"Well, I am very glad," cried the minister, arising and
giving his hand. "And as for burdening me with your
affairs, no one has a better right, you know, since you
released me from the persecution of Washington and
the friends of the Wainwrights. May good luck follow
you both forever. You, in my opinion, are a very, very
fortunate man. And, for her part she has not done too
badly."

Seeing that it was important that Coleman should have
his spirits pacified in part, the minister continued:
"Now, I have got to write an official letter, so you just
walk up and down here and use up this surplus steam.
Else you'll explode."

But Coleman was not to be detained. Now that he had
informed the minister, he must rush off somewhere,
anywhere, and do - he knew not what.

All right," said the minister, laughing. "You have a
wilder head than I thought. But look here," he called,
as Coleman was making for the door. "Am I to keep
this news a secret?"

Coleman with his hand on the knob, turned im. pressively. He spoke with deliberation. " As far as I am concerned, I would be glad to see a man paint it in red letters, eight feet high, on the front of the king's palace."

The minister, left alone, wrote steadily and did not even look up when Peter Tounley and two others entered, in response to his cry of permission. How ever, he presently found time to speak over his shoulder to them. "Hear the news?"

"No, sir," they answered.

"Well, be good boys, now, and read the papers and look at pictures until I finish this letter. Then I will tell you."

They surveyed him keenly. They evidently judged that the news was worth hearing, but, obediently, they said nothing. Ultimately the minister affixed a rapid signature to the letter, and turning, looked at the students with a smile. "Haven't heard the news, eh?"

"No, Sir."

"Well, Marjory Wainwright is engaged to marry Coleman."

The minister was amazed to see the effect of this announcement upon the three students. He had expected the crows and cackles of rather absurd merriment with which unbearded youth often greets, such news. But there was no crow or cackle. One young man blushed scarlet and looked guiltily at the floor. With a great effort he muttered: "Shes too good for him." Another student had turned ghastly pate and was staring. It was Peter Tounley who relieved the minister's mind, for upon that young man's face was a broad jack-o-lantern grin, and the minister saw that, at any rate, he had not made a complete massacre.

Peter Tounley said triumphantly: "I knew it!"

The minister was anxious over the havoc he had wrought with the two other students, but slowly the colour abated in one face and grew in the other. To give them opportunity, the minister talked busily to Peter Tounley. "And how did you know it, you young scamp?"

Peter was jubilant. "Oh, - I knew it! I knew it I I am very clever."

The student who had blushed now addressed the minister in a slightly strained voice. "Are you positive that it is true, Mr. Gordner?"

"I had it on the best authority," replied the minister gravely.

The student who had turned pale said: "Oh, it's true, of course."

"Well," said crudely the one who had blushed, she's a great sight too good for Coleman or anybody like him. That's all I've got to say."

"Oh, Coleman is a good fellow," said Peter Tounley, reproachfully. "You've no right to say that - exactly. You don't know where you'd. be now if it were not for Coleman."

The, response was, first, an angry gesture. "Oh, don't keep everlasting rubbing that in. For heaven's sake, let up. - Supposing I don't. know where I'd be now if,it were not for Rufus Coleman? What of it? For the rest of my life have I got to -"

The minister saw. that this was the embittered speech of a really defeated youth, so, to save scenes, he gently ejected the trio. " There, there, now ! Run along home like good boys. I'll be busy until luncheon. And I - dare say you won't find Coleman such a bad chap.'"

In the corridor, one of the students said offensively to Peter Tounley: "Say, how in hell did you find out all this so early?"

Peter's reply was amiable in tone. "You are a damned bleating little kid and you made a holy show of yourself before Mr. Gordner. There's where you stand. Didn't you see that he turned us out because he didn't know but what you were going to blubber or something. - you are a sucking pig, and if you want to know how I find out things go ask the Delphic Oracle, you blind ass."

"You better look out or you may get a punch in the eye!"

"You take one punch in the general direction of my eye, me son," said -Peter cheerfully, "and I'll distribute your remains, over this hotel in a way that will cause your, friends years of trouble to collect you. Instead of anticipating an attack upon my eye, you had much better be engaged in improving your mind, which is at present not a fit machine to cope with exciting situations. There's Coke! Hello, Coke, hear the news?

Well, Marjory Wainwright and Rufus Coleman, are engaged. Straight? Certainly! Go ask the minister."

Coke did not take Peter's word. "Is that so?" he asked the others.

"So the minister told us," they answered, and then these two, who seemed so unhappy, watched Coke's face to see if they could not find surprised misery there. But Coke coolly said: "Well, then, I suppose it's true."

It soon became evident that the students did not care for each other's society. Peter Tounley was probably an exception, but the others seemed to long for quiet corners. They were distrusting each other, and, in a boyish way, they were even capable of maligant things. Their excuses for separation were badly made.

"I - I think I'll go for a walk." "I'm going up stairs to read." "Well, so long, old man.' "So long." There was no heart to it.

Peter Tounley went to Coleman's door, where he knocked with noisy hilarity. "Come in I" The correspondent apparently had just come from the street, for his hat was on his head and a light top-coat was on his back. He was searching hurriedly through some, papers. "Hello, you young devil What are you doing here?

Peter's entrance was a somewhat elaborate comedy which Coleman watched in icy silence. Peter after a long,and impudent pantomime halted abruptly and fixing Coleman with his eye demanded: "Well?"

"Well - what?." said Coleman, bristling a trifle.

"Is it true ?"

"Is what true ?"

"Is it true?" Peter was extremely solemn. "Say, me bucko," said Coleman suddenly," if you've come up here to twist the beard of the patriarch, don't you think you are running a chance?"

"All right. I'll be good," said Peter, and he sat on the bed. " But - is it true?

"Is what true? "

"What the whole hotel is saying."

"I haven't heard the hotel making any remarks lately. Been talking to the other buildings, I suppose."

"Well, I want to tell you that everybody knows that you and Marjory have done gone and got yourselves engaged," said Peter bluntly.

"And well? " asked Coleman imperturbably.

"Oh, nothing," replied Peter, waving his hand. "Only - I thought it might interest you."

Coleman was silent for some time. He fingered his papers. At last he burst out joyously. "And so they know it already, do they? Well - damn them let them know it. But you didn't tell them yourself ?"

"I!" quoth Peter wrathfully. "No! The minister told us."

Then Coleman was again silent for a time and Peter Tounley sat on the. bed reflectively looking at the ceiling. "Funny thing, Marjory 'way over here in Greece, and then you happening over here the way you did."

"It isn't funny at all."

"Why isn't it?"

"Because," said Coleman impressively, "that is why I came to Greece. It was all planned. See?"

"Whirroo," exclaimed Peter. "This here is magic."

"No magic at all." Coleman displayed some complacence. "No magic at all. just pure, plain - whatever you choose to call it."

"Holy smoke," said Peter, admiring the situation. "Why, this is plum romance, Coleman. I'm blowed if it isn't."

Coleman was grinning with delight. He took a fresh cigar and his bright eyes looked at Peter through the smoke. "Seems like it, don't it? Yes. Regular romance. Have a drink, my boy, just to celebrate my good luck. And be patient if I talk a great deal of my-my-future. My head spins with it." He arose to pace the room flinging out bis arms in a great gesture. "God! When I think yesterday was not like to-day I wonder how I stood it." There was a knock at the door and a waiter left a note in Coleman's hand

"Dear Rufus:- We are going for a drive this afternoon at three, and mother wishes you to come,

if you. care to. I too wish it, if you care to. Yours,
"MARJORY."

With a radiant face, Coleman gave the note a little
crackling flourish in the air. "Oh, you don't know what
life is, kid."

"S-steady the Blues," said Peter Tounley seriously.
You'll lose your head if you don't watch out."

"Not I" cried Coleman with irritation. "But a man must
turn loose some times, mustn't he?"

When the four, students had separated in the corridor,
Coke had posted at once to Nora Black's sitting room.
His entrance was somewhat precipitate, but he cooled
down almost at once, for he reflected that he was not
bearing good news. He ended by perching in awkward
fashion on the brink of his chair and fumbling his hat
uneasily. Nora floated to him in a cloud of a white
dressing gown. She gave him a plump hand. "Well,
youngman? "she said, with a glowing smile. She took a
chair, and the stuff of her gown fell in curves over the
arms of it.,

Coke looked hot and bothered, as if he could have
more than half wanted to retract his visit. " I-aw-we
haven't seen much of you lately," he began, sparing.
He had expected to tell his news at once.

No," said Nora, languidly. " I have been resting after
that horrible journey - that horrible journey. Dear,
dear! Nothing,will ever induce me to leave London,
New York and Paris. I am at home there. But here I
Why, it is worse than living in Brooklyn. And that
journey into the wilds! No. no; not for me! "

Stephen Crane

"I suppose we'll all be glad to get home," said Coke, aimlessly.

At the moment a waiter entered the room and began to lay the table for luncheon. He kept open the door to the corridor, and he had the luncheon at a point just outside the door. His excursions to the trays were flying ones, so that, as far as Coke's purpose was concerned, the waiter was always in the room. Moreover, Coke was obliged, naturally, to depart at once. He had bungled everything.

As he arose he whispered hastily: "Does this waiter understand English?"

"Yes," answered Nora. "Why?"

"Because I have something to tell you-important."

"What is it?" whispered Nora, eagerly.

He leaned toward her and replied: "Marjory Wainwright and Coleman are engaged."

To his unfeigned astonishment, Nora Black burst into peals of silvery laughter, " Oh, indeed? And so this is your tragic story, poor, innocent lambkin? And what did you expect? That I would faint?" -

"I thought - I don't know -" murmured Coke in confusion.

Nora became suddenly business-like. "But how do you know? Are you sure? Who told you? Anyhow, stay to luncheon. Do - like a good boy. Oh, you must."

Coke dropped again into his chair. He studied her in some wonder. "I thought you'd be surprised," he said, ingenuously.

"Oh, you did, did you? Well, you see I'm not. And now tell me all about it."

"There's really nothing to tell but the plain fact. Some of the boys dropped in at the minister's rooms a little while ago, and, he told them of it. That's all."

Well, how did he know?

"I am sure I can't tell you. Got it first hand, I suppose. He likes Coleman, and Coleman is always hanging up there."

"Oh, perhaps Coleman was lying," said Nora easily. Then suddenly her face brightened and she spoke with animation. "Oh, I haven't told you how my little Greek officer has turned out. Have I? No? Well, it is simply lovely. Do you know, he belongs to one of the best families in Athens? Hedoes. And they're rich-rich as can be. My courier tells me that the marble palace where they live is enough to blind you, and that if titles hadn't gone out of style - or something - here in Greece, my little officer would be a prince! Think of that! The courier didn't know it until we got to Athens, and the little officer - the prince - gave me his card, of course. One of the oldest, noblest and richest families in Greece. Think of that! There I thought he was only a bothersome little officer who came in handy at times, and there he turns out to be a prince. I could hardly keep myself from rushing right off to find him and apologise to him for the way I treated him. It was awful! And -" added the fair Nora, pensively, "if he does meet me in Paris, I'll make him wear that title down to a shred, you can bet. What's the good of having a title unless you make it work?"

CHAPTER XXIX

COKE did not stay to luncheon with Nora Black. He went away saying to himself either that girl don't care a straw for Coleman or she has got a heart absolutely of flint, or she is the greatest actress on earth or - there is some other reason."

At his departure, Nora turned and called into an adjoining room. "Maude I" The voice of her companion and friend answered her peevishly."What?"

"Don't bother me. I'm reading."

"Well, anyhow, luncheon is ready, so you will have to stir your precious self," responded Nora. "You're lazy."

"I don't want any luncheon. Don't bother me. I've got a headache."

"Well, if you don't come out, you'll miss the news. That's all I've got to say."

There was a rustle in the adjoining room, and immediately the companion appeared, seeming much annoyed but curious. "Well, what is it ?"

"Rufus Coleman is engaged to be married to that Wainwright girl, after all."

"Well I declare!" ejaculated the little old lady. "Well I declare." She meditated for a moment, and then continued in a tone of satisfaction. " I told you that you couldn't stop that man Coleman if he had feally made up his mind to -"

"You're a fool," said Nora, pleasantly. "Why?" said the old lady. Because you are. Don't talk to me about it. I want to think of Marco."

"'Marco,'" quoted the old lady startled.

"The prince. The prince. Can't you understand? I mean the prince."

"'Marco!'" again quoted the old lady, under her breath.

"Yes, 'Marco,'" cried Nora, belligerently. "'Marco,' Do you object to the name? What's the matter with you, anyhow?"

"Well," rejoined the other, nodding her head wisely, "he may be a prince, but I've always heard that these continental titles are no good in comparison to the English titles."

"Yes, but who told you so, eh?" demanded Nora, noisily. She herself answered the question. "The English!"

"Anyhow, that little marquis who tagged after you in London is a much bigger man in every way, I'll bet, than this little prince of yours."

"But - good heavens - he didn't mean it. Why, he was only one of the regular rounders. But Marco, he is serious I He means it. He'd go through fire and water for me and be glad of the chance."

"Well," proclaimed the old lady, " if you are not the strangest woman in the world, I'd like to know! Here I thought -"

"What did you think?" demanded Nora, suspisciously. "I thought that Coleman -"

"Bosh!" interrupted, the graceful Nora. "I tell you what, Maude; you'd better try to think as little as possible. It will suit your style of beauty better. And above all, don't think of my affairs. I myself am taking pains not to think of them. It's easier."

Mrs. Wainwright, with no spirit of intention what. ever, had sit about readjusting her opinions. It is certain that she was unconscious of any evolution. If some one had said to her that she was surrendering to the inevitable, she would have been immediately on her guard, and would have opposed forever all suggestions of a match between Marjory and Coleman. On the other hand, if some one had said to her that her daughter was going to marry a human serpent, and that there were people in Athens who would be glad to explain his treacherous character, she would have haughtily scorned the tale-bearing and would have gone with more haste into the professor's way of thinking. In fact, she was in process of undermining herself., and the work could have been. retarded or advanced by any irresponsible, gossipy tongue.

The professor, from the depths of his experience with her, arranged a course of conduct. "If I just leave her to herself she will come around all right, but if I go 'striking while the iron is hot,' or any of those things, I'll bungle it surely."

As they were making ready to go down to luncheon, Mrs. Wainwright made her speech which first indicated a changing mind. " Well, what will be, will be," she murmured with a prolonged sigh of resignation. "What will be, will be. Girls are very headstrong in these days, and there is nothing much to be done with them. They go their own roads. It wasn't so in my girlhood. - We were obliged to pay attention to our mothers wishes."

"I did not notice that you paid much attention to your mother's wishes when you married me," remarked the professor. "In fact, I thought -"

"That was another thing," retorted Mrs. Wainwright with severity. " You were a steady young man who had taken the highest honours all through your college course, and my mother's sole objection was that we were too hasty. She thought we - ought to wait until you had a penny to bless yourself with, and I can see now where she was quite right." "Well, you married me, anyhow," said the professor, victoriously.

Mrs. Wainwright allowed her husband's retort to pass over her thoughtful mood. "They say * * they say Rufus Coleman makes as much as fifteen thousand dollars a year. That's more than three times your income * * I don't know. * * It all depends on whether they try to save or not. His manner of life is, no doubt, very luxurious. I don't suppose he knows how to economise at all. That kind of a man usually doesn't. And then, in the newspaper world positions are so very precarious. Men may have valuable positions one minute and be penniless in the street the next minute. It isn't as if he had any real income, and of course he has no real ability. If he was suddenly thrown out of his position, goodness knows what would become of him. Still stillfifteen thousand dollars a year is a big incomewhile it lasts. I suppose he is very extravagant. That kind of a man usually is. And I wouldn't be surprised if he was heavily in debt; very heavily in debt. Still * * if Marjory has set her heart there is nothing to be done, I suppose. It wouldn't have happened if you had been as wise as you thought you were. * * I suppose he thinks I have been very rude to him. Well, some times I wasn't nearly so rude as I felt like being. Feeling as I did, I could hardly be very amiable. * * Of course this drive this afternoon was all your affair and Marjory's. But, of course, I shall be nice to him."

"And what of all this Nora Black business?" asked the professor, with, a display of valour, but really with much trepidation.

"She is a hussy," responded Mrs. Wainwright with energy. "Her conversation in the carriage on the way down to Agrinion sickened me!"

"I really believe that her plan was simply to break everything off between Marjory and Coleman," said the professor, "and I don't believe she had any grounds for all that appearance of owning Coleman and the rest of it."

"Of course she didn't" assented Mrs. Wainwright. The vicious thing!"

"On the other hand," said the professor, " there might

be some truth in it." "I don't think so," said Mrs. Wainwright seriously. I don't believe a word of it."

"You do not mean to say that you think Coleman a model man ?" demanded the professor.

"Not at all! Not at all!" she hastily answered. "But * * one doesn't look for model men these days."

"'Who told you he made fifteen thousand a year? asked the professor.

"It was Peter Tounley this morning. We were talking upstairs after breakfast, and he remarked that he if could make fifteen thousand, a year: like Coleman, he'd - I've forgotten what-some fanciful thing."

"I doubt if it is true," muttered the old man wagging his head.

"Of course it's true," said his wife emphatically. "Peter Tounley says everybody knows it."

Well * anyhow * money is not everything."

But it's a. great deal, you know well enough. You know you are always speaking of poverty as an evil, as a grand resultant, a collaboration of many lesser evils. Well, then?

"But," began the professor meekly, when I say that I mean -"

"Well, money is money and poverty is poverty," interrupted his wife. "You don't have to be very learned to know that."

"I do not say that Coleman has not a very nice thing of it, but I must say it is hard to think of his getting any such sum, as you mention."

" Isn't he known as the most brilliant journalist in New York?" she demanded harshly.

"Y - yes, as long as it lasts, but then one never knows when he will be out in the street penniless. Of course he has no particular ability which would be marketable if he suddenly lost his present employment. Of course it is not as if he was a really talented young man. He might not be able to make his way at all in any new direction."

"I don't know about that," said Mrs. Wainwright in reflective protestation. "I don't know about that. I think he would."

"I thought you said a moment ago -" The professor spoke with an air of puzzled hesitancy. "I thought you said a moment ago that he wouldn't succeed in anything but journalism."

Mrs. Wainwright swam over the situation with a fine tranquility. " Well - I - I," she answered musingly, "if I did say that, I didn't mean it exactly."

"No, I suppose not," spoke the professor, and despite the necessity for caution he could not keep out of his voice a faint note of annoyance.

"Of course," continued the wife, " Rufus Coleman is known everywhere as a brilliant man, a very brilliant man, and he even might do well in - in politics or something of that sort."

"I have a very poor opinion of that kind of a mind which does well in American politics," said the professor, speaking as a collegian, " but I suppose there may be something in it."

"Well, at any rate," decided Mrs. Wainwright. "At any rate -"

At that moment, Marjory attired for luncheon and the drive entered from her room, and Mrs. Wainwright checked the expression of her important conclusion. Neither father or mother had ever seen her so glowing with triumphant beauty, a beauty which would carry the mind of a spectator far above physical appreciation into that realm of poetry where creatures of light move and are beautiful because they cannot know pain or a burden. It carried tears to the old father's eyes. He took her hands. "Don't be too happy, my child, don't be too happy," he admonished her tremulously. " It makes me afraid - it makes me afraid."

CHAPTER XXX

IT seems strange that the one who was the most hilarious over the engagement of Marjory and Coleman should be Coleman's dragoman who was indeed in a state bordering on transport. It is not known how he learned the glad tidings, but it is certain that he learned them before luncheon. He told all the visible employes of the hotel and allowed them to know that the betrothal really had been his handiwork He had arranged it. He did not make quite clear how he had performed this feat, but at least he was perfectly frank in acknowledging it.

When some of the students came down to luncheon, they saw him but could not decide what ailed him. He was in the main corridor of the hotel, grinning from ear to ear, and when he perceived the students he made signs to intimate that they possessed in common a joyous secret. "What's the matter with that idiot?" asked Coke morosely. "Looks as if his wheels were going around too fast." Peter Tounley walked close to him and scanned him imperturbably, but with care. "What's up, Phidias?" The man made no articulate reply. He continued to grin and gesture. "Pain in oo tummy? Mother dead? Caught the cholera? Found out that you've swallowed a pair of hammered brass and irons in your beer? Say, who are you, anyhow?" But he could not shake this invincible glee, so he went away.

The dragoman's rapture reached its zenith when Coleman lent him to the professor and he was commissioned to bring a carriage for four people to the door at three o'clock. He himself was to sit on the box and tell the driver what was required of him. He dashed off, his hat in his hand, his hair flying, puffing, important beyond everything, and apparently babbling his mission to half the people he met on the street. In most countries he would have landed speedily in jail, but among a people who exist on a basis of jibbering, his violent gabble aroused no suspicions as to his sanity. However, he stirred several livery stables to their depths and set men running here and there wildly and for the most part futiltiy.

At fifteen minutes to three o'clock, a carriage with its horses on a gallop tore around the corner and up to the front of the hotel, where it halted with the pomp and excitement of a fire engine. The dragoman jumped down from his seat beside the driver and scrambled hurriedly into the hoiel, in the gloom of which hemet a serene stillness which was punctuated only by the leisurely tinkle of silver and glass in the dining room. For a moment the dragoman seemed really astounded out of specch. Then he plunged into the manager's room. Was it conceivable that Monsieur Coleman was still at luncheon? Yes; in fact, it was true. But the carriage, was at the door! The carriage was at the door! The manager, undisturbed, asked for what hour Monsieur Coleman had been pleased to order a carriage. Three o'clock! Three o'clock? The manager pointed calmly at the clock. Very well. It was now only thirteen minutes of three o'clock. Monsieur Coleman doubtless would appear at three. Until that hour the manager would not disturb Monsieur Coleman. The dragoman clutched both his hands in his hair and cast a look of agony to the ceiling. Great God! Had he accomplished the herculean task of getting a carriage for four people to the door of the hotel in time for a drive at three o'clock, only to meet with this stoniness, this inhumanity? Ah, it was unendurable? He begged the manager; he implored him. But at every word. the manager seemed to grow more indifferent, more callous. He pointed with a wooden finger at the clock-face. In reality, it is thus, that Greek meets Greek.

Professor Wainwright and Coleman strolled together out of the dining room. The dragoman rushed ecstatically upon the correspondent. "Oh, Meester Coleman! The carge is ready!"

"Well, all right," said Coleman, knocking ashes from his cigar. "Don't be in a hurry. I suppose we'll be ready, presently." The man was in despair.

The departure of the Wainwrights and Coleman on this ordinary drive was of a somewhat dramatic and public nature, No one seemed to know how to prevent its being so. In the first place, the attendants thronged out en masse for a reason which was plain at the time only to Coleman's dragoman. And, rather in the background, lurked the interested students. The professor was surprised and nervous. Coleman was rigid and angry. Marjory was flushed and some what hurried, and Mrs. Wainwright was as proud as an old turkey-hen.

As the carriage rolled away, Peter Tounley turned to his companions and said: "Now, that's official! That is the official announcement! Did you see Old Mother Wainwright? Oh, my eye, wasn't she puffed up! Say, what in hell do you suppose all these jay hawking bell-boys poured out to the kerb for? Go back to your cages, my good people -"

As soon as the carriage wheeled into another street, its occupants exchanged easier smiles, and they must have confessed in some subtle way of glances that now at last they were upon their own mission, a mission undefined but earnest to them all. Coleman had a glad feeling of being let into the family, or becoming one of them

The professor looked sideways at him and smiled gently. "You know, I thought of driving you to some ruins, but Marjory would not have it. She flatly objected to any more ruins. So I thought we would drive down to New Phalerum." Coleman nodded and smiled as if he were immensely pleased, but of course New Phalerum was to him no more nor - less than Vladivostok or Khartoum. Neither place nor distance had interest for him. They swept along a shaded avenue where the dust lay thick on the leaves; they passed cafes where crowds were angrily shouting over the news in the little papers; they passed a hospital before which wounded men, white with bandages, were taking the sun; then came soon to the and valley flanked by gaunt naked mountains, which would lead them to the sea. Sometimes to accentuate the dry nakedness of this valley, there would be a patch of grass upon which poppies burned crimson spots. The dust writhed out from under the wheels of the carriage; in the distance the sea appeared, a blue half-disc set between shoulders of barren land. It would be common to say that Coleman was oblivious to all about him but Marjory. On the contrary, the parched land, the isolated flame of poppies, the cool air from the sea, all were keenly known to him, and they had developed an extraordinary power of blending sympathetically into his mood. Meanwhile the professor talked a great deal. And as a somewhat exhilarating detail, Coleman perceived that Ms. Wainwright was beaming upon him.

At New Phalerum-a small collection of pale square villas-they left the carriage and strolled, by the sea. The waves were snarling together like wolves amid the honeycomb rocks and from where the blue plane sprang level to the horizon, came a strong cold breeze, the kind of a breeze which moves an exulting man or a parson to take off his hat and let his locks flutter and tug back from his brow.

The professor and Mrs. Wainwright were left to themselves.

Marjory and Coleman did not speak for a time. It might have been that they did not quite know where to make a beginning. At last Marjory asked: "What has become of your splendid horse?"

"Oh, I've told the dragoman to have him sold as soon as he arrives," said Coleman absently.

"Oh. I'm sorry * * I liked that horse."

"Why? "

"Oh, because -"

"Well, he was a fine -" Then he, too, interrupted himself, for he saw plainly that they had not come to this place to talk about a horse. Thereat he made speech of matters which at least did not afford as many opportunities for coherency as would the horse. Marjory, it can't be true * * * Is it true, dearest * * I can hardly believe it. - I -"

"Oh, I know I'm not nearly good enough for you."

"Good enough for me, dear?

"They all told me so, and they were right ! Why, even the American minister said it. Everybody thinks it."

"Why, aren 't they wretches To think of them saying such a thing! As if-as if anybody could be too -"

"Do you know -" She paused and looked at him with a certain timid challenge. " I don't know why I feel it, but-sometimes I feel that I've been I've been flung at your head."

He opened his mouth in astonishment. Flung at my head!

She held up her finger. "And if I thought you could ever believe it!"

"Is a girl flung at a man's head when her father carries her thousands of miles away and the man follows her all these miles, and at last -"

"Her eyes were shining. "And you really came to Greece - on purpose to - to -"

"Confess you knew it all the time! Confess!" The answer was muffled. "Well, sometimes I thought you did, and at other times I thought you - didn't."

In a secluded cove, in which the sea-maids once had played, no doubt, Marjory and Coleman sat in silence. He was below her, and if he looked at her he had to turn his glance obliquely upward. She was staring at the sea with woman's mystic gaze, a gaze which men at once reverence and fear since it seems to look into the deep, simple heart of nature, and men begin to feel that their petty wisdoms are futile to control these strange spirits, as wayward as nature and as pure as nature, wild as the play of waves, sometimes as unalterable as the mountain amid the winds; and to measure them, man must perforce use a mathematical formula.

He wished that she would lay her hand upon his hair. He would be happy then. If she would only, of her own will, touch his hair lightly with her fingers - if she would do it with an unconscious air it would be even better. It would show him that she was thinking of him, even when she did not know she was thinking of him.

Perhaps he dared lay his head softly against her knee. Did he dare?

As his head touched her knee, she did not move. She seemed to be still gazing at the sea. Presently idly caressing fingers played in his hair near the forehead. He looked up suddenly lifting his arms. He breathed out a cry which was laden with a kind of diffident ferocity. "I haven't kissed you yet -"

Choose from Thousands of 1stWorldLibrary Classics By

Ada Leverson
Adolphus William Ward
Aesop
Agatha Christie
Alexander Aaronsohn
Alexander Kielland
Alexandre Dumas
Alfred Gatty
Alfred Ollivant
Alice Duer Miller
Alice Turner Curtis
Alice Dunbar
Ambrose Bierce
Amelia E. Barr
Andrew Lang
Andrew McFarland Davis
Andy Adams
Anna Sewell
Annie Besant
Annie Hamilton Donnell
Annie Payson Call
Annonaymous
Anton Chekhov
Arnold Bennett
Arthur Conan Doyle
Arthur M. Winfield
Arthur Ransome
Atticus
B.H. Baden-Powell
B. M. Bower
Baroness Emmuska Orczy
Baroness Orczy
Basil King
Bayard Taylor
Ben Macomber
Bertha Muzzy Bower
Bjornstjerne Bjornson
Booth Tarkington
Boyd Cable
Bram Stoker
C. Collodi
C. E. Orr
C. M. Ingleby
Carolyn Wells
Catherine Parr Traill
Charles A. Eastman
Charles Dickens
Charles Dudley Warner
Charles Farrar Browne

Charles Ives
Charles Kingsley
Charles Klein
Charles Lathrop Pack
Charles Whibley
Charles Willing Beale
Charlotte M. Braeme
Charlotte M. Yonge
Charlotte Perkins Stetson
Clair W. Hayes
Clarence Day Jr.
Clarence E. Mulford
Clemence Housman
Confucius
Cornelis DeWitt Wilcox
Cyril Burleigh
D. H. Lawrence
Daniel Defoe
David Garnett
Don Carlos Janes
Donald Keyhoe
Dorothy Kilner
Dougan Clark
Douglas Fairbanks
E. Nesbit
E.P.Roe
E. Phillips Oppenheim
Edgar Rice Burroughs
Edith Van Dyne
Edith Wharton
Edward J. O'Biren
Edward S. Ellis
Edwin L. Arnold
Eleanor Atkins
Eliot Gregory
Elizabeth Gaskell
Elizabeth McCracken
Elizabeth Von Arnim
Ellem Key
Emerson Hough
Emily Dickinson
Enid Bagnold
Enilor Macartney Lane
Erasmus W. Jones
Ernie Howard Pie
Ethel Turner
Ethel Watts Mumford
Eugenie Foa
Eugene Wood

Evelyn Everett-green
Everard Cotes
F. H. Cheley
F. J. Cross
Federick Austin Ogg
Ferdinand Ossendowski
Francis Bacon
Francis Darwin
Frances Hodgson Burnett
Frances Parkinson Keyes
Frank Gee Patchin
Frank Harris
Frank Jewett Mather
Frank L. Packard
Frank V. Webster
Frederic Stewart Isham
Frederick Trevor Hill
Frederick Winslow Taylor
Friedrich Kerst
Friedrich Nietzsche
Fyodor Dostoyevsky
G.A. Henty
G.K. Chesterton
Gabrielle E. Jackson
Garrett P. Serviss
Gaston Leroux
George Ade
Geroge Bernard Shaw
George Durston
George Ebers
George Eliot
George MacDonald
George Meredith
George Orwell
George Tucker
George W. Cable
George Wharton James
Gertrude Atherton
Grace E. King
Grace Gallatin
Grant Allen
Guillermo A. Sherwell
Gulielma Zollinger
Gustav Flaubert
H. A. Cody
H. B. Irving
H.C. Bailey
H. G. Wells
H. H. Munro

H. Irving Hancock
H. Rider Haggard
H. W. C. Davis
Hamilton Wright Mabie
Hans Christian Andersen
Harold Avery
Harold McGrath
Harriet Beecher Stowe
Harry Houidini
Helent Hunt Jackson
Helen Nicolay
Hendrik Conscience
Hendy David Thoreau
Henri Barbusse
Henrik Ibsen
Henry Adams
Henry Ford
Henry Frost
Henry James
Henry Jones Ford
Henry Seton Merriman
Henry W Longfellow
Herbert A. Giles
Herbert N. Casson
Herman Hesse
Homer
Honore De Balzac
Horace Walpole
Horatio Alger Jr.
Howard Pyle
Howard R. Garis
Hugh Lofting
Hugh Walpole
Humphry Ward
Ian Maclaren
Inez Haynes Gillmore
Irving Bacheller
Israel Abrahams
Ivan Turgenev
J.G.Austin
J. Henri Fabre
J. M. Barrie
J. Macdonald Oxley
J. S. Fletcher
J. S. Knowles
J. Storer Clouston
Jack London
Jacob Abbott
James Allen
James Andrews
James Baldwin

James DeMille
James Joyce
James Lane Allen
James Lane Allen
James Oliver Curwood
James Oppenheim
James Otis
James R. Driscoll
Jane Austen
Jens Peter Jacobsen
Jerome K. Jerome
John Burroughs
John Cournos
John F. Kennedy
John Gay
John Glasworthy
John Habberton
John Joy Bell
John Kendrick Bangs
John Milton
John Philip Sousa
Jonas Lauritz Idemil Lie
Jonathan Swift
Joseph A. Altsheler
Joseph Carey
Joseph Conrad
Joseph E. Badger Jr
Joseph Hergesheimer
Joseph Jacobs
Julian Hawthrone
Julies Vernes
Justin Huntly McCarthy
Kakuzo Okakura
Kenneth Grahame
Kenneth McGaffey
Kate Langley Bosher
Kate Langley Bosher
Katherine Cecil Thurston
Katherine Stokes
L. A. Abbot
L. T. Meade
L. Frank Baum
Latta Griswold
Laura Lee Hope
Laurence Housman
Leo Tolstoy
Leonid Andreyev
Lewis Carroll
Lilian Bell
Lloyd Osbourne
Louis Tracy

Louisa May Alcott
Lucy Fitch Perkins
Lucy Maud Montgomery
Lydia Miller Middleton
Lyndon Orr
M. Corvus
M. H. Adams
Margaret E. Sangster
Margaret Vandercook
Margret Penrose
Maria Edgeworth
Maria Thompson Daviess
Mariano Azuela
Marion Polk Angellotti
Mark Overton
Mark Twain
Mary Austin
Mary Catherine Crowley
Mary Cole
Mary Hastings Bradley
Mary Roberts Rinehart
Mary Rowlandson
M. Wollstonecraft Shelley
Maud Lindsay
Max Beerbohm
Myra Kelly
Nathaniel Hawthrone
Nicolo Machiavelli
O. F. Walton
Oscar Wilde
Owen Johnson
P.G. Wodehouse
Paul and Mabel Thorne
Paul G. Tomlinson
Paul Severing
Percy Brebner
Peter B. Kyne
Plato
R. Derby Holmes
R. L. Stevenson
R. S. Ball
Rabindranath Tagore
Rahul Alvares
Ralph Henry Barbour
Ralph Waldo Emmerson
Rene Descartes
Rex Beach
Rex E. Beach
Richard Harding Davis
Richard Jefferies
Richard Le Gallienne

Robert Barr
Robert Frost
Robert Gordon Anderson
Robert L. Drake
Robert Lansing
Robert Lynd
Robert Michael Ballantyne
Robert W. Chambers
Rosa Nouchette Carey
Rudyard Kipling
Samuel B. Allison
Samuel Hopkins Adams
Sarah Bernhardt
Selma Lagerlof
Sherwood Anderson
Sigmund Freud
Standish O'Grady
Stanley Weyman
Stella Benson
Stephen Crane
Stewart Edward White
Stijn Streuvels
Swami Abhedananda

Swami Parmananda
T. S. Ackland
T. S. Arthur
The Princess Der Ling
Thomas A. Janvier
Thomas A Kempis
Thomas Anderton
Thomas Bailey Aldrich
Thomas Bulfinch
Thomas De Quincey
Thomas H. Huxley
Thomas Hardy
Thomas More
Thornton W. Burgess
U. S. Grant
Valentine Williams
Various Authors
Victor Appleton
Virginia Woolf
Walter Camp
Walter Scott
Washington Irving
Wilbur Lawton

Wilkie Collins
Willa Cather
Willard F. Baker
William Dean Howells
William le Queux
W. Makepeace Thackeray
William W. Walter
Winston Churchill
Yei Theodora Ozaki
Yogi Ramacharaka
Young E. Allison
Zane Grey

www.ingramcontent.com/pod-product-compliance
Lightning Source LLC
Chambersburg PA
CBHW021313250626
47155CB00002B/515